JOHN D. MacDONALD
"One of our best craftsmen!"
The San Francisco Chronicle

JOHN D. MacDONALD
"A masterful writer!"
The Chicago Tribune

JOHN D. MacDONALD
"An expert storyteller!"
The New York Times

JOHN D. MacDONALD
"The best novelist in America!"
Pete Hamill, *The New York Daily News*

Fawcett Books
by John D. MacDonald

John D. MacDonald

AREA OF SUSPICION

(Specially revised by the author)

FAWCETT GOLD MEDAL • NEW YORK

To the memory of
JOSEPH THOMPSON SHAW

A Fawcett Gold Medal Book
Published by Ballantine Books

Copyright © 1954, 1961 by John D. MacDonald Publishing, Inc.

A shorter version of this book appeared in Collier's under the title MY BROTHER'S WIDOW.

ISBN 0-449-13099-1

Printed in Canada

First Fawcett Gold Medal Edition: June 1961
First Ballantine Books Edition: April 1983
Fifth Printing: December 1988

Chapter 1

I woke with the feeling of disorientation an unfamiliar bed gives you, woke in a room too small, and too still. It took long seconds to remember this was George Tarleson's cruiser, the "Vunderbar," to remember I had borrowed it yesterday noon, Saturday noon, telling George I had fishing on my mind. Actually my motive had been to get away from the Tarleson's usual noisy week-end house party.

My bachelor beach cottage is a few hundred yards from their big house at Indian Rocks Beach. It is a good little party house, and when I bought it four years ago, I wanted the gay life—and got it. The cottage was the setting for a party that lasted one year. The personnel changed, but the party went on. For the next two years the parties were shorter, but just as loud. I endured them. During this past year, my fourth in Florida, I tried to escape whenever possible.

So yesterday noon I had borrowed the cabin cruiser from George, and cast off just in time to avoid the unwanted company of a brown and Bikinied maiden who had decided it would be jolly to shanghai herself. She stood in pigeon-toed wistfulness on the dock and watched me out of sight.

I trolled north, glad to be alone, and at dusk I found a

secluded, mangrove-bordered bay near Dunedin Isles and dropped the hook far enough from shore to avoid the bugs.

So this was an April Sunday and I had slept long and well. I pulled on swimming trunks and padded out onto the deck. The day was still and gray and silver. Mullet leaped and ripples circles outward. The water was clear and deep. I balanced on the stern rail and dived, and the water washed away the last mistiness of long hard sleep. I swam straight and fast until I was winded, then rolled and floated. The "Vunderbar" was a blue and white toy resting on a display window mirror. This year I was sun-darkened, as during other years, to the shade of waxed mahogany, hair and eyebrows bleached lighter than my skin. But during other years it had been a veneer of health over a permanent condition of either hang-over or a fine high edge. I was back in shape, a testimonial to the abuse the human body will take without permanent damage, and being in shape again was a minor satisfaction which, more and more often, was balanced against vague, unwelcome stirrings of discontent.

Midge and George Tarleson had thrown the standard party. My group, I suppose, making a busy project out of idleness, giving dedicated attention to a new terrace, or a trip to Nassau, or non-objective art—junior grade—or a meaningless affair. When I felt superior or contemptuous, I told myself all my own little make-work projects in the area were also just so much window-trimming. There was no need for me to do anything except play. I had my inheritance—my nice bundle of eight thousand shares of Dean Products stock, the family enterprise. And every year the dividend was just about eight dollars a share.

It had been the usual party and Midge Tarleson had tried to pair me off with somebody whose motives were not as transient as my wariness likes to have them. She had been pretty enough, but she wore a lost look, and her prettiness was something she wanted to trade for security.

Once I had told Midge Tarleson just enough of my emotional history to give her a yen to cure me. She thinks marriage is a cure. But, to her exasperation, my playmates are the little sun-tanned beach girls who want to keep all alliances informal. I want no lost-looking ones.

Mine was the Great American Dream achieved. Money and idleness. But with it had come a sense of guilt, as though I were accused of some unspecified crime. And I guessed that my playmates, when they were alone, felt the same way. Hence our perpetual and turbulent parties. It was as though we had all begun to have a faint aroma of decay. The world was spinning toward some unthinkable destination, and we sat in the sand with our buckets and castles.

In spite of the restlessness it caused, it was better to be alone—a condition I was arranging with increasing regularity. Alone where gulls teetered on the wind, and made bawdy shouting, and the stingarees leaped high and came down with hard clap of gristled wings against the water.

As I swam back to the "Vunderbar" I heard a gutty droning. I looked south down the channel and saw a speedboat swing gracefully around the channel marker. I hauled myself up over the stern of the "Vunderbar," shaded my eyes against the sky's pale glare and recognized Jigger Kelsey's hot little sixteen feet of mahogany hull with its one hundred horses. Jigger was behind the wheel with two women sitting near him. One of them waved and I recognized Midge.

For a moment I had a quick, inward twisting of alarm, an almost superstitious certainty that something had gone very wrong. But it faded quickly. I had left the party, so here was Midge bringing me a piece of it so that I wouldn't be lonely. There would be a shaker of rum sours aboard, and an account of the fun I was missing.

Jigger made a sweeping turn and came alongside, reversing the motor, judging the distance nicely. He stood up and caught the rail of the "Vunderbar." "You're a tough guy to find, Gev," he said, his grin white in the tan face. "Don't you ever use that ship-to-shore?"

I tried to give the imitation of a man welcoming friends. The girl in the middle was the one with the lost gray eyes. But she looked at me quite absently and resumed her silent study of Jigger's broad brown shoulders.

"How did you find me?"

"I sent out a general call," Midge said, "and one of the charter boats reported seeing the "Vunderbar" at anchor up here."

I frowned at Midge. "General call?"

She climbed deftly over the rail, ignoring my out-stretched hand. Midge is a tall, thin woman with dusty black hair and a pallor the sun never changes. She always looks incongruous in casual beach clothes.

"Thanks loads, Jigger," she said. Jigger gave a mock salute and shoved off and dropped into the seat. His boat was planing before it had gone twenty yards. The girl sat very close to Jigger. The bow wave sparkled, the drone faded out of the morning, leaving a white wake in a long curve around the channel marker.

"What's up, Midge?" I gave her a cigarette. "George want the boat back?"

"No. But it was very anti-social of you to take off like this. You act like a hermit lately, Gev."

"So you came out to tell me that?"

She sat in a fishing chair, hiked one knee up and hugged it. "Oh, not just for that."

"This is your woman-of-mystery mood." I made my tone light and casual. I knew Midge well. I knew that the more interesting the news, the longer it would take her to get to it. It all tied in with the twist of fear I had felt when I saw Jigger's boat.

I thought about Ken, my brother, and felt the guilt in me again. Not the old guilt of having run out on him years ago, but a new guilt. His previous letters to me had been reserved, cool. But there had been recent ones. Odd letters. Full of vague hints of trouble, oblique statements about the plant, about his wife. Yet nothing definite or positive.

And there was another odd thing about his letters. They now rambled on about old days, old times, long before our trouble. Like the time at the lake we went searching for the lost Harrison girl and became lost ourselves. It was odd for him to bring up those old days, as though he were trying to recreate the warmth between us. I could try to deny that warmth, but it was still there. That sort of thing can't really be killed.

Midge made a ceremony of inspecting the burning tip of her cigarette. I waited for her to speak, concealing my impatience.

"Sooner or later," I said, "you're going to have to tell me. I've got all day too."

She made a face. "There's a man waiting. He says it's important. He's a stuffy type. I think he disapproves of me. His name is Fitch."

"Fitch!" It shocked me. I wondered what on earth Lester was doing in Florida. I couldn't imagine him taking a vacation—or looking me up if he did. He belonged entirely to the world I had given up.

"He says it's important, and whatever it is, I guess the phone call was about the same thing."

"Maybe I should know about that too," I said with forced patience.

"Oh, that was a long-distance from Arland yesterday. It came right after you sneaked off in the boat."

"I didn't sneak off. George loaned it to me. Who phoned?"

"I took it and explained we couldn't get in touch with you and didn't know when you'd be back." She took her long dramatic pause and said, "It was your brother's wife, Gevan."

Maybe I could have successfully kept my expression blank and bland if I'd never told Midge about the whole mess. Perhaps not. Even after four years it was much too close, too vivid, too hurting. I had to turn my back and that, of course, told Midge precisely what she wanted to know, confirmed all the rest of it, and made me resent her.

The thought of Niki phoning me was like a knife. Niki phoning, and Lester Fitch coming to see me. Maybe it was just a new angle on the old game of trying to get me to go back into the firm, back to that life that had become

5

impossible four years ago. But that didn't fit. The method seemed implausible. Niki would never be a part of any such sales attempt—not if she wanted it to succeed. I felt the dread I'd had when I'd seen Jigger's boat bearing down on me.

Midge came up beside me and put cold fingers on my arm. She is a woman with little warmth. Yet she needs warmth. She gets what she needs by becoming involved in the emotional problems of others. She knew my problem and I was sorry I had ever told her, because her interest is too avid.

"That man wouldn't tell me what he wants. He just kept saying it's important, Gevan. He didn't want to ride with Jigger, so I said I'd bring you back. He got in on the plane this morning. So apparently he started right after they found out they couldn't get you by phone."

"Take over, Midge, and I'll get the hook."

The starters whined and the motors caught as I pulled in the wet line, hand over hand. I swashed the gunk off the anchor and laid it in place on the bow. Midge eased the "Vunderbar" around and headed toward the channel on the outgoing tide.

I went below and changed to a shirt and slacks. When I came back up she was just making the turn into the open Gulf.

"Do you think they want you to go back?" she asked.

"I don't know. They stopped asking me a long time ago."

"Maybe you should go back, you know."

"It's so gay here, Midge. Who'd want to leave?"

"Be serious! You know as well as I do what's wrong. You're going sour, Gev. You tried to get over her. You tried all the methods and now you've stopped trying and you're going sour."

I looked at her dark, avid eyes, and saw the flick of tongue tip across her underlip. This was her meat.

"Once upon a time, Midge, I told you too damn much about my life. I'm not a soap opera for your private

6

pleasure. Tune in tomorrow and find out if Gevan can find happiness."

She smiled. "I'm not going to let you make me angry, my friend," she said firmly.

I moved away and stood at the stern, watching the boil of the wake. There was little point in restating my position to Midge, or to myself. After my father died I had taken over the job of running Dean Products. I'd been too young for the job—too young and inexperienced. But sometimes, when you have to grow fast, you can do it. Two years at Harvard Business School had given me the theory. But practice is another animal. At Harvard they don't have any course in how to react to men your father, and your grandfather, hired. To them you are a punk, and there can be great joy in tripping you up.

It had scared me, but I stayed with it, and got up every time I was thrown, and one day I found out I was enjoying it. Maybe you enjoy any skill you acquire. You learn that the raw materials most important are not the special steels, that the production equipment most important is not the stolid rows of machine tools. Your material and your equipment are human beings, and you learn their strengths and their weaknesses, and how to make them part of a production team. Then the rest comes easier. The shoes had looked too big and the steps too long, but after a time I could match the stride and we showed a profit, and that was good because it was a measure of how well I was doing.

Then Niki came along, fitting into my life in a way that made wonderful sense. Niki, who would inevitably be my wife and bear our children and live with me in a house that would be warm and good with love.

Girl and Job. Work in itself cannot be both means and end. There must be some person to whom you can bring your small victories and be rewarded.

But twelve hundred nights ago I walked down a rainy street toward her place, walked with the bumping heart the thought of seeing her always gave me. I walked in, not thinking to knock or call out, and that was neither guile nor rudeness, but the same eagerness which had made me walk so quickly from my car.

I walked in on her and saw my brother's hands, strong against the sheen of her housecoat. I saw her on tiptoe in his arms, with upturned mouth and all the long ripe lines of her held by him in the instant before she turned to look at me with the drowsy, tousled look of a woman lost in kissings.

We were to have been married that month.

There are pictures you keep with a peculiar vividness in your mind, the very good ones and the very bad ones. There was the look of his hands on her, and the way she stumbled aside when I pushed her so I could get at him, and the look in his eyes as he stood there making no attempt to block or dodge the blow that broke his mouth. There was no memory of the things I said to the two of them before I walked back out into the rain. Nor any memory of the walk, or, much later, of driving the car back to my place.

During that week I found out that I could not go on. I couldn't adjust myself to the role of the betrayed, the strong silent type who contents himself with Job alone now that Girl is gone. I might have managed it if it had been someone else who had taken her from me. But Ken and I had been close. I had come to think of us as a good team, his practical, methodical steadiness compensating for my weakness of trying to move too fast, too soon. If it had been someone else who took her from me, hate would have been less complicated. I might have been able to recreate my interest in, and dedication to, Dean Products. But my brother had stolen the satisfactions of my work in the same moment he had stolen Niki Webb.

I walked out and the presidency went to Ken. He wrote often at first, asking me to come back. I read the first few letters, destroyed the rest unread. Later he did not write as often. The hand that signed the letter was a hand I had seen against the blue of her housecoat. And it was the hand which had put the ring on Niki's finger.

The beach house at Indian Rocks was a new world and I tried to keep everything out of that world which could start me thinking of what-might-have-been. When I was least charitable with myself I would think of it as a four-year sulk. But when the sun was bright and the beach girls' laughter was warm in their throats, and the portable radios were picking up the Latin rhythms of the Havana stations—then it all seemed desirable and good.

The "Vunderbar" churned south, paralleling the coast. There was a change in the silver-gray day. Gusts came out of nowhere, riffled the water and faded into stillness. There was a yellowish hue in the west, a threat of storm—that sort that appears before the storm clouds can be seen. In moments a day can change just enough for the atavistic warnings to occur, that prickling at the back of the neck, a crawl and pull of flesh.

I looked at the yellow cube that was the Fort Harrison Hotel at Clearwater, landmark for local navigation, and thought about Lester and told myself they just wanted me to go back. The last annual report to the stockholders had told of an increasing load of government contracts—and the plant expansion, added shifts, increased tool procurement. That was all it was. New management stresses. A desk for Gevan Dean.

I told myself all that and didn't believe it.

I couldn't get it out of my mind that something had gone terribly, desperately wrong.

"You know we don't want you to leave," Midge said suddenly. "George and I. You know that."

"Thanks, Midge. I won't go back there."

"You say that. I feel lonesome already." Her laugh had a thin nervous flutter. "We've had good times."

"Yes."

"But not many lately, Gev. Not many at all."

I didn't answer her. Far ahead of the "Vunderbar" a school of fish were striking bait, hitting like bonito, sending the gouts of spray up as though a machine gun was being fired at the water. Gulls whooped and dipped. The Gulf had an oily look and the ground swell had begun to build up. Far out the charter boats were through trolling, were heading home, running for shelter.

And I had not heard Niki's voice in four years . . . .

Chapter 2

Lester Fitch wore a dark gray suit, a white shirt, sedate-figured tie. In his felt hat, and with the sun glinting on the perfect prisms of his glasses he was completely out of key with the beach and the sea as he walked beside me down the sand road to my house.

I have contempt and pity for Lester. I have watched him with others, watched the excellence of his imitation of a sincere young lawyer who is going places in his profession. His act is unsure when he is with me, and perhaps with anyone else who remembers him from high school. He probably wishes no one could remember. He was one of those blubbery, ungainly kids with acne, who grew too fast and who seems to exist in order to be persecuted. He could not run fast enough to avoid torment, and had no strength to match his growth. His cry of pain and outrage was an adenoidal bellow. With those of us who remember him from then, he tries very hard to be the manly lawyer, but the mask is always slipping a bit, exposing the wariness and uncertainty underneath.

He had watched me somberly while I hosed down the "Vunderbar," looking more than ordinarily ill at ease. I had concealed my impatience to know what had brought him down, and made the routine job last. The rich leather of his

10

briefcase glowed in the pale and ominous light of the day. When I was through he said he'd rather talk at my place. He walked there, beside me, as out of place in Indian Rocks as one of our tanned beach girls would have been in the raw April of Arland.

We went into my small, cypress-paneled livingroom. I had left the windows closed and the air was musty, sea-damp. I opened them wide. Lester sat on the couch and put the briefcase beside him and placed his felt hat carefully on the briefcase. He crossed his legs and adjusted his trouser crease. He seemed intent on little routines, and the whole act was wrong. I didn't know how it was wrong until I realized how he would have acted had it been an attempt to get me back into the firm. Then he would have been full of false affability, full of chat about what a nice little place this is, and you're looking well, old boy. Instead of joviality, he was acting like a lawyer awaiting an unfriendly verdict.

"Niki tried to get in touch with you by phone yesterday, Gevan," he said, on a faint annoying note of accusation.

"So I was told. And you flew down. I was told that too. Now you're supposed to tell me why?"

He polished his glasses on a bone-white handerchief. His naked eyes looked mild and helpless. Usually it is possible to guess which part Lester is playing, which mask he has selected from his limited supply. This one bothered me because I couldn't guess what effect he was trying to create.

He put the glasses on, and his smile was something that came and went quickly and weakly, a smile of nervous apology. My unreasoning forebodings had made me as nervous as he acted. I said harshly, "Get to the point! What do you want?"

"Gevan—I don't know how to—Gevan, Ken's dead."

I walked to the window and looked out at the sand road, at the beach, and the oiled gray of the Gulf. The swells curled and broke. The wind had freshened. Pelicans, in single file, glided by, somber and intent. Two husky boys in blue trunks were practicing handstands. They could have been brothers.

11

Kendall Dean is dead.

One word. A heavy word, like something falling. It did a strange thing. It changed him from a man I thought I hated back into my kid brother. Kid brother, dead at thirty-one. It awakened all the deep, warm things of long ago, all the things I had pushed out of my mind so I could think of him only as a male who had taken my woman from me, so I could deny brotherhood and recognize only the hate and the resentment.

The hate had been strong. But one word took it away. One word brought back the good days, those good, lost summers. He was a face weeping in the window that first day when I was taken to school, because he was not old enough to go, and the days would be lonely for him without our games and projects. Cave, treehouse, hideout, secret rites of many memberships, codes and plots and complicated wars.

I remembered the day the roan threw him and broke his arm, and I walked him home and he would not cry.

I thought of him as my kid brother, and felt a terrifying remorse that we had not spoken in four years, that I had not written him, that the last thing I had done to him was hit him heavily in the mouth and knock him down. I had blamed him, and it was all changed. It had been Niki who had stolen something from me. Stolen the last four years of my brother. All dead now. Mother, father, sister, brother. Sister dead at seven, and all I could remember of her was the way she looked once, running down a wide lawn as fast as she could run, as though she ran away that day from our familiar world.

Now it seemed Niki had stolen half my life and all of his. Too many deaths. He had been the last one who gave a damn what happened to me, what I did, whether or not I was happy. I had told myself I hated him, but I had not realized these past four years that the very awareness of his existence had been a tie with all the good years.

The two boys ceased their handstands and walked down

12

the beach, one of them carrying a yellow beach ball. An old woman in a black bathing suit bent over, fingering a pile of shells. The wind flapped the skirt of her bathing suit against suet-legs and the wind came through the window and I could smell rain and dampness in it.

Lester touched my shoulder and it startled me. I turned and he pulled his hand back.

"I—didn't mean to break it to you so—bluntly."

"How did it happen?"

"It was one of those crazy, pointless things." There was anger in his voice. "It happened just after midnight Friday night, Gevan. Lord, that seems weeks ago. He and Niki were having a quiet evening. She went to bed, but she wasn't asleep when it happened. Ken was taking a walk around the place. The police think he surprised a prowler. Somebody shot him in the back of the head. It killed him instantly."

I stared at Lester. "In the back of the head!"

"It's such a senseless waste," he said. "It's the sort of thing that's always happening to people you don't know. You read about it in the papers. You think what a bad break, but it doesn't touch you, because it never happens to people you know."

"When is the funeral?"

Lester looked at his watch. "A lot of company people want to attend, of course. And things are so rushed at the plant that it was decided they'd have it today. About three hours from now. Niki is terribly, terribly shocked, as you can well imagine. It shocked the whole city. He had a lot of friends, Gevan."

"I know." I sat down. He had a lot of friends because he was a good man. The news changed the look of my world. My livingroom was alien, as if I had wandered into a place where strangers lived. I got up to make myself a drink. I asked Lester if he wanted one. He asked for a light one. I made mine stiff. A prowler with a twisted mind and a finger on a trigger. There would be quite a few stiff drinks, but I knew there wouldn't be enough of them.

13

As I brought the drinks, Lester was opening his briefcase. The zipper made a secretive sound. I put the drink beside him and said, "What have you got there?"

His specialized knowledge gave him assurance. He was out of the world of bad tidings, and back in his garden of torts and writs. Assurance brought back his air of patronizing efficiency. "You know I hate to bother you with this sort of thing at a time like this, Gevan. But it's best to get the details taken care of. I have a plane connection to make. But if you'd rather not, of course, we can—"

"Let's see what you've got."

He handed me a paper, saying, "I need your signature on this for the probate court. Under the terms of your father's will, as Ken died without issue, his share of the trust fund reverts to you. Ken's will, of course, leaves everything to Niki. You can have another lawyer check this, but—"

I read it carefully. He uncapped a pen and handed it to me at precisely the right moment. If he had been handling the personal legal affairs of Ken and Niki, he had acquired a pleasantly profitable account. I signed it and gave it back to him.

He handed me another bit of paper. I saw that it was a standard proxy form. It was made out to Niki, to Mrs. Kendall Dean.

"This will require more explanation," he said.

"I should think so." I hadn't voted my shares since I had left.

He shrugged. "Actually it's a case of finding someone acceptable to you, Gevan. We didn't think you'd care to—have me vote it."

I stared at him and he flushed and looked down and did some unnecessary rearrangement of the papers. I knew that he was remembering, as I was, that day years ago when he had come to me with a choice and tainted little scheme that involved a "friendly" salvage officer and a rigged auction of some army surplus material. He'd presented it as though he were doing me a favor, letting me in on it. He was trying to scrape up enough financial backing to swing the whole purchase. He came to see me on a day when I had no time for soft answers and no patience with such schemes. I had told him in blunt words what I thought of the plan, the salvage officer, and Lester Fitch, until he wheeled with flaming face and ran from my office.

"What's all this 'we' talk, Lester?" I asked him softly.

"We? Oh, I see what you mean. Through Ken I've been doing quite a bit of state tax work for the firm, and I've been made a member of the board—pro tem—to be confirmed at the next meeting."

"Niki too, I suppose?"

"She'll sit in on the emergency meeting a week from tomorrow. An open meeting. Board and shareholders. Notices will go out tomorrow."

I looked at the proxy form again. "That doesn't explain why you want this, Lester."

He gave me a condescending glance, big business talking to a beach boy. "You've made it definite that you don't want to come back, Gevan. It was talked over. We—everyone decided when we couldn't contact you in time to make the—ceremony, you'd rather have it handled this way than come up and attend the meeting yourself."

It took a few moments to get my attention back to what he was saying. I had drifted off again into memories of Ken.

I stared at Lester. "I don't want to seem dull. But the questions I've been asking sound reasonably simple to me. Why do you want a proxy form signed? For what purpose?"

He waved a large white hand. "Oh, that's not something so terribly special, Gevan. It's one of the usual rows. A minority group trying to clobber management. We need a show of strength."

"What minority group? What do they want?"

He sighed, patiently. "You've been out of touch, Gevan. I'll have to give you some background on this. If you happened to glance at the annual report you must have—"

"I read it with interest."

"Good!" he said. "Splendid! That saves time. We've just been awarded another twenty-five million's worth. We

15

have so much government work a Colonel Dolson—a fine officer—has been stationed at the plant with his staff. For some time Colonel Dolson has felt that Ken, quite frankly, wasn't big enough to handle the new picture. He told me quite confidentially that he had spoken to Ken about stepping down in favor of Stanley Mottling some time ago. Ken had seemed in favor of the suggestion and had said he would think it over."

"Stanley Mottling? Just who the hell is Stanley Mottling?"

He raised his eyebrows. One of those oh-come-now expressions. "Don't you know about him? Ken brought him in as executive vice-president. Amazing man. Enormously capable. It's a credit to Ken that he located him and brought him in. A world of experience, believe me. Exactly the sort of man to put Dean Products on its feet."

"I wasn't aware that it had been knocked off its feet."

"You don't realize the tremendous problems involved in setting up entirely new production—"

"I'm just a poor cracker-boy."

He smiled uneasily. "I was about to say, in the quantity that they've been loading on us. With Ken gone, Niki and I—and the Colonel, of course—feel that Stanley should take over with the least possible delay. In fact, we're grateful that he's available and willing. But Mr. Karch, from the bank, as board chairman, has been rocking the boat. He's been organizing the other shareholders and putting them squarely behind old Walter Granby to take over."

"Any firm could do much worse. Walter is shrewd and able."

Lester shook his head. "He *was* shrewd and able. He's failed badly in the four years you've been gone. You'd be shocked to see him. But even at his best, Gevan, or—and I say this in complete honesty—at your best, neither of you could measure up to Mottling. We need your shares behind Mottling to confirm Ken's wishes and keep little people from upsetting the apple cart. I'm pretty certain they won't go as far as a mismanagement suit. It will be enough just to vote Granby down. A suit like that wouldn't stand a chance, not when you stack it up against Mottling's record.

"If this Mottling is so hot, why the opposition?"

"Jealousy. Unwillingness to keep up with the times. Inability to comprehend that Dean Products is in the big time."

"I seem to remember that Dean Products was in the big time ten years ago."

He gave me a hush-hush tone of voice, leaning forward. "Gevan, we've been entrusted with the production of— some very crucial items. I'm not permitted to say more than that."

"Why should Walter buck Mottling? Walter is bright."

"He lives in his own world these days."

I flicked my cigarette into the small littered fireplace and turned back toward Lester. "It seems so damn fast, Lester. Too damn fast. Ken was killed on Friday. This is Sunday. And here you are with a proxy form."

"You have absolutely no idea of the tremendous pressure on the firm," he said solemnly. I wondered if he knew how he sounded. I sensed anxiety. All right, so Lester had deeded his heart and soul to the company and become a very dedicated young man. But that did not fit my understanding of Lester Fitch. Maybe they were giving him a bonus or something for coming back with the signed proxy.

"I don't want *anybody* voting my shares. You or Niki or Karch or anybody else."

He looked at me sadly and shook his head. "I'd hate to think you'd apply emotional reasoning to anything this important, Gevan."

I suspected it was a phrase he had thought up on the plane ride down, complete with rehearsed head-shaking.

"Exactly what does that mean?"

He coughed and fiddled with the strap on his briefcase. "If you weren't being emotional about it, you'd have no objection to Niki. That seems clear to me."

"Don't oversimplify. If it's this important that my stock be voted, I should vote it myself."

The light caught his glasses in such a way I couldn't see his eyes behind them. "Maybe I have oversimplified it. I didn't realize that now you'd have such a much better reason for coming back." The insinuation was unmistakable, and unmistakably nasty.

I reached him in one stride, caught the front of his coat and lifted him up off the couch. His briefcase slid to the floor. I had my right fist back, I saw the mouth go slack, and saw behind his frightened eyes a lumbering lout bleating his way across the playground with the pack shrill behind him. I pushed him back onto the couch. He sat on his hat, mashing it. It wasn't worth hitting him. He'd used a snide and clumsy weapon. The very crudeness of it was perhaps an index of his anxiety.

"I know I shouldn't have said—"

"Shut up, Lester," I said wearily. "Just go away. Go catch your plane."

He thumbed his hat back into shape. "I'll leave the proxy form with you."

I turned away. "What are you going to do?" he asked.

"Go back and tell them you don't know what I'm going to do."

I heard him go to the door. He said, "I'm—very sorry about Ken. When you get over the emotional shock and give this some rational thought, Gevan, you'll see that the best . . ."

I turned toward him. He swallowed, and fixed his hat and left. The wind banged the door shut. I saw him going down the road, holding his hat brim. He looked back. His face was too pallid for this land. The two boys had come back. They had a girl with them. Her yellow suit matched the beach ball. One of them slung the ball at her. Her back was turned. I heard the thin squeal and watched her chase him, agile and brown.

I stretched out on the couch and went back through all the years, like looking at old photograph albums. The world had been a safe place then, full of high, square automobiles, full of sailboats and ponies and summer camps.

But the depression had put an end to the extra things. Other firms had folded, but Dad had held Dean Products together with guts and bare hands. I remember how he would sit with us at dinner, silent, his face very old. The bad years lasted a long time.

In 1939 Dean Products got an order from the British Purchasing Commission for Bren machine-gun mounts. Ken and I got all heated up over the war. We were going for sure. But in my past was that year in Arizona and the healed scars were too impressive on the X-ray plates. And when the checked Ken they found sugar, and he went on a diabetic's diet. Healthy kids.

So it was college then, and the feeling of being left out. There were all kinds of uniforms and training programs around the colleges. I went on to Harvard Business School. After I got out I went into the firm and got a full year of shop experience before Dad's stroke, coma, and death. The war was over and things had eased, and I guess they made me boss man because there didn't seem to be any specific damage I could do. Scared witless, I concealed it behind what was supposed to be a confident manner. Walter Granby helped. They all helped. I found out how reins can feel good in your hands, and a profit is a good thing to make because it shows you how well you've been doing. When I found Niki I knew that she had been the one thing missing . . . .

The phone rang and I reached over and picked it up after the first ring. "Mr. Dean, sir? One moment, please. Arland is calling."

I knew who it had to be before she spoke, and I knew precisely how her voice would sound. "Gev?"

"Hello, Niki." You couldn't say that and let it go at that. There had to be more. The standard words. "I'm sorry about Ken, Niki."

"It's so—so unfair. That's all I can think. So unfair."

"I know."

"I'm lost, Gev. Just terribly lost and alone. I want to

crawl away and hide. But there's all these business things I don't understand. I just talked to Lester. He said you're upset."

"About Ken. And Lester irritated me."

"He shouldn't have gone down there. He thought it would be all right after we couldn't get in touch with you yesterday."

"I supposed he told you I refused to sign the proxy."

"I don't know what he said. I hardly listened to him. Oh, Gevan, it's raining here like it would never end. Fat gray rain. What do they say—a good day for a funeral?" The sound she made was half-sob, half-laugh.

"Easy Niki."

"Lester didn't know whether you're coming up here or not. Maybe you should come up here, Gev. I—I want to see you."

Yes, you want to see me. To check on the damage, maybe. Ken never would have touched you without invitation. Bitch.

I kept thinking of how she would look. Four years older now. Sitting with her fingers white on the telephone, a strand of that black hair swinging forward, to be thrown back with the familiar, impatient gesture. In the right light her hair would glint violet and blue. Her eyes were a strange blue, darker when she was troubled or aroused. Now she would be staring into an empty distance, her white teeth set into the roundness of underlip, and she would be wearing black . . .

I could sense the pull of her, the sheer physical pull that could moisten my palms, shorten my breath, even when she was fifteen hundred miles away. I remembered my finger tips on the silk of her cheek, remembered how when my arms were around her I could feel, under my palm, the slow warm sliding of her muscles under the warmth of her back.

"Like Lester said," I told her harshly, "I haven't decided."

"I'm sorry I said that. I wasn't thinking. I haven't any right to ask you to come up here, or ask you for anything, Gevan."

"You have a right to ask. You were my brother's wife. I want to do anything I can for you, naturally."

Her voice became fainter and there were noises on the line. I had to strain to hear her. ". . . all this company business. I don't know. I have to leave soon, Gev. Good-by."

"Good-by, Niki." I went to the window. The rain came out of the west. It wasn't fat and gray. It was in wind-driven sheets. I shut the windows on the west. The kids were gone from the beach. A brown palm frond slid across the sand road with the wind.

No point in going up there. Nothing I could do. Nothing I could do about the four wasted years. They don't give you two chances. Not on the biggest table in the house. They make you pass the dice.

No adolescent urge for vengeance would hasten the capture of the prowler by the police. Stay here, Dean, and keep on with the routines of four years.

If I went up there, Ken wouldn't come striding toward me out of the rain, an inch shorter than I, a few inches broader. A husky guy with nice eyes. Always a bit shy. He had always followed my lead. Even, I thought mockingly, with Niki.

I looked at my watch. The services would begin soon. The plot was on a hill. There were cedars there. The big granite stone said Dean. Three generations there. Now Kendall. If Niki never married again, she would be there one day. And I would, too. Strange reunion on the green hill.

The wind rattled the jalousied windows and I told myself again that I would not go back.

But on Tuesday, after too many restless, aimless hours, too many drinks and toubled dreams, George Tarleson drove me across Courtney Campbell Causeway to catch a flight from Tampa International. And George seemed to be driving too slowly.

Chapter 3

The city of Arland, population four hundred thousand, is constricted by two conical hills into a crude figure eight. In the waist of the eight is the downtown section, three bridges across the river, a convergence of railroad lines and national highways. The north half of the eight is industrial—slum land, saloon land, ptomaine diners along the highways, shops and railroad sidings and tarry belch of smoke, complete with city dump, littered streets, candy stores where you can place a bet.

The southern half is old residential, with high-shouldered Victorian, shoebox post-Victorian, and Grand Rapids Gothic sitting too close together on quiet, shaded streets. The new subdivisions clamber up the southern slopes of the two hills and spread south into the flatlands.

I fastened my seat belt on order and I cupped my hands against the glass and looked down at the north end of the city, trying to spot the hundred acres of Dean Products, Incorporated. But the night lights were confusing, mazed by the shower that whipped against the wings and fuselage. Down there somewhere was the original plant building, sitting in fussy matronly dignity, overshadowed by the saw-toothed roofs of World War I construction, the pastel oblongs of World War II expansion. Modern offices had been completed in '42, fronting on Shambeau Street, and the offices in the tiny wing of the original plant building had been turned over to the representatives of the procurement branches of the armed services.

During any period of armament the government looks primarily for those contractors who can cut heavy metal to close tolerance. That means having the precision machine tools, the men to run them, the men to set them up, the engineering staff to lick the bugs, and the executive control to keep the whole operation moving. Military production is full of bastard threads and tolerances down to a ten thousandth and metallurgical specifications that give ulcers to promising young engineers.

In both wars Dean Products acquired the reputation of being able to machine anything—from aluminum optical fittings so light they had to be hand-shimmed in place with tin foil, to traverse rings for medium tanks, to bases for coastal defense rifles. We made few complete assemblies. But we were prime subcontractors for Rock Island Arsenal and Springfield, and for boys like G.E. and the Chrysler Tank Arsenal and Lima Locomotive.

During that second war the totalitarian nations operated their war production on the basis of freezing design and then making no changes until the production order was complete. Not so with our people. Mandatory changes came in by the bale. Each change would effect all future production. We won the war. So the system must be okay. But there are a lot of executives underground who would be walking around today if it hadn't been for the load it placed on them. My father was one of them.

The plane slowed as the wheels came down. The runway lights streamed by and we were down and the plane slowed quickly. We taxied to the terminal. The rain was coming down. Women trotted toward the entrance with newspapers over their heads. The unaccustomed collar had rubbed my throat raw. The feeling of excitement and anticipation that I had felt on the way up from Florida did not die now that I was home. It became more intense. In a strange way it had been easier to believe Ken dead while I was in Florida. Thoughts of him kept slipping into my mind through unguarded doorways. Transition by aircraft is unreasonably abrupt. The scene changes too fast. Yet there was no overlapping. Florida was gone as though it had never happened. It was like walking out of a movie into the dark rainy streets of Arland in April, pausing for that wrench of readjustment and then turning in the right direction and letting the sunlight of the movie fade out of your mind.

At last I got my suitcase and I shared a cab into the heart of town, to the Gardland Hotel. The streets were wet tunnels, lined with neon. I could sense how the town was. Hopped up. Every night is Saturday night. The heavy industry cities get that way when plants put on the extra shifts. It was like the forties. I knew how it would be. The factory girls in slacks, the bars lined three deep, the juke jangle, blue spots on the girl doing the trick with the parrots, green floodlights on the tank where the girl was doing the underwater strip. The high-priced call girls with their hatboxes and miniature dogs. The too-young tramps with tight skirts and mouths painted square. That's when the town jumps and the big cars get sold on time, and you can hear in the night the bingle-bang of ten thousand cash registers.

But I had seen Arland when the streets were dreary with broken shoes, hacking coughs, and panhandlers. I had seen the empty houses. I had seen sharp winter winds blowing the drifters by the closed joints. The heavy metal towns are feast or famine.

Now it was feast, and in the rain-bright night the town was licking its chops, clapping grease-bitten hands and saying, "Let's have us a time!"

The lobby of the Gardland Hotel looked like a movie set for a society mob scene. Everybody seemed to be hurrying in purposeless circles, and they all wore earnest, worried faces. People sat on stacks of luggage looking doleful. I stood near one of the lines at the reservation desk and heard the clerk saying, "Sorry, we don't have a thing, sir. Next, please? No reservation, sir? Sorry we don't have a thing."

I went to the assistant manager's desk. In a moment he came hurrying back, looking like a distracted penguin. "Yes, sir?"

"Is Mr. Gardland in his office?"

"If you're after accommodations, sir, I can assure you that it will be useless to—"

"Would you mind phoning his office and giving my name?"

"Not at all, but—"

"Tell him Gevan Dean wants to see him for a moment."

"Dean?" His eyes seemed to focus on me for the first time. He murmured into the phone. He hung up and said, "The door is beyond the cashier's windows, the last door at the end of—"

I told him I knew where it was. Joe Gardland came out of his office and halfway down the short hallway. His face lighted up. He is a small, plump, balding man, younger than he looks, with shrewd eyes. If they weren't shrewd eyes, the Gardland would long since have been absorbed into one of the big chains. Purchase or stock transfer would have made Joe permanently, independently wealthy, but he preferred being the king of his own domain.

He pumped my hand. "My God, Gevvy! My God! Not since Miami two years ago. What a hassle that was! Come in."

We went into his office. A pretty girl in waitress uniform sat nervously on a straight chair near the desk. He went to her and put an edge in his voice. "Is it clear now?"

"Yes, Mr. Gardland."

"Shall I send you back to work?"

Her eyes brightened. "I—I was hoping you would."

"Run along then. And watch it. Understand?"

She stood up and smiled and said, "Gee, I'll certainly—"

"Run along."

She hurried to the door and smiled again at him over her

shoulder and shut the door behind her as she left. He looked ruefully at the door. "Should have tied the can to her. Getting soft, I guess. Sit down. Scotch? . . . How do you want it? . . . On the rocks coming up." As he busied himself at the office bar, chinking the ice into the outsized old-fashioned glasses, he said, without turning around, "Sorry as hell about Kenny. A damn shame."

He brought me my drink. "That's why I came up, Joe."

"I'm damn glad they nailed the guy who did it."

"What!"

"Hell, didn't you know that?"

"I just got into town."

"Then you wouldn't. They grabbed him around noon in a rooming house in the north end. It's in the evening papers. Record as long as your arm. He's all sewed up."

"I'm glad they got him," I said.

"It sort of surprised me, Gev," he said, looking down into his glass.

"That they got him? Have the cops gotten that bad?"

"I didn't mean that. It's not my place to say anything. Look, forget I opened my mouth."

"What do you mean, it's not your place? Whose place would it be, Joe? We've been friends a long time. Don't start something like that and then try to back away from it."

He sat down behind his desk. He looked embarrassed. "A man sees a lot in this business. Maybe he adds two and two too often. And makes a fool habit of getting six."

"What about Ken?"

He looked at me. "I had it all tabbed as suicide. Now wait a minute. I thought he'd worked it out in some tricky way, maybe for the insurance angle or something. And I was going to keep my mouth shut. Now don't look so sore. I know he wasn't the suicide type. He definitely wasn't until this past year."

"And this past year?"

Joe shrugged. "It's a pattern. Came in every day at four-thirty. Eight, nine, or ten stingers. Got very sedately loaded and sat around with ghosts in his eyes. Everybody knew he was on his way out at the plant. He was coming apart. After a while he'd get up and go home. Walking a chalk line, walking like somebody with a big bundle of trouble balanced on his head."

"The plant never meant that much to him. He didn't have enough yen to be top dog, Joe."

"Not when you knew him. Hell, that didn't sound very good. Your own brother."

"It's accurate, Joe," I said briskly. "I used to know him. Now I keep thinking of the four years. I was a damn fool."

"A woman like that can make anybody act like a damn fool."

"Is that an excuse?"

"Knock it off, Gevvy," he said gently. "It's spilled milk. Stirring it with a stick turns it into the self-pity pitch. Everybody is in some sense a damn fool. Anyway, you don't have to believe me. Be in the Copper Lounge tonight about eleven. I'll introduce you to a little girl who knows more than I do. She's a cutie and she sings for me and her name is Hildy Devereaux."

"Was he playing around?"

"That word covers too much ground, Gevvy. They were friendly. If they were ever in the hay, it wasn't here. I would have had a report." He looked suddenly older. "Need a bed?"

"I left the bag with the bell captain. Haven't tried for a room yet."

He picked up the phone and asked for the desk. "Ralph? What are we holding?" He listened for a moment. "Okay. A Mr. Gevan Dean goes in the suite on eight. Send a boy to my office with the key and the card."

Joe built us another drink. The boy came. I signed the card and described my bag and told him where I left it and asked him to bring the key back to me. We had some aimless talk about old times and old places. The boy came back and I tipped him. Joe went with me to his office door. "It's a hell of a world, Gev. I'll miss Kenny. He was one of the nice people."

27

It was nearly eleven when I went into the Copper Lounge. Business was very very good. Low lights gleamed on the bar, on the bare shoulders of women, on the forward-leaning, soft-talking, intense faces of their men. A girl in silver lamé sat at a little pastel piano in the light of a subdued spot, doodling old tunes, chatting and smiling up at a heavy man who leaned on the piano, a drink in his hand.

I found a stool at the bar and ordered a drink. The bits and pieces of conversation around me were in the tradition of boom town. It was the same record that had been played in the early forties.

"So we finally got it in carload lots out of Gulfport after Texas City turned us down . . ."

". . . told them if they wanted to hit their delivery dates on the nose, they could put on another shift like we had to . . ."

". . . the last time I was home it was the middle of February and how the hell do I know what she's doing while I'm being bounced all over the damn country . . ."

". . . look, why doesn't George bring the plane to Cleveland and that'll give us an extra day in Chicago . . ."

". . . so they furnish hotel suites complete with girls and then have a hell of a flap if you won't set delivery ahead to . . ."

This was the same record they'd played many years ago. I looked around at the male faces at the bar. Tension in the mouth, eyes moving quickly, pencil whipped out for a fast sketch on the back of a bar tab. ". . . Like this, see? Then you use extruded plastic for the sleeve, see? Then you don't have to sweat out deliveries on the metal stampings."

Operators. Angle boys. The expense-account boys. A lot of them were chasing the fast buck and the special privilege. But there were just as many who were in it because they loved the tension, the pressure, the excitement of it. In the old wars of long ago the sutlers were scorned. But not in these wars. A hundred-ton press is worth two battalions. One physicist can be worth two allies. The equations are new.

The girl at the piano bowed off into the gloom to a polite spattering of applause. A sallow man took her place and the spot slid away from him, moved ten feet to focus on a girl who stood at a microphone. She was small and she had long brown hair and gold tones in her skin and big, brown eyes. She bit her lip and smiled in an appealingly nervous fashion. She stood there until the conversations quieted down.

There was something helpless about her that made you want to give her your attention. She nodded in the direction of the piano, took a short, unobtrusive introduction, and then sang.

A ballad about loneliness and longing. The lyrics were tired and flat, but her voice, low and tender, and her manner, intimate and warm, gave the words a personal meaning to every man in the Copper Lounge. She was a pro and she was good and she didn't corn up the gestures or wag her body around the way amateurs do. Yet you were aware of her body, aware of the good lines of it. The dress was clever. Like a kid's first formal when you half looked at it, but then you saw how, in the fit and cut, it was very daring.

While I was adding my share to the loud applause, Joe Gardland edged in beside me and asked, "Like our Hildy?"

"Very choice, Joe. Very special."

He flagged a waiter and said, "Give Mr. Dean that deuce by the wall, Albert." He turned back to me and said, "Take the table, and I'll bring Hildy over after her turn."

After her songs were over, I saw her coming through the tables toward me, smiling. I stood up. She said, "I'm Hildy. Joe couldn't bring me. He had to send me." A waiter held her chair. "Ken spoke of you often, Gev."

At close range her features had that flavor of boldness typical of entertainers. She was no longer a shy child singing tender for the people. Entertainers are a separate breed. They have their own language and customs and tribal mannerisms. Any other person is enough to form an audience. I often wonder what they do when they are completely alone—or if they ever are.

"It was nice of you to come over."

"I sing the words other people write, Gev. It doesn't leave me any of my own to tell you how terribly sorry I am about Ken."

"Thank you, Hildy," I said, and my tone may have been a bit stuffy. "You sing other people's words very nicely indeed."

She tilted her head a bit on the side. "Thank you. I guess you're a lot like him, aren't you? You're kind of standoffish right now. Looking at me as if I were 'the other woman.'"

Some re-evaluation of Hildy was in order. "I don't know what my reaction is to you, Hildy. Mostly I don't know exactly what to say. Joe said Ken was troubled. I thought maybe—"

"Some of the trouble was me? I don't think so. He was a friend. We talked. If he'd wanted to put us on a different basis, I don't know what I would have said. It just never came up." She smiled a bit bitterly. "Which can be called a new experience for Hildy. Being given no chance to say no, I mean. I don't know yet if I liked it. I guess I did. He needed somebody around who didn't make any demands."

"That doesn't fit so well. Ken was never a moody guy."

"I never saw him otherwise, Gev. Something was nibbling him. I tried to get him to talk it out. He talked, but not enough. Ever."

"Did you ever get any clues?"

She had a pleasant trick of raising one eyebrow. Her arms were round, and her skin had that golden tone. "He carried his drinks pretty well. Too many drinks. One night he went over the edge a little too far. That was the night he told me dead men didn't have any troubles. You know the way a drunk talks. He said it like it was a big discovery. I told him he was being morbid. And he said that he could tell the medical profession what it felt like to be torn in half. That didn't make much sense to me. I got him into a cab and sent him home. The next night he was worried about what he might have said to me. He acted relieved when I told him he hadn't said anything I could understand."

"Torn in half. Funny thing to say. The only way it makes sense is if you think of it as being some decision he had to make and couldn't make. Like Solomon threatening to chop the baby in two hunks."

She drew on the table top with her thumbnail and stared at the little paper tent which advised us to order a Gardland sour. "I read once a out a lab where they trained rats to find their way out of mazes. Then they'd put them in a maze with no way out. The rats would finally lie down and chew their own feet."

"Was Ken about to do that?"

"Something like that. A guy with no way out. I wanted him to talk it out. I thought it would help. But he seemed to like just being with me, and he wanted me to stay in type. Sweet, dumb little songstress. So that's what I was, most of the time. When I stepped out of character it bothered him."

I reached over and put my hand on hers. "I'm glad you were around, Hildy."

She pulled her hand away slowly. "Don't, please. You'll make me cry and I don't want to. Let's get back to our guessing game, Gev. Was it wife trouble? I know there was trouble at the plant, but it didn't seem to bother him that he wasn't running the show out there."

I thought of Niki leaving me for Ken. And then, perhaps, leaving Ken for somebody else. I thought of her voice on the phone. It didn't seem possible. And yet, the night before I had found her with Ken, she had been all eagerness in my arms. All soft words and sighs. Maybe neither of us had known Niki.

"I don't know, Hildy. I just don't know."

"Sometimes the love bug is a virus, and after a while you go dead inside."

"I know that," I said softly.

She studied me for a few moments, head tilted again, eyebrow raised. "Is your whole family messed up?"

I saw then what Ken had seen in her: that capacity for

warmth and understanding which seems, always, to be the product of a very special kind of heartbreak. She said, "You're a stronger one than he was. You're not as much like him as I thought. Now I know why he missed having you around."

"Did he say that?"

"Yes, he said that, Gevan. And said he didn't blame you for not being around."

"Don't kid me, Hildy. I should have been around and I wasn't."

I wanted to believe what she said about Ken. I had to believe it.

She looked at her small jeweled watch. "I've got to go sing for the people, Gev."

She stood up and I stood up too. She was a very small girl. She looked up at me, biting her lip, speculative. I said, "You'll be back?"

"We've said what we had to say about Ken. And all you can give me now is a load of some of your own trouble, Gev."

"I wouldn't want to do that."

"You'd do it without trying to do it."

"You see a lot, don't you?"

"I guess. And this whole thing has made me feel older than hills. Old enough and tired enough so I don't want any new trouble. Come back some time, Gev. When things are straightened out for you, and when we can have some laughs."

"I will, Hildy."

Her hand rested in mine for a moment and this time her smile was shy. I watched her walk toward the mike, her small back very straight, her brown hair bobbing against her shoulders with the cadence of her walk. I left while she was singing about a love that would not die, her eyes glistening in the subdued spotlight. Her voice followed me out the door.

Dreams kept waking me up that night, and fading before I could grasp them. Each time I woke up I knew that Niki had been in the dream. But the words she had said were lost.

Chapter 4

The nine-o'clock telephone call interrupted my morning shower. Lester Fitch greeted me in a mellow, oiled voice and informed me that he would be pleased to purchase my breakfast for me.

I stood dripping, holding the phone. "Gevan?" he said.

"I'm here."

"Oh, I thought we were cut off. I'll wait right here in the lobby. I didn't get much chance to brief you on the current status of things at the plant."

That was just a bit too much. I didn't want my head patted by Lester Fitch, and I didn't want to listen to his large editorial we. It's odd how much of our lives we spend being polite to people in whom we have absolutely no interest. 'No' is a word which, if said at the right moment, is the greatest time-saving device in the world. I said it.

"What was that?" he asked, shocked and plaintive.

"No, Lester. Don't wait." I hung up.

It was Wednesday morning. If Lester knew, then Niki would know, and Mottling would know, and they would be interested in finding out who I intended to back. I was interested in knowing that myself. I told myself it was the reason I had come up, to make an investigation on my own. Duty to the family firm and all that. Four years of indifference, and then a sudden burst of dedication. But, last night, Joe and Hildy had given me another problem. Maybe there would be no answer to that one. Maybe it was locked forever in the dead brain of my brother. Sooner or later I would have to see Niki. But I wasn't ready yet.

Perversely, turning down Lester had improved my morning mood. I rode the elevator below the lobby floor just in case Lester might be hanging around in hopes of my changing my mind. I went out through the grill and up the steps onto Pernie Street. The rain had washed the air. The day sparkled. It felt good to be back where most of my life had happened. Even Pernie Street had a special meaningfulness. My high school class held the graduation ball at the Hotel Gardland. Ken was a sophomore when I was a senior. He attended too, and I couldn't remember the name of his date. Mine was named Connie Sherman. Somebody had a bottle and Ken and I nibbled on it a few times in the men's room. Later we took the girls down to the grill when the dance was folding. I had parked my car, a beat-up old Olds as big as a hearse, in a lot down Pernie Steet, so we went out the Pernie Street entrance.

There were some boys there we didn't know, probably North Side High, hanging around to make trouble with the southsiders. Some of them had tried to crash the dance earlier and were tossed out. As we came out, one of them, in the shadows, made a remark about Ken's date. It was very explicit and anatomical. Ken turned toward them and his date tugged at him and told him to ignore it. I didn't want trouble, not with the girls there. I think Ken was going to turn away, but he never got a chance. The sucker punch sent him sprawling. I shoved Connie toward the doorway. She used her head and grabbed Ken's date by the arm and they ran inside. Ken bounced up as one of them tried to kick him and grabbed the leg and spilled the guy on the sidewalk. Then I couldn't see what was happening because I was suddenly very busy. Somebody banged me under the eye and I swung back and missed and the scrap moved into the shadows. It was very confusing. I hit somebody solidly and got kicked in the leg. There was grunting, and the sounds of blows, and then I heard somebody making that distinctive sound of trying to suck air back into the lungs after getting hit in the pit of the stomach. I wondered with part of my mind if it was Ken. Somebody ripped my coat and I got hold of a wrist and heaved and sent somebody spinning out across the curb into the lights. Then there was a police whistle and men running out of the hotel. The ones we were fighting ran down Pernie Street. The police were going to take us in, but Connie was very convincing about what happened. We were a mess.

I remember how we got laughing so hard in the car I could hardly drive. My eye was puffed shut by the time we got home. And by the time the story got around school, there were nine of them and Ken and I had knocked out at least five. We smiled in silent, manly modesty, and I felt disappointed when the last saffron hues had faded from my eye.

That was one of the memories. The city was full of them. And the countryside where bike tires had purred, and we had known where to get horse chestnuts. Ken was in the memories. I returned to a present tense, a world in which Ken no longer lived. If his death had any reason or purpose, I had to find it. I had to find out why life had become tasteless to him, why his recent letters had been so troubled, oblique, almost disjointed. Niki and Ken and plant politics and the brute hammer of lead against skull. I wanted it all sorted out, and I thought of the trite analogy of a jigsaw puzzle. But this was one of those where pieces are missing. I sensed that they were all there, but too many of them were turned face down, so that I could not see the colors.

I had a drugstore breakfast and walked eight blocks through the women shoppers to Police Headquarters. I told the desk sergeant my name and said I wanted to talk to whoever was in charge of the investigation of the murder of my brother. He turned me over to a uniformed patrolman who took me down a hall, across an open court, and into another wing of the big building. We went up a flight of stairs and into a big room. There were long rows of oak desks, with men working at about half of them. The patrolman led me down to one. The small wooden sign on the desk said Det. Sgt. K. V. Portugal. The patrolman bent over and murmured something to him. Portugal glanced at me and gestured toward the chair pulled up beside his desk. I sat down. I thanked the patrolman and he walked away.

Portugal kept working, not rudely, but with air of a man getting routine details out of the way so he could talk in peace. He glanced at reports, scrawled his initials, dropped them in his 'out' basket. I guessed his age at about forty. He was a pallid, heavy man, and he looked as if his health was poor. His hair was a scurfy brown, and the flesh of his face hung loose from his cheekbones and the bridge of his nose, sagging in folds against his collar. He breathed heavily through his mouth and his fingers were darkly stained with nicotine. He finished the last document, and looked at me. His chair creaked. He took the cigar from his ash tray and relit it, turning it slowly over the flame of the kitchen match.

"You're the brother, eh? A sorry thing, Mr. Dean. A mess. Glad we could wrap it up so fast. What can we do for you?"

"I flew in last night. I read the newspaper account. I thought you could tell me the details."

"A phone tip came in. If it wasn't for informants, this business would be a lot rougher than it is." His voice was wheezy and pitched high. "We sent a squad car over to the north side and picked up this Shennary fella. We've got two witnesses to testify that Shennary left his room around ten Friday night and didn't come back until nearly two. The gun was in his room. Thirty-eight automatic. Hadn't been cleaned since it was fired."

He grunted as he bent over and pulled open the bottom drawer of his desk. He took out a Manila folder and opened it, took out a glossy print, and placed it in front of me. He used his pencil as a pointer.

"This here is a microphotograph from ballistics. This is the test slug, and this is the slug out of your brother's body. See how it's a perfect match. This Shennary is a punk. Picked up three times for armed robbery and did time twice. He was wanted for violation of parole. Here's his pretty face."

He slid the mug shot on top of the ballistics print. I picked it up. There was a double photograph, full face and profile, with a reproduction of fingerprints underneath, with print classification, and a reproduction of a typed slip giving vital statistics and criminal record. He looked to be in his middle twenties. He had dark eyes, deeply set, a lantern jaw, overlong, dark hair, and black brows that met above the bridge of his nose. He looked weak, shifty, sullen, and unremarkable. Looking at his face made Ken seem more dead, more completely gone.

"Paroled, you said?"

Portugal leaned back and frowned at his cigar and relit it. "I'm just a cop, not a social worker, Mr. Dean. Some people think they all ought to serve full time. I wouldn't blame you if you think so, seeing how this one killed your brother. But a lot of them get the parole and straighten out. It's exceptions like this Shennary who spoil it for the others. He must have convinced the parole board he was going to be okay, or he wouldn't have been out. He's a guy without pressure or contacts to do him any good. So he turns out to be a little man with a big gun and bad nerves, and that's too bad for him and for your brother."

"Could I get a look at him?"

Portugal shrugged. "If you want to, I guess so."

"I don't want to bother you."

"No trouble. Come on."

We went down the stairs and across the court to another wing. Portugal walked heavily, leaning forward, teeth clamped on the cigar. His suit was red-brown, shiny in the seat, the jacket wrinkled and hip sprung. An armed patrolman ran the elevator. Portugal asked for the top floor. There was a bull's-eye window in the door at the top floor and a man looked through at us and unlocked the door. The man grinned at Portugal and, as he went back to his green steel desk, said, "Aces back to back. Don't you ever get tired?"

"Ralphie, you know you can't beat aces with a pair of ladies. We are calling on my pal, Mister Shennary, esquire."

When the elevator went back down, the man called Ralphie unlocked the cell-block door. "Call me if Mr. Shennary wants his pillow fluffed up, or hot tea or anything."

Shennary was in the end cell on the left. The plaster walls were painted a pale blue. The window was covered with heavy mesh. He glanced up and got up from the bunk and came over to the door, wrapping thin, dirty fingers around the bars. He wore a gray outfit cut like pajamas.

"How are you on this lovely morning, Wally?" Portugal asked him.

Shennary glanced at me and back at Portugal. Obviously I meant nothing to him. His knuckles were white where he gripped the bars. "You get the right guy, did you?"

"You're it, Wally. Let's not kid each other."

"How many times I got to tell you it wasn't me? How many times, copper?" His voice was thin and high and it trembled.

"You're coming apart, Wally. Your nerves are going bad."

"Get that lawyer back here. Get him to come back. I've been telling you it's a frame. It stinks."

"This is the brother of the man you killed, Wally."

Shennary looked at me for long moments. He shook his head. "Don't let them give you that, mister. They're making it easy for themself. That's all it is. Look, I'm a loser. These guys, all they think about is keeping the books clean. Wrap everything up. So they grab the first guy the can find and that's me. Honest, I never in my life saw that gun until they take it out from under my shirts. That blond copper found it. That place hasn't got decent locks.

Anybody could put it there. Even the copper that found it. Look, mister, I'm not a moron. If I shoot anybody, I get rid of the gun, don't I? That figures, doesn't it? And I get out of town, don't I?"

"You were drunk," Portugal said heavily. "Pig drunk."

"Is there a law now a guy can't drink?"

"If he's on parole, there is. And you don't have a job, and you had a couple of hundred dollars. Where did that come from?"

"I confessed! I told you! So I knocked over a supermarket a couple weeks ago. Send me up for that. But no murder rap. You got to listen to me. Lita can tell you where I was. I told you all that. Why don't you listen to her?"

Portugal turned toward me. "Seen enough?"

I nodded. Shennary's voice followed us down the cell block, shrill and frightened. "Mister, they won't work on it because it's easier this way. And they don't care if they get the right guy. They just get somebody and make it stick and then the books are clean. Don't let him tell you. . . ."

We rode down the elevator. It had shaken me. I guess Portugal sensed that. He said, "They all go into that song and dance. 'Honest it wasn't me. There's some mistake.' That's the way their minds work."

When we walked into the courtyard Portugal said, "We think he was casing those fancy Lime Ridge houses and your brother surprised him. Wally was liquored up and jumpy and so he fired. They all put on an act. He'll crack before the trial and give us a statement."

"When will the trial be?"

"One of the assistant D.A.'s was over this morning and approved the file. We're closing him out and trial will be in the fall sometime."

"Who is that Lita he was talking about?"

"Girl friend. Italian girl. Lita Genelli."

"Where could I find her?"

He eyed me a bit warily. "Look, Mr. Dean, you're not falling for that act, are you? I see it all the time."

"No—I just wonder what kind of a man he is. Why he'd do a thing like that. I want to see what she's like."

"She's a dumb kid who wants to be a heroine like in the movies and swear Shennary was with her all the time."

"I really would like to talk to her."

He was obviously reluctant. He sighed audibly. "Okay, she's a car hop at a drive-in on the South Valley Road. It's called The Pig and It. They got a big pig on their sign, all made of neon."

"Thanks, Sergeant."

He picked a bit of cigar leaf off his underlip and rolled it in his fingers. "That's okay, Mr. Dean. We always feel kind of responsible when people like you get knocked off by some punk."

I watched him as he walked back toward his wing of the building. He looked tired, worn, shrewd, and disenchanted. I decided I'd have better luck looking the Genelli girl up later in the day. That would give me some time to find out what was going on at the plant, to learn the facts in the Mottling-Granby tussle. There were two good sources of reliable information and the first one was Tom Garroway, a smart young production engineer. I had promoted him twice before I left four years ago.

I called the plant from a drugstore booth near Police Headquarters and asked the main switchboard to connect me with the engineering offices. I asked the girl there if she could give me Mr. Garroway.

"Mr. Garroway left the firm some time ago, sir," she said. "Can I connect you with someone else?"

"This is a personal matter. Could you tell me where I can locate Mr. Garroway?"

"Please hold the line a moment, sir." She was gone for thirty seconds and came back on the line. "Hello? Mr. Garroway is with the Stringboldt Corporation in Syracuse, New York, sir. He left over five months ago."

I thanked her and walked slowly back to the hotel. It bothered me that Tom was gone. He was smart enough to know he had a good future with Dean Products, and he was the sort of man that companies must attract if they hope to maintain a competitive position. He was one of those intuitive engineering brains, the kind that have that extra sense which enables them to cut through to the heart of a problem, instinctively avoiding all those promising bypaths that lead nowhere. And though he was sometimes hard to control, he had a nice leadership talent.

There was a note waiting for me at the desk. It was in a sealed silver-gray envelope, addressed in Niki's familiar scrawl. I sat in one of the lobby chairs and held it to my nose. There was a faint perfume. I ripped it open: *Gev—Lester told me you're in town. Can't tell you how glad I am that you decided to come home. Most anxious to see you. I'll expect you for a drink at four-thirty at the house.—Niki.*

I crumpled the note, then smoothed it out and read it again. There was no uncertainty in it. Just the confident assumption that I would do exactly as she wished. I was expected to forget the rainy night of four years ago.

I remembered the first time I had seen Niki. That too had been a time of rain. One of those December afternoons when dusk comes at three. I came out of the offices, heading for my car, ducking my head against the misty rain. The girl came up to me, slim and dark, with a raincoat belted around her, rain beads caught in her hair.

"If your name is Dean, I have a question," she said. She looked and sounded angry. In a job spot like that you are always running into cranks. She didn't look like one.

"Come in out of the rain, then, and ask your question. I'm Gevan Dean."

"I like the rain. And I don't like a brush-off, and I'd like to know what you have to do to make an appointment with that Personnel Manager in there. If he says no, I'll accept that. But I don't want to be told no by some little sheep-eyed receptionist."

"Did you make an appointment?"

"I tried to."

I looked at her. She stood there in the rain, purse strap looped around her waist, hands shoved deep in the slash pockets of the raincoat, feet planted, eyes of hot blue like a gas flame. Very much girl. Very completely girl.

It started right there. She came with me and we talked it over at a little rainy-afternoon bar. I ignored my scruples and saw that she got the job she wanted. I knew it made a certain amount of office gossip, and marked her as my protégée, which meant she had to be better than good at her work.

She turned out to be crisply efficient, superbly trained. She wore neat black and navy suits, starched white blouses. But the sedateness of her office uniform seemed only to enhance the proud, free swing of her body when she walked down a corridor. She hit the office males like a pickax dropped from a roof. They found excuses to go to her desk, lean over her and repeat unnecessary instructions.

In that little bar she had told me her history. Orphaned at fifteen, she had lived with second cousins in Cleveland until she could make her own way. She had resigned her job in Cleveland because her married employer had begun to make a damn fool of himself, and she said she had picked Arland almost at random, and picked Dean Products because she wanted to be in a big firm, not in some small office again.

I kept seeing her around the offices. She always had a small grave smile for me, merely polite, with no connotation of intimacy. After I would see her, and then try to look at the papers on my desk, there would be a retinal image of her, as though I had looked at a bright light, and she would stride across the neatly typed papers, her skirt tightening across her hips with each stride, breasts high and firm under the starchy white blouse, dark hair alive against the nape of her neck.

One day I walked down the hall and she was at the water fountain. I walked toward her and she turned to face me as she straightened up, almost running into me, stepping back, saying, "Oh! I'm sorry, Mr. Dean."

"Would you go out with me? Tonight?"

"Would that be—wise, Mr. Dean?"

"I don't know about that. I don't care much, I guess. You don't have to say yes because I got you the job. You know that. You only have to say yes if you want to."

"I—I think I'd like to."

After that I saw more of her and thought more about her. There is an unwritten law about office girls. I ignored it. She had a small apartment. I tried to stay there with her, but she would have none of that. I realized I wanted to be married to her. I can't remember how I asked her. But I know she said yes, and after that the world was a very fine place. I spent too many hours a day thinking about her. She kept working, of course, and scrupulously avoided any familiarities in the office, yet the news was all over the plant, and the wolves gave up.

Then I found her in Ken's arms and I had not seen her since that night. And today I could see her at four-thirty, I could call on the widow, and have a drink with her, and look at the woman who had come between Ken and me and turned us into strangers for the last four years of my brother's life. She had lived with my brother in that house. It angered me to be summoned. Yet I knew I would go. Just to look at her again. Just to try to understand.

As I rode up to eight I remembered how we had planned the honeymoon, that night sitting in the car, the radio on, dash lights glowing green. The British West Indies, and I thought how it would have been, the long still nights, with the flavor of the day's sun still caught in her hair. Joe Gardland had told me two years ago in Miami that Ken and Niki had honeymooned in the Pacific Northwest. I was glad they hadn't gone to the islands.

I unlocked the door to my suite and went in. I stood and felt an odd prickling at the back of my neck. There is a special flavor about a room which is occupied, or where somebody has recently been. There is some atavistic instinct in us which quickens the senses. I found myself on tiptoe as I went to the bedroom door and glanced in. I looked in the bath and then, feeling a bit ridiculous, I yanked the closet door open.

I was alone, but I felt positive someone had recently left. I looked at my unpacked belongings. Everything seemed in order. But I realized that if somebody had been waiting to attack me, he would hardly have forewarned me by disarranging my clothing.

I felt in actual physical danger. Then it receded. Just because I had begun to see myself as the bold investigator of a murder, there was no reason to add all the other aspects of melodrama. I began to whistle. It sounded too loud in the room.

I ran water into the wash basin. I looked into the mirror and found myself looking over my shoulder out into the bedroom behind me. I made a face at myself in the mirror. Steady, boy.

Chapter 5

It was nearly noon when, from my hotel suite, I got the call through to Tom Garroway in Syracuse. It had taken them fifteen minutes to locate him out in the shop. It made me remember the times I had tried to find him, and the uselessness of trying to teach him to leave word where he'd be.

He came on the line. "Gev! It's damn good to hear your voice. Say, I read about Ken in the papers. I was going to write you. A damn shame, Gev. A sweet guy."

"Thanks, Tom. Can you talk or do you want to call me back?"

"I can talk. What's up?"

"Why did you leave? You had a good deal here."

"I know that. After you left, I got lonesome."

"Let's have it, Tom."

"Okay. When Mottling came into the picture it ruined things."

"How?"

"I don't like people leaning over my shoulder. I want to be given something and a chance to work it out my own way. If I had to spit, I had to make out a request in triplicate and get Mottling's initials on it. I could feel an ulcer

45

coming. Do it this way. Don't do it that way. Do it my way not your way, and report on the hour."

"No way to handle bull-headed Garroway."

"You're damn well told. This is a good outfit, Gev. Fine people. Hot problems. But I want you to know this. The day you toss out Mottling I'll come running back if you want me to. And two bits says Poulson and Fitz will come back too."

"Are *they* gone?"

"Man, yes. Where have you been? Mottling really took over. He pushed your brother around too. I don't know why Ken stood for it. Mottling and that tin soldier Dolson are thick as thieves. The next step is to hoist Grandby out of there; then all the old guard will be gone. I'm not sentimental about it, Gev. If you were a knuckle-head, I'd say stay the hell out. But you're one Dean who's entitled to run Dean Products. Why don't you take over again?"

"It's a little late for that, Tom."

"Hell, I'll come back and teach you the ropes. You can be a trainee. One of Garroway's bright young men."

"I'm a beachcomber. There's something with a real future."

His tone changed. "Seriously, Gev. No joke. I almost wrote you a few times. There's a smell around there. Like something crawled under the buildings and died. Maybe I should have stayed and fought. But it was safer to land another job. Give some thought to going back in there, Gev. Those years were good. I'd like it to be the way it used to be."

I thanked him. The odds were against my going back in. I hung up and called room service and ordered a sandwich sent up. I thought of what he had said. Even thought I'd tried to deny it for four years, when I had quit, I'd felt as though both hands had been cut off at the wrist.

Sure, it was just another corporate entity that would keep churning along whether Gevan Dean was there or not.

But I missed it. I missed the hot stink of coolant and oil, that rumble and chatter and screech of the production areas, where metal is peeled sleekly back from the high-speed cutting edges, and the turret lathes and automatic screw machines squat heavily and busy themselves with their robot operations. And it had been good to go into the shipping department and smell the raw wood of the big packing cases, and see the fresh-paint stencils which said DEAN PRODUCTS.

When the pressure was off, I'd go down to Receiving and watch the materials coming in, the sheets and the bar stock, the castings and forgings, the billets and pigs. Raw and semi-fabricated items would come in; they would leave as complete assemblies, machined, assembled, inspected, crated. It all started when some prehistoric genius squatted on his haunches and chipped out an ax head and lashed it to a piece of wood. It must have given him a good satisfaction when he swung the completed tool. And there was a satisfaction in directing the skilled operation that made Dean Products tick, which turned materials into something that could be hefted, used. The skill was the value you added.

I remembered how it used to be with my father. When a new item was going into production, his desk top would be littered with machined component parts. He'd spend a lot of time picking them up and turning them over and over in his hands, holding them just so, so the light would turn machined steel surfaces into tiny mirrors. There was always a pair of coveralls hanging in his office closet and he was supposed to put them on before he went out into the production areas. But something would go wrong and he would forget and go bulling down and wade into the trouble and get grease smeared. Then Mother would give him a mean time, and so would his secretary, old Miss Brownell.

Remembering Miss Brownell made me think of my second valid source of information. When ancient Miss Brownell had finally retired, I asked Hilderman to recommend someone from the stenographic pool, someone I could take into my office on trial. Hilderman had sent Joan Perrit to me, and I wondered if he had suddenly acquired holes in the head. She was nineteen, and gawky and nervous, and she plunged around the office with such a reckless desire to please that I was in constant fear she would fracture herself on the furniture or fall out the window. She was painfully shy. But she could make a typewriter sound like small boys running and holding sticks against a picket fence. And she could take down and transcribe every mumble and grunt in a ten-man conference where everybody interrupted everybody else.

Technical excellence was just part of her arsenal of talents. Inside of a month she knew my style of expressing myself so perfectly that I couldn't tell which letters I had dictated and which ones I had told her to handle. And she managed to fend off the pests, even those who would have gotten by Miss Brownell, without ever offending anybody, and without ever shooing away anyone that I wanted to see. She had schedules and timetables and appointments neatly filed away in her pretty head, and each morning when I came into the office there would be a typed notation on my desk, placed with geometric exactness atop the mail I should see. That notation would tell me not only the fixed appointments, but what was likely to come up.

She was a sweet kid, with dark red hair and a look of virginal freshness. She was so loyal it was embarrassing. On the morning I dictated my letter of resignation, she had to leave the office. She was gone a full ten minutes, and when she came back her eyes were reddened and swollen, but her voice was level and calm again as she read back to me the last sentence I had dictated.

I got her on the phone and her voice was just the same as on that last day. "I heard you were in town, Mr. Dean."

I wondered how much four years had changed her. "I wonder if I could talk to you, Miss Perrit."

"Of course, Mr. Dean. When?"

"Say this evening. After dinner sometime."

"Will nine o'clock at the corner of Martin and Lamont be all right? In front of the leather shop." I agreed. Though her voice had not changed, I knew she undersrtood I wanted information. Thus the quickness of her response was an indication she felt there was information to be given. I trusted her judgment.

After lunch I looked up car rental agencies in the phone book and found one quite close to the hotel. I rented a new Chevrolet sedan. I drove by the house where I was born, and headed south out of the city. At The Pig and It I found that Lita Genelli was off duty. I drove through the countryside for a time, parked near a place where we had always had family picnics. But they had changed everything. The elms and willows were gone. The area had been graded and filled. The pool where I caught the six-pound brown trout was gone. They had straightened and widened the highway, and there was a big drive-in movie where Ken and I used to play at being Indian scouts, trying to wiggle through the sun-hot grass until we were close enough to yell and leap out. I remembered the way the grass used to smell, and the way the picnic potato salad tasted, and the time Ken had tied the braids of a female cousin to a tree limb, and the way the line had hissed in the water when the brownie had taken the worm.

Now there was a stink of fast traffic, and a disheveled blonde on the drive-in ads, and a roadside place where they sold cement animals painted in bright colors.

And I kept glancing at my watch and thinking about Niki. A bitter excitement kept lumping in my throat. I drove slowly, and it was exactly four-thirty when I drove through the gateposts of the house Ken had built for Niki in the Lime Ridge section. The driveway was asphalt, and it was wide and satiny and curving. It led up the slope toward the house, to a turn-around and a parking area near the side entrance.

It was the house I would have wanted to build for her. A long, low white frame house, in an L shape, with a wide chimney painted white, with black shutters, with deep eaves. The spring grass was clipped to putting green perfection. High cedar hedges isolated the property from the neighbors. The three-car garage was separated from one wing of the house by a glassed-in breezeway, and beyond the garage was an apartment affair which I imagined belonged to the help. The house sat quiet and content in the spring sun, and it looked like a house people could be happy in.

There were two cars parked near the garage. One was a big fin-tailed job in cruiser gray, and the other was a baby blue Jag convertible with the top down. Both cars had local licenses, and I guessed the big one had been Ken's and now both of them were Niki's. And the house was Niki's, and all the manicured grounds, and all the cedar hedges. A very fine take for the lass who had stood in the rain with her eyes ablaze on that December afternoon. Such thoughts helped still my nervousness.

I pressed the bell at the side door and a pretty little Negro maid in a white uniform let me in and took my hat, murmuring that I should go straight ahead into the living-room and she would tell Mrs. Dean I was here. It was a big room, and quiet. Low blond furniture upholstered in nubbly chocolate; lime yellow draperies framing a ten-foot picture window that looked down the quiet expanse of the lawn. A small bar had been wheeled to a convenient corner. There were fresh flowers, built-in shelves of books in bright dust jackets, wall-to-wall neutral rug. I lit a cigarette and tossed the match behind the birch logs in the fireplace. I looked at book titles. I looked out the window. The room was empty and silent, and I could hear no sound in the house. I felt the jitters coming back. I looked out the big window and wondered if they had stood there in the evening, his hand on her waist, her head on his shoulder, before going to their bed. And had they read any of the books aloud? And had he gotten up to poke at the fire while she sat in uxorial contentment. . . .

"Gevan!" she said. She had come into the room behind me and I had not heard her. I turned, my mind foolishly blank, staring at her as she walked tall toward me, her hands outstretched, smiling.

Four years had changed Niki. The years had softened the young tautness of her figure. Her waist was as slim as ever, but under the strapless dress of some bright fabric, there was a new warm abundance of breast and hip. Her cheeks were the familiar flat ovals and her mouth was the same as it had been, deeply arched, sensuous and imperious.

She moved in the same gliding walk like the pace of some splendid animal. She walked toward me for an endless time while, with all senses sharpened, I heard the slither and whip of the hem of the heavy skirt and scented her familiar perfume.

"You've changed your hair," I said inanely.

"Oh, Gevan, what a sparkling greeting!" When she said my name I saw the remembered way she said the v, white teeth biting at her underlip, holding the consonant sound just a bit longer than anyone else ever did.

I tried to take one of her hands and shake it in polite formality, but her other hand found my wrist, long warm fingers wrapping tightly around it, and she stood like that, smiling at me, tall and rounded, that black hair sheening like spilled ink.

"It's nice to see you, Niki." My voice was husky.

She closed her eyes for a moment. "It's been a bit too long," she said as she released my hand and turned away with an uncharacteristic awkwardness. I saw she shared my nervousness. It made her more plausible, made her more believable as the girl who had said she would marry me so long ago. She had betrayed me, and in her manner was awareness of that. Somehow, I had fallen into the habit of attributing to her a perfect poise, a bland denial of any guilt. To see her now, unsure of herself, uncertain of her ground, even perhaps a bit afraid of me, destroyed that false image of her. It was right she should feel guilt. In some obscure way she had destroyed Ken. She was the evil luck of the Dean brothers. And the warmth I felt for a few moments faded.

Perhaps she sensed that. She turned with a controlled smile and said, "You're looking preposterously healthy, Gevan."

"I'm a beach boy. A muscle-flexer."

"With no dissipations? I'm quite good at martinis these

days." It made me remember the burnt-acid abominations she had mixed for us long ago.

"Prove it."

I sat and watched her at the small bar. The room was silent. Ice tinkled. She measured with small girl intentness. She swirled the cocktail in the crystal bubble of the shaker, poured carefully, brought me the first drink. I stood up and took it and sipped. "You're better than you used to be," I said.

She sat opposite me with her drink. We were walking a polite and formal line. On either side were quicksands.

"You have a very nice home, Niki."

"It's too big, actually. Ken wanted a big house. I'll sell it, I guess."

"And then what?"

"Go away. Get sort of—straightened out. And come back here. Stanley says I should take an active interest in the company."

The silence grew. It was not a comfortable silence. There was a tingling to it, a nervous suspense. I liked her hair better the way she used to wear it. The present effect made her face look more fragile, but it also gave her a look of false composure.

"Do you like Florida, Gevan?"

"Very much."

"You'll go back, I suppose."

"Yes, of course."

And again there was the silence of the big room. She sipped her drink. I saw her round throat work. She looked down into her glass, frowning. "We could talk and talk and talk and never say a thing—if we keep on this way."

"This is the safe way."

She looked up sharply. "Is it? Then I'll say it. I should never have married Ken."

The silence came back but it was altered. It had changed.

"Don't step out of character," I said. "Remember, you're the shattered widow."

"I know I hurt you. I know how badly."

"Do you?"

"Don't try to hurt back. Not right now. Later, but not right now. Let me say this."

"I'll listen to you."

"Six months after I married him I knew it was a mistake. But he loved me, and I'd hurt enough people. I tried to make him as happy as I could."

"Not very successfully, from what I hear."

"Then you know how he was the last few months. I couldn't help that, Gevan. I tried. God, how I tried! But he—sensed how it had all gone wrong. He guessed I was pretending. But I never told him I regretted marrying him."

I set my empty glass aside. "That raises a pretty question, Niki. Why did you marry him?"

"For a long time I didn't know why I did that—dreadful thing to you. To us. Because what we had was so good, Gevan. So right for us. I finally figured it all out."

"With diagrams?"

She leaned forward. "You and I are both strong people, Gevan. Terribly strong. Dominants, I guess you call it. Ken was weaker. He needed me. He needed strength. He appealed to something—maternal, I guess. You would never need me that way. My strength seemed to respond to his weakness. He made me feel needed."

"And I didn't."

"Not in the same way. It was so queer the way it began. It crept up on us. We weren't expecting it. And then it got worse and worse and we had to find some time and place to tell you how it was with us. We were going to tell you that same night when you walked in. But having it happen that way made it all sort of nasty. I'll never forget that night, or the way you looked."

"It hasn't exactly slipped my mind, Niki."

"I want to be honest with you. I've had to be dishonest for so long. I'll tell you how it is. I miss him. I miss him dreadfully. He was sweet. But I didn't love him. So I can't miss him the same way I've missed you for four years. I can't look at you while I say this. If things had gone on, Ken and I would have separated. And then—darling, I would have come to you and begged forgiveness. I would have come to you on any basis you wanted." She lifted her head then and looked directly at me. "I would have come to you, Gevan."

I looked back into her eyes. They looked darker. "Is that supposed to help?" I asked her.

"It's too late, isn't it?" she asked. Her voice was soft and remote. It was less question than statement, an acceptance of a mistake which had forever changed our special world. "Much too late," she said, turning away from me.

I knew how quickly and how easily I could reach her. The impulse brought me to my feet before I could bring it under control, my empty glass bounding and rolling on the silence of the rug. She sat with her head turned away from me. I saw tendons move in the side of her throat. Except for that small movement, she did not stir for the space of ten heartbeats. Then, with a careful precision she put her glass on the table and rose to her feet with a remembered effortlessness and came over to me, her eyes downcast, smudged by the darkness of her lashes. I heard a hush of fabric and a hiss of nylon. She stopped, inches from me, and slowly raised her glance until, with the mercilessness of a blow without warning, she looked into my eyes.

After that instant of recognition her eyes lost their focus; her mouth trembled into slackness and her lips, wet-shining, seemed to swell as they parted. Her head lolled, heavy, sleepy, on the strong and slender neck, and her knees bent slightly in her weakness. Her body seemed to become flaccid, heavier, sweeter, softer with the inadvertent arching of her back, and there were tiny, almost imperceptible, movements of which I knew she was, as she had told me long ago, completely unaware, small, rolling pulsations of belly, hip and thigh.

With us it had been a strong and a compulsive attraction, a grinding feverish spell that always began in this humid hypnotic way, building to an urgency that made frantic use of the nearest couch or bed or rug or grassy place. It was always beyond thought and plan, and in a shamefully few moments she had taken me back into our rituals as though nothing had ever come between us. I found I was grasping her by the upper arms, in an ancient sequence, closing my hands with a force that twisted and broke her mouth and propelled the heat of her breath against my throat in a long hawing sound of pain and wanting. Under the strength of my hands I felt the warm sheathings of firm muscles as she strained to break free. It was one of our contrived delays. She rolled her head from side to side with an almost inaudible moan. I knew how violently she would come into my arms the instant I released her, how harsh and glad would be her cry, how astonishingly strong her arms would be, how hotly sweet the heavy mouth would taste, how all of her tallness would be in urgent, rhythmic, helpless movement.

Tires made a droning sigh on asphalt and stopped outside. A car door slammed. I held her until I felt the straining go out of her arms, and then I released her. I watched her come back to the objective world. Her mouth healed itself and her eyes became quick and her body straightened and tightened into formality. After a purely animal sensation of fury at my loss, I felt all the gladness come. I knew I would not have stopped. Nor could she. By accident I had been delivered from a sweaty interlude that would have shamed me beyond my ability to forgive or excuse myself.

She touched her hair and looked at her watch. "It's Stanley Mottling," she said. "I forgot I'd asked him to stop by." She tilted her head and looked at me in a challenging way, arched and roguish. "It isn't really too late, darling."

"For a moment I almost forgot it was. Go greet the nice man. What does he drink? I'll start fixing it."

I was puddling the sugar in a teaspoon of water when Stanley Mottling came in. No one had described him to me. I had expected one of those hard-jawed, little terrier types, with nerves drawn tight and sharp and quick. Mottling ambled in and was introduced. He was vast and rangy,

tweedy and shaggy. He looked sleepy . . . a young forty
with mild, watchful eyes, and, in tweeds that looked slept
in, there was an upper drawer flavor to the way he looked
and handled himself. He was at least six-four, and his
handshake was firm.

"Nice to know you, Mr. Dean. Damn shame it had to
take a mess like this to bring you back here. Hope we can
get along as well as Ken and I did."

I said trite things while I tried to figure him out. The guy
was likable. He had charm and ease of manner without
seeming to be conscious of either. He also seemed very
much at home. Though he had been in the room only a few
moments, he had the air of host rather than guest.

I took the drinks over and he sat facing Niki and me on
the other couch. The two couches were at right angles to the
fireplace with a squat cocktail table between them.

We said pleasant nothings while I decided on one fast and
definite gambit which might teach me something about the
man.

"I was disturbed, Mr. Mottling, to learn Tom Garroway
left us."

He nodded. "It was a hell of a shame. A good man. The
kind we ought to make a special effort to keep. If there'd
been less pressure, I would have tried to re-educate him. He
was spoiled."

"Spoiled! For what?"

He smiled. "Mr. Dean, you've just let yourself in for a
short lecture on one of my pet management theories. I feel
that industrial techniques have advanced beyond the point
where any one man can be given a production problem to
work out in his own way. I believe in operation on a team
basis. Suppose, for example, I have a tool-design problem,
a tricky cutting edge for high-speed operation. I want to
form a team consisting of a mechanical engineer, a
metallurgist, and a practical shop man to lick it. It saves
time because what they come up with will have a minimum
of bugs. If it is a quantity situation, I want somebody from
purchasing on the team too, so that they'll specify some-

thing we can get without too much delay. Tom Garroway wouldn't work that way. And I didn't have time to re-educate him."

It was one of those things that sounds perfectly plausible if you say it fast enough. A fine theory—and I didn't like it. "Same problem with Fitz and Poulson?" I asked casually.

His eyes narrowed just a bit, and for a moment the real Mottling spoke. "I keep men around me who work with me, Dean, not against me." The real Mottling was a most impressive organism. Cold, direct, tough, and ruthless. A deity who would countenance no atheism. Then the mask was back, and he was again, a big, shambling, tweedy guy, mild and amiable, pipe smoker, bird dog fancier.

"I understand you've made yourself quite a record, Mr. Mottling."

He shrugged. "A lot of luck. I've managed to go into companies where they've been too close to some very obvious problems. Too close to them to be objective about them. And pointing out the obvious is no indication of genius."

"Then we had an obvious problem too?"

"Very. Your grandfather set up certain organizational matters in accordance with his own theories of management. Your father left those unchanged and added more superstructure of his own. Then you and your brother glued on some more. As a result there were no clear-cut lines of responsibility and authority. The place was running by ear, or by tradition, I suppose you could say."

It was a callous dismissal of everything my father had done, of the way he had held the firm together during the dark days when competitors were going into receivership with monotonous regularity. I felt annoyance and Niki made a half-gesture that caught my eye. I glanced at her and saw on her face a reflection of my own distaste for that approach. I felt close to her in that moment, then wondered if her annoyance was based on her desire to have Mottling make the very best of impressions on me. That made me feel cool toward her again, cool and wondering what her stake was—in Mottling.

"It may have been running by ear, as you say, but running as a successful and profitable enterprise," I said. "You are aware of that."

He smiled, patronizing me. "Of course. We can't afford to continue on that basis. I've been clearing out the dead wood, redefining lines of responsibility and authority, setting up standard production controls and ratios of accomplishment. All under your brother, of course. Now, whether I follow through with the program is up to you. From what I've seen, you did an adequate job when you were here. Within, of course, the handicaps under which you had to work. I believe you should let me show you what I've done so far. Then you will have the facts. Facts which will be important to you in any decision you may make."

It was very direct, a broadside with heavy weapons, yet it had gotten him neatly over the hurdle. Niki leaned back, her expression bland and interested. I sensed relief in her. A proprietary relief. It was possible she had succumbed to a virus which is rare among beautiful women—the power drive in an industrial sense. Obviously she could not go down there and head up the company. But if she had a capable alter ego, under full control—a man like Mottling—that would mean that her protestations of lack of knowledge about the firm and the work and the legal angles were a smoke screen to keep me from guessing her true purpose. If Mottling could be controlled, by the use of her obvious feminine weapons—and Ken had become relatively immune to them. . . .

"Why did Ken bring you in here in the first place?" I demanded, trying to match his directness.

"He saw the expansion coming, saw how space age contracts would grow. And he sensed the job would outgrow him. He had given up trying to get you back here. He had to find someone. I was recommended to him. I happened to be relatively free. He gave me almost complete authority. It was a sound management decision on his part."

"And I should do the same, I suppose?"

He grinned, spread his big hands in a quick gesture. "I didn't say that. I said you should check the facts."

The man was likable. "That seems fair enough. One thing bothers me, though. If you're doing so well, why should you have so much opposition from one group of shareholders?"

Mottling frowned and loaded a pipe, slowly and carefully. "It's a bit difficult to explain, Mr. Dean. In spite of the size of Dean Products, it has always had the flavor of a local concern. Local ownership. Local talent. And, forgive me, the usual low-pressure operation that invariably accrues from such background. I've been ruthless. I am an outsider. I keep the pressure on. Their response is emotional. To them I am a foreigner coming in here, pushing nice people around. Mr. Karch, who has been instrumental in organizing the minority stockholders, and getting the backing of your uncle with his block of stock, is annoyed because I fired his son, who was incompetent. Granby, I am afraid, is a symbol of the comfortable past. I'm a symbol of the uncomfortable future. The human animal resents change."

He was so sweetly reasonable. He made it all fall into place. Then he proved his timing was excellent. He glanced at his watch. "I'm afraid I've got to go back to the office."

"Oh, Stanley!" Niki said.

"Can't be helped, Niki. Very nice to have seen you, Mr. Dean. And thanks for the chance of telling you, a little bluntly I'm afraid, exactly how I feel about the job. Can I expect to see you in the morning?"

"I'll probably be over. I don't want to get in your way. I'll just poke around, if that's all right with you."

"I think that would be the best way. I don't want you to get the impression that I want to edit the trip in any sense. I don't believe you'd let me do that anyway."

We shook hands and Niki walked him to the door. I heard the low murmur of their voices in the hallway. They were both delightfully plausible. I wondered if they were congratulating each other on how well Gevan Dean had been handled. I wondered if they were setting a time and place for their next assignation. There was an undercurrent of closeness between them, of uniformity of viewpoint, as though, somehow, they were members of the same club, knew the grip and the password and the club songs. Maybe between them it was very simple. A big profitable company is a nice thing to pick up and walk off with.

I resented feeling as if I had been an audience of one at a special play put on by competent actors. I resented being steered. I resented liking the guy. I resented being able to look at Niki and still want her. I resented knowing I should leave here, too.

She came back and I heard his car going down the drive. "Do you like him, Gevan?"

"Very impressive."

"And terribly nice. He's let down his hair with me. He told me that he hates to hurt people, but he had learned that it has to be done to get a job done."

"Protesting too much, wasn't he?"

"Please don't be nasty, Gevan. And when you go to the plant, please try to understand his position. You'll need a special pass to get into C Building. From Colonel Dolson. And I'm positive that if you give the Colonel a chance he will speak very highly of Stanley."

"What goes on in C Building?"

"Oh, it's some kind of a secret contract. I don't know what they're making. I remember Ken saying they had to buy an awful lot of special equipment for that contract, and Colonel Dolson came the day the contract was signed, and a security officer, a Captain Corning, arrived the same week. I guess there's a big military staff there now."

"Niki, who recommended Mottling to Ken?"

"I haven't the faintest idea, Gevan."

I frowned down at my drink. "I'd like to know."

Her voice changed. "Let's not talk about the plant and Mottling and all that."

"Put some violins on the sound track, and we can talk about us."

She sat beside me. She leaned far forward, the black hair

60

spilling to one side. I saw the tiny dark V of soft hair at the nape of her neck, the shift of muscle under the creamy skin of her shoulder as she crooked her arm, resting her forehead on her forearm. She was close to me. I wanted to lay my hand against her smooth back, run my finger tips up to the nape of her neck, feel the warmth of her and the breathing. She was near me, warm, very alive—somehow more immediate than life, and more dramatic. The stillness had changed again. We were back in a soundless world. I saw her faint shudder.

"Tears?" I asked.

She gave an abrupt nod and did not speak. She did not seem real to me. She seemed more like something I used to dream. I put my hand on her shoulder. I felt the starting tremor of her, and that stillness in her as though she had stopped breathing. I remembered all those beach house nights, when I would be alone and think of Ken and her together, and torture myself by envisioning them in all the gaudy forms of love, all her animal torments.

I knew once again that all this breathing aliveness was mine to take. She had married Ken. This was their house. He lay in earth between bronze handles on padded satin. I took my hand away. She stood up in one unbroken movement, in one sleek flex of thighs, turning away from me to go to the mantel, her back to me. I put my empty glass on the coffee table. It made a decisive click in the silence of the room.

I stood up and she turned. Her mouth looked soft, but there was an expression on her face that seemed to hint of conspiracy—as though we had again come closer during this time of silence. I resented it.

"I'll be running along."

"But you'll come back, Gevan." It was half question and half statement of fact.

"If there's anything to discuss, Niki."

She smiled then. A woman-smile, full of conquest. It made me feel young, crass and inexperienced. The advantage had passed to her, and that was something I had not intended should happen.

I walked down the hallway. The maid brought me my hat. I drove down the curving driveway. I slowed and glanced back. She stood in the big window, watching me leave. There was an immobility about her, as though she planned to stand there for a very long time, as though the next time I came up the drive she would be standing in exactly that same place, waiting for me. I wondered if I would have the strength not to come back. Ken married her and was killed, and though it made no sense, I knew I had to hold her emotionally responsible for it, had to keep my awareness of that blame, or there was no power that would keep me from returning. She would wait there for me, and she had made it very clear.

I drove too fast. This was happening the wrong way. It should have happened the way she had told me it might, for them to drift apart and for her to come to me. That would have been simple. Make her pay for the lost years. Make her humiliation complete, and then build from there. But Ken had died and everything was confused. It could never be clear cut now. In death, he sat silently between us, as though I had reached around him to place my hand upon her.

Chapter 6

At nine o'clock I double-parked in front of the leather store. Joan Perrit was looking into the display window. I touched the horn ring and she turned and came quickly across the sidewalk, between two parked cars. I reached over and opened the door for her. She slid in quickly, smiling, pulled the door shut, and then held her hand out without hesitation. The street lights touched her face. She had grown into a woman. There was no formlessness in her face. It was cleanly structured, the bones delicate and good.

"It's nice to see you, Joan."

"I'm glad you came back, Mr. Dean." Her voice was softer, pitched lower than I remembered. "I'm sorry about your brother. It was a terrible thing." She had new poise and assurance.

I turned the corner slowly. "Is there some place we can go and talk, Joan?"

"Go out South Cleveland, Mr. Dean. There's a little bar just over the city line that's nice."

It seemed odd to have her beside me. It was a relationship not possible when she had worked for me. I had planned a sort of jovial avuncular approach to ease the nervous intentness I expected. But she was relaxed, smartly dressed, decisive. I stopped for a red light, and she leaned forward and pushed in the dash lighter, opened her purse to find cigarettes. I looked at her and liked the sheen of the dark red hair.

"You better call me Gevan, Joan." That sounded banal, and made me realize I was less at ease than she was.

"I guess I already do, subconsciously. Anyway, it doesn't seem strange, Gevan. I'm Perry, mostly, to my friends. Joan or Joanie at home. I'm more used to Perry."

"Perry, then. You understand, of course, that I wouldn't have done this if you were Mottling's secretary. But the switchboard gave me Granby's office when I asked for you."

"Isn't that six of one and half a dozen of the other?"

"I guess so. I didn't think of it that way. But you *did* agree to meet me."

"I would have done that no matter who I was working for, Gevan."

"How do you mean?"

"I'm still your secretary at heart, I guess. The girl's first big job, or something. After you left, I was sent back to the stenographic pool. Then when Mr. Granby's girl left, he requested me. But—I think of you as part of the company, and I think of personal loyalty as being first to you, Gevan." She laughed and it was a good sound. One of those warm laughs that fill the throat. "When I think of what you put up with before I learned the score!"

"You learned fast."

"That's the place ahead, on the left."

I waited for oncoming traffic, then cut across and parked diagonally in front of the place. It was small, with soft lighting, hushed piano, well-dressed customers, help that moved with professional competence. I left my hat at the tiny checkroom and followed her down between the tables to a table for two. I saw how she walked, saw how tangle-footed awkwardness had been transmuted into leggy grace. The waiter took her gin and tonic order and mine for Scotch on the rocks. She glanced around the room as she took off her gloves. I held a light for her cigarette and looked directly into her eyes, realizing that it was perhaps the first time I had ever really looked at her. Her eyes shifted away and I thought I saw a slight trembling of her cigarette as she lifted it again to her lips.

"You're so tan, Gevan. You make all these people look bleached. As if they've been left out in the rain."

"I remember a vacation when you came back with a good tan."

"I'm lucky. Most redheads just burn and burn and peel and peel. I remember that vacation. I didn't even want to take it. I was afraid the plant would fall down or something if I went away."

"Officious?"

"Well—earnest." She lifted her glass. I looked at her ring finger and saw it was unadorned, and my mild pleasure surprised me.

"Should I start earning my drink?" She asked me.

"Go ahead, Perry."

She frowned and stubbed out her cigarette. "It isn't terribly complicated. Mr. Mottling came in and from the first day, he started getting hold of the reins. He pushed your brother out of the way, and your brother didn't seem to mind. He seemed relieved, almost. Mr. Mottling fired everybody in sight who disagreed with his policies. He couldn't fire Mr. Granby, because Granby is an officer of the corporation. But the conflict between them was very obvious months ago. Your brother's death brought it out into the open. The battle lines were already set. By Saturday, the day after your brother's death, both sides started to move. Mrs. Kendall Dean is backing Mr. Mottling. The Chairman of the Board, Mr. Karch, with your uncle on his side, is backing Walter Granby. The meeting is set for next Monday morning. And you actually hold the balance of power, Gevan. Both sides are going to try to get you to vote with them. I don't know if there's been any pressure yet. I mean aside from Mr. Fitch going down there with that proxy form. I knew that wouldn't work."

"How did you know that?"

"When I worked for you, I knew what you thought of Mr. Fitch. And I knew—why you left, of course. And I know how you like to know all the facts before you make a decision. So I knew it wouldn't work."

"That's more than they knew. There was some pressure today, Perry. Niki asked me out. She arranged for Mottling to arrive while I was there."

"What do you think of him, Gevan?"

"Very impressive. What do you think of him?"

"A secretary's opinion?"

"The opinion of an orderly mind, Perry."

She turned her glass slowly, her lips pursed. "I think he's a good executive. If he has a weakness, it's with people. He gets results, but gets them through fear instead of loyalty."

"I'd think that would make him less effective."

"It doesn't seem to. But there's one thing—" She smiled over at me. "It's too vague to talk about."

"Hunches are pretty valid sometimes."

"Gevan, I read all about him in the paper when he came here. The things he'd done. The jobs he's had. He's had bigger jobs than this one, Gevan. He's got a good reputation. I just don't see why he should be so—well, so tensed up about Dean Products. It doesn't seem as if there could be enough at stake for him. But I shouldn't be sitting her talking about things on the management level. I'm out of my depth and you know it."

"I'm not too sure. If you were me, would you support Granby?"

"No."

"Mottling then, in spite of this feeling you have about him?"

"No, Gevan. Neither of them. Mr. Granby is financial. The plant needs a production man at the top. He knows that, so I'm not being disloyal."

"Then who?"

She tapped a cigarette on the back of her hand. Her voice was utterly calm. "You, of course."

"Now wait a minute—"

'The whole Granby vote could be switched to you in a minute, Gevan."

"I haven't got a tenth of Mottling's experience. I've spent four years getting out of practice."

"I haven't been swimming in two years. I don't think I'd drown if I went tomorrow. I think you owe it to yourself, Gevan, but more than that you owe it to the firm."

"Maybe you've forgotten why I left," I said angrily.

"Oh, everybody remembers why you left, Gevan. Your brother stole your girl and you went marching off in a big dramatic huff."

"My God, that makes it sound juvenile!"

"Wasn't it—just a little?" she asked mildly.

"My personal life isn't up for discussion," I said.

I saw the quick hurt in her eyes and felt ashamed of myself.

"You asked me for my opinion, Gevan."

"I know, but—"

"And I couldn't give my opinion without saying something personal. I'm sorry if it bothered you. Not way down deep sorry. Just surface sorry, because I still think your relationship to Niki is pertinent. It effects what will happen at the plant."

I know I glared at her. Her eyes didn't waver. I managed a weak smile. "Okay, Perry. I asked your opinion and got it. Thanks."

Her answering smile was good. "I don't want to push my luck, Gevan, but do you still feel the same way about—her?"

"I don't know. I came back with the idea of—hating her, I guess, but that word is a little too strong. I saw her. Whatever it was in the beginning—in the very beginning—attraction, desire, what have you—that's still there."

I ordered another round. Her smile was a twisted thing, a look close to pain. "I used to hate her, Gevan. And that word is too weak."

"You! Why?"

She looked away. "I guess it's a common thing. Getting a massive crush on the first boss you have all to yourself. A kid crush. An office infatuation. My God, I was young, Gevan. If you'd asked me to jump out the window, I wouldn't have waited to raise the sash. When you started going out with her, everybody knew it. Everybody knew you'd gotten her the job. It hurt when you started taking her out. But I told myself it was just one of those things. You'd get tired of her. Nothing to worry about. Did it show, Gevan? What I was feeling?"

"I thought you used to blush a lot and knock things over, but I didn't think of that reason."

"I used to think it showed. And I used to think you were laughing at me. Maybe telling your friends about the kid stenographer with the crush on her boss."

"It didn't. And I wouldn't have told anyway."

She balanced her chin on her fist. "Oh, I had it all worked out. A real script. One day you were suddenly going to look at me: I mean *really* look at me. And you would be astounded such incredible charm and beauty had been underfoot all this time and you'd been too blind to see it. You would make a speech, and I would simper, and then we would clinch and walk into the sunset together."

"Perry, I never—"

"I was an awful little fool, Gevan. Every night I prayed that tomorrow would be the day. But it never was, of course. I thought I was going to die when I heard about the engagement. That was a dreadful winter and spring. You know, you used to ask me clumsy questions—about girl things. Colors and so on. And I knew you were buying things for her. I couldn't stop hoping you two would bust up. Then you did. It was like the sun coming out. I lay on my bed and laughed out loud, I was so happy. But you went away."

"And you got over it."

"Not quickly, Gevan. I wrote you fifty letters and tore them all up. I dreamed of running away and coming to see you. How do crushes die, anyway? I don't know. You have to dream so many useless dreams and get so many pillows damp, and walk just so far in the rain, and then one day you are over it, and it is all like something pressed in a book and you know how ridiculous you've been. Gevan, it was partly your fault, because you were so very nice with me when I was green. So gentle and understanding. So very patient. You know, I used to feel actually physically dizzy when you'd call me into the office."

"Good Lord!" I said.

She laughed. "Oh, *don't* look so alarmed. I'm not the same person I was."

It wasn't easy to adjust to this new Joan Perrit. I had seen her as a shy, awkward, nervous girl. I had never seen or suspected the spirit underneath. While she had told me about herself, she had become completely alive, her face mobile, gestures quick, voice vibrant.

"I wish I'd known it at the time."

"No you don't, Gevan. I was a very silly girl."

"Then maybe I wish it was still going on."

She tilted her head. "Isn't that a rather odd thing to say?"

"I'm sorry. I spoke before I thought. I guess you have all that—affection focused on somebody else by now."

"Actually, no."

"But I'd think you'd want to have—" I stopped just short of working myself into an impossible corner and realized she was laughing at me, and I blushed.

"The place for the working girl is home," she said, looking at her watch. I signaled the waiter. She told me her address and how to find it. It was a narrow, quiet street in an old residential section. We had a last cigarette in the car. She said, *"Do* think seriously about coming back to work, Gevan. I think of you down there in Florida, and I think of what a waste it is."

"I've been out too long. I just want to stay around long enough to swing my vote in the right direction, and then I'll go back. I—I'd like to see you again before I go back, Perry."

"Why?"

The blunt question irritated me. "Because maybe I had a good time tonight."

"Much to your surprise? Good night, Gevan. Don't bother to walk me to the door."

She shut the car door and was gone. The hall light in the house was on. I saw her silhouetted against it, saw the door open. She turned and waved and went into the house. I drove slowly away, thinking about her. It was both amusing and flattering to know how she had once felt. She had changed into a handsome, poised young woman. It was odd to learn you had lost something you never knew you had.

I found the street I wanted and turned south, toward the South Valley Road.

Chapter 7

It was midnight when I got to The Pig and It. It was a small white building, garishly lighted, set in the middle of a huge, floodlighted parking area. A juke, amplified beyond all reason, blared from speakers set on posts. There were a few dozen cars in the lot. A damp night wind was blowing and the car hops looked chilly, full of false bravado, in their crisp little mid-thigh skirts, white boots, Russian blouses, and perky hats.

A blonde one came up to my car window with order pad and I said, "Is Lita on tonight?"

"Yeah. You wanner?"

"Please."

"Sure thing," she said and walked toward the other girls, rolling heavy hips. A dark girl came toward the car. She was small-bodied, and her legs were thin. She came to the car window and looked in at me. Her dark eyes were large in her white face and her expression was one of surly indifference.

"You want something with me?"

"If you're Lita Genelli, I do."

"That's me, mister. What's on your mind?"

"My name is Dean, Lita. Gevan Dean."

She looked blank for a moment and then her eyes went

wider, and she bit her lip. "Dean! Jesus! It was your brother who—say, what do you want with me?"

"I talked to Walter Shennary. Sergeant Portugal told me you tried to give Shennary an alibi. I wondered if you were telling Portugal the truth or lying to him. I want to be certain they've got the man who murdered my brother."

"Hold it a sec," she said. She hurried toward the building to see the clock inside. She hurried back. "I want to talk to you, but I can't talk here." She dug into the pocket of her short red skirt, pulled out a handful of change, found a key in with the change, and handed it to me. Our hands touched. Her fingers were cold. "You go a hundred yards down the road, down that way. It's the Birdland Motel. This is my key. It's number nine. The next to the last one on the far end, the right end as you're facing the place. Park right in front. Nobody will bother you. Go right on in and wait for me. I'm supposed to be on till one, but it's a slow night and maybe I can get off quicker. Make yourself at home, Mr. Dean. There's liquor and soda and ice in the kitchen. Turn on the radio if you want, and read the magazines. Please, will you wait for me?"

"Okay, Lita."

"Remember, it's number nine and nobody will bother you."

She stepped back, hugging herself against a raw wind as I drove out. I parked where she told me to. Red neon told the world there was no vacancy. My headlights illuminated liverish-yellow stucco, small sagging wooden stoops, windows with discouraged curtains, a window box full of dead stalks.

I let myself into a dark room that smelled of dust and perfume, of laundry and stale liquor, of bedclothes and girl. I used a match to find the light switch beside the door. It turned on a ceiling light with a single bulb and the bodies of bugs in the reflector. Her bed was a studio couch and she had left before making it. On the table near it was a coffee cup with coffee dried in the bottom of it. There were the charred black lines of forgotten cigarettes on the edges of the furniture. The room had an unkempt, cluttered look, a look of stale loves and brutal hangovers.

On a chair was a stack of newspapers, and the top one was the paper containing the account of my brother's murder. ARLAND EXECUTIVE SLAIN. *Prowler Shoots Kendall Dean,* with a picture of Ken, taken long ago, with half-smile and quiet eyes.

I read the accounts, then looked at the room. In the glow of the overhead bulb it was a grubby place. A man like Portugal could understand this place. A man could go out from a place like this with a gun in his hand and his belly full of rye. The room made me feel quixotic. I could tell myself that I could understand these people, but I knew I didn't. And I wanted to leave, and be content with Portugal's shrewdness, but I had gone so far that, even assuming Shennary's guilt, it would be a needless act of cruelty toward the girl. She wanted her man free. I still wondered what sort of person she was. I made certain the blinds were closed. I began a bungling, amateurish search of the room.

I found letters in the top drawer of a maple-finish dressing table. I hesitated for a moment, and then took them over to where the light was better. I read a few of them. They were nearly all penciled on cheap stationery, and addressed to her at the Birdland Motel or The Pig and It. They all had a pattern:

Lita, baby—The rig busted at Norfolk and I missed the Buffalo load, so I won't see you as soon as I figured. I got a load to K. C. now and maybe there I can get one to Philly which will bring me by there and you know I will be stopping so be on the lookout for me honey. We had us a time and I'm looking forward to seeing you soon again.

They were signed Joe and Al and Shorty and Red and Pete and Whitey, and they bore dirty thumbprints and they were mailed from all over the East. And they were all over two months old.

She owned cheap bright clothes, and a large collection of cosmetics in elaborate jars and bottles. I could learn nothing else about her. I turned on a table lamp with a red shade and turned off the overhead light. It made the room look better. I turned the small radio on low to a disc jockey program.

It was twenty to one when she opened the door and came in and shut it against the force of the night wind. She looked cold, and her car-hop uniform looked forlornly theatrical.

"Gee, I'm sorry I couldn't get off sooner. I was worried you'd be gone. I was glad when I saw the car. Jesus, it's getting cold. I'm all goose bumps. Didn't you make yourself a drink? I'll fix you one, hey? I got to get these goddamn boots off. My feet are killing me. I need a drink bad." She talked with hectic vivacity, being the gay hostess.

I agreed to a drink and she slumped into the kitchenette. Over the rattling of the ice tray, she called out to me, "I've been going nuts trying to get somebody to listen to me. I'm glad you came by, believe me. I know Wally didn't shoot anybody. He wouldn't kill anybody. If I thought he had it in him to kill anybody, I wouldn't have nothing to do with him, Mister Dean. He was right here with me when he was supposed to be killing your brother. But can I prove it? Can he prove it?"

She came out with the drinks and handed me mine and plopped down on the unmade studio couch. The drinks were stiff. They looked like iced, black coffee. She pulled off her boots and sat on the bed, Buddha-fashion, adjusting the skimpy red skirt as a casual concession to modesty. The light came through the red lamp shade and made bloody highlights along her lean cheek, on her small arm and knee.

"I suppose," I said cautiously, "they think you'd try to give him an alibi anyway."

"That clown Portugal laughed in my face. It would be okay, maybe, if he didn't have a record."

"And they hadn't found the gun in his possession."

"In his room. Not on him," she said firmly. "There's a big difference. Anybody could put it there. I'll tell you how it was. I was off. We drove out here and we stayed here. We got here about ten. We had some laughs and some drinks. He was going to stay all night. Then, you know, drinking and all, we got yelling at each other about something. So he took off. And I know that was right around two o'clock, and he was drunk and I worried about him driving. We got fighting about him not reporting to the parole officer the way he was supposed to. The thing is, nobody saw him here but me."

"He told Portugal he robbed a supermarket a while back."

"Sure. He confessed that because this murder thing has him scared bad. He got six hundred bucks. It wasn't armed robbery. He busted a back window and got in and pried open a drawer. They can't drop him too hard for that. Not more than three years, maybe."

She talked about it as an expected business risk. I stared at her. She didn't look over eighteen. "How did you get mixed up with anybody like Shennary?"

She stared back at me. "Don't think he tried to kid me. He told me right off he had a record and he was on parole. I kidded myself he was going to play it straight from now on. He was just another date. He knew I'd done some playing around. It was for kicks. Then . . . Oh, hell, I really started to go for him. You can't help a thing like that. I knew he was no good. Mean temper. Thought everybody was down on him. Knocked me around when he felt like it. But we'd make up, and then I'd do anything for him. That's something you don't figure out in your head, Mr. Dean."

"What kind of a man is he, really?"

"Like I said, he thinks everything is against him and so he acts hard. But he's soft underneath. Likes kids and dogs and things like that. He just started out wrong. I guess I did too. We were brought up three blocks apart on the north side, but we never knew each other, him being older. That's funny, isn't it? He wouldn't kill anybody, Mr. Dean, unless maybe he had to keep from getting killed himself."

"Is he bright?"

She shrugged. "Too bright to hold onto a gun if he killed somebody with it, if that's what you mean."

"I don't see how you can ever convince Portugal that he was here with you."

She drained the last of her drink and wiped her mouth on the back of her hand. "Look, Mr. Dean. They don't want to try to think straight about it. I didn't tell the sergeant this. Maybe I should have. Come over here." She went over to the bureau and pulled the second drawer all the way out and stood holding it. "Now light a match and look back in there."

I did. There was an automatic back there, held in place by a strip of heavy rubber that had been thumbtacked to the wood. I straightened up.

She replaced the drawer, banging it shut. "That's his. He didn't want it over at his place in case he got picked up or something. He thought it would be better here. So why would he have another one over there? Does that make sense?"

I had to agree that it seemed odd.

"Another thing," she said. "He told me how he worked. Never with anybody. Always alone. He said it was safer. So I ask you, who sent in that phone tip? How would anybody know? Forget he was right here all the time. Just imagine he *did* shoot your brother. How would anybody know that if he was alone?"

She looked at me with defiance and shrewdness. "You see," she said, "it's like Wally figures. He's an easy answer, and the killing is off the books. They don't *want* to listen to anything that makes sense. He has to lose on that supermarket thing. He knows that. Will you laugh if I tell you something?"

"I don't think so, Lita."

"Make you another drink first?"

"No thanks."

"I'll make me one." She made it quickly and came back in her bare feet and sat as before. "I've been working on Wally. In my own way." She seemed shy. "I wanted to marry the guy. And I don't want to marry a crook. I think in another week or so I could have gotten him to turn himself in. Look at this." She padded to the bureau, dug around in the top drawer, and brought back something I'd missed in my search, a small blue bankbook with gilt lettering. "Go ahead. Look at it."

There were no withdrawals. There were deposits of two and five and nine and eleven dollars. The total was just under nine hundred. I handed it back to her.

"That's what we kept fighting about, but he was weakening. Sooner or later I was going to make him see that we could give back the money he took and turn himself in and maybe he could get off with just serving the rest of the sentence he was paroled from, and that's only two years. Two years more. Or suppose it's five? I can take that. So can he. But I can't take it if they clip him with this murder thing. I—can't."

"I don't see how—"

"Mr. Dean, you're a big man in this town. Anybody named Dean is big in this town. They got to listen to you. You can go to the Chief of Police or the Mayor of the District Attorney or somebody and say you're not satisfied. Say you want more detective work on it. They'll listen and maybe they'll find out who it was and get off Wally's back."

"I'm not so sure they'd listen, Lita."

"I'd sure appreciate it if you'd try."

I didn't answer. She'd made a pretty good case for Shennary, but at the same time I could remember what Portugal had said. I didn't want to make a fool of myself, and yet . . .

She took the bankbook back to the drawer, and then, on her slow and thoughtful way back toward the daybed, paused, turned, looked at me in a strange, still way. A rumble of trucks shook the room. She touched the center of her upper lip with the sharp pink tip of her tongue, nervous, speculative.

She took one slow step toward me, then came the rest of the way with a tumbling haste that seemed a product of shyness. She scrambled onto my lap, thudding with an unexpected force and heaviness against me, then quickly curling and fitting herself against me, her fingers cold at the nape of my neck, bare knees hooked over the arm of the chair, drawing small lines on the side of my throat with the edges of her teeth.

"You could help," she whispered. "You could help Wally and me so much! You can have anything you want, if you'll just help us."

With her free hand, with great deftness, she caught my right hand and lifted it, turned it, cupped it strongly against a breast of astonishing abundance in comparison to all the rest of her. There was an odor of fried meat caught in her hair, mixed with some flower scent. I did not want her. Her scrambling assault had been such a surprise to me; my mind was working too slowly as I sought some kind of rejection that would not wound her pride. It was a tawdry little sacrifice, but it had meaning to her.

As I sought some gentle gambit that would end it, I found myself becoming ever more conscious of the female warmth and weight of her against me. She made an intent series of practiced little motions and adjustments, a click of snap fastenings and a slither of fabric just as her mouth— surprisingly fresh and sweet—came up to meet mine, so that in the beginning of the kiss, fabric pulled aside and the bare warm roundness of her breast seemed to burst into my hand, which no longer required the pressure of hers to hold it there. There were other tuggings and graspings and adjustings, such an agile and continuous shedding of what she wore that it left the long kiss uninterrupted.

It was in some way that defied explanation, more of an innocence than a sexuality. She was a gamine child, playing some involved game at which she excelled. There was an intentness about her, which must have paralleled the same humorless energy she had brought to her games of hopscotch and jacks too few years ago.

Sexual rationalizations and excuses are sick, sly and agonizingly strong. I had begun to tell myself that no one need ever know about this, that it was a simple and meaningless way to ease all the tensions Niki had aroused. This spindly busy animal I held did not have to have a name or an identity.

"You'll help Wally," she murmured, her mouth against mine.

Without breaking the kiss, she turned in a limber way, knelt astride me in the chair and murmured, "Carry me over there," knowing of my readiness. As I ran my hands up the bare, spare, smooth lines of her back, they touched the jutting bony wings of her shoulderblades, and she was suddenly a pathetic starveling, and, in self-derision, my hungers collapsed and I knew it could not happen.

I put my hands on her narrow waist and lifted her up and out and away from me, and sat her out there on my knees, facing me. She had stripped to a pair of threadbare peach panties. She was so thin the insides of her thighs were concave. The light glowed red through the shade onto washboard ribs and the unlikely breasts, high, round and plump. A sheaf of dark hair screened one eye. She palmed it back and stared at me, alert as a bird. Here were no sultried paintings, no race of breath and heart, no tumid lollings.

"What the hell's the matter with you?" she demanded.

"This isn't a very good idea," I said.

"It's been pretty popular lately."

"I don't want to . . . complicate matters, Lita."

She gave me a lewd, angelic smile, half seen in the ruby light as she perched there, shameless as a child. "Complicate? I had the idea it was going to be real easy." Her eyes narrowed. "You make me look real good, don't you? You make me feel like I was some kind of tramp."

"Hush now, Lita. Look at me. Was Wally really here that night? Tell me the truth."

As I held her balanced there, my hands on her waist, she straightened her shoulders, lifted her chin. Slowly and solemnly she crossed herself. "I swear he was. I swear to Jesus and his Holy Mother that Wally was here with me while your brother was being shot, right here in this room, Mr. Dean, and may I burn forever in hell if I'm lying."

In that moment we were no longer strangers. I believed her. I was certain Portugal was wrong. Somebody else had killed my brother. Not Walter Shennary. Somebody far more clever."

"I believe you," I told her, "and I'll help all I can."

Tears stood in her eyes, shiny in the red of the light. "Now," she said in an uncertain voice, "where were we when you interrupted us?"

"Let's skip it, Lita. It's a gesture you don't have to make."

Tears spilled. "The way it was before, Mr. Dean. I was conning you. Now it's a way to say thanks. What else do I have I could give you anyhow? And now . . . it'll be more like with love, you know?"

Beauty can emerge in the most grotesque and unexpected places. Beauty is involved with dignity. With this cheap girl in this drab room, perched so ludicrously at my arm's length, there should have been no dignity—but there was. Far more, in fact, than I had encountered with any of the random beach girls of the four lost years, even the ones who spilled Neiman-Marcus beach wear onto my rush rug and murmured their lust-talk with that precision and word choice refined during the Smith and Wellesley years, and sweetened their bodies at an outlay of forty dollars an ounce, while they co-operated with me in my futile campaign to bury all the nerve-end memories of Niki under so many layers of sensation that no sudden memory of her could bring back the pain.

Lita tilted her head with a simian shrewdness. "But you don't wanna anyhow," she said, and sighed, and slid back away from me and walked to a cardboard closet and took out a lavender rayon robe and put it on, and zipped it from hem to throat. I stood up, when she picked up a cigarette and went to her and held the light.

"I should get the idea I'm such a big prize bonus deal," she said with a weary irony. "You can do better, hey?"

"It isn't that. You see what I mean by things getting too

complicated. We'll have to work together on your problem. And mine. Let's just stick to that."

She looked at me with that special hostility of class antagonism. "People like you do too goddamn much thinking."

"Lita, I like you. I like you very much. So let's see what we can do to help Wally. I'm certain he didn't kill my brother."

We moved to the door. When I took the knob to open it, she stayed me by putting her hand on my wrist. She looked up at me, tiny and intense, the dark hair unkempt. In spite of the $9.98 sophistication of the robe, she looked about twelve years old.

"Either way, Mr. Dean," she said, "I'm going to be without him. If you try and it doesn't work, I'm without him forever. If you help him, he still does time for the supermarket thing. Either way it goes, I owe you. After it's settled, I'll be right here, except when I'm working or visiting him. I lived it up maybe too much before I met him. That's over. I told him so, and I mean it. I'm going to be lonely. I know how guys figure. There'd be no claims on you. No fuss and no trouble, and I wouldn't con you for nothing. And the way it is, I wouldn't feel trampy. I'll fix this place up so it's a better place to come to. I think you'd like that. So when it's over, anytime you want a place and a girl, with nobody pressuring you or able to find you, and nothing you have to do or say unless you feel like it, you got a permanent rain check good any time."

I clasped her fragile shoulder and bent and kissed her lightly on the mouth. We smiled at each other. There was nothing else we had to say to each other.

When I turned my car lights on they shone brightly on her as she stood in the doorway, shoulders hunched against the cold, her hands cupping her elbows, the red lamp glow silhouetting her. She squinted into the light and waved good-by as if I were a hundred yards away instead of five. I backed out and drove toward the city.

I believed her. Portugal would not call me a fool in so

many words. But I could guess at the expression he would wear. I drove to the hotel garage through the late city, remembering the look in Lita's dark eyes.

If Shennary hadn't killed Ken, the whole structure of a clumsy killing collapsed. Clumsiness became cleverness. The gun hidden in his room. Premeditation, cunning, motivation. It made the night and city seem darker. Something mysterious called They. Why had They killed him? How could his existence bother Them?

There is a sickness in murder. It made a sickness in the city, and made me think, perversely, of the Gulf in pre-dawn grayness, the sudden hard strike on the trolled lure, the dip of the rod tip, the singing of the reel, the breath-taking silver of the tarpoon at the height of his leap. Later the sun would come up and the Gulf would be blue and the terns would dip and waver on the morning wind, white as bone, squabbling like picnic children. I had left all that and I had begun to walk along a narrow place. Too narrow to turn around.

I stood in the dark hotel room and looked at the faint pinkness of neon against the overcast. It looked like a fire beyond the horizon. The emotional climate of the city was pre-storm—a stillness and a brassiness and winds out of nowhere that flickered and faded into stillness. I remembered a girl who had been visiting the Tarlesons over a year ago. I remembered the late afternoon when we had been on the beach, she and I, in front of my place, and the strange excitement with which we watched the storm moving in off the Gulf.

The day had been like a wire pulled tight, full of expectancy. We waited there, watching it come until the last possible moment, then grabbed the beach things and ran for my place, the first fat thunderous drops driving against our bare backs, lightning breaking the sky, and we laughed as we ran.

I remembered how dark the day became. We ran through the beach house, shutting windows. We turned on lights but the storm put the lights out. We were children in an attic.

We made love while the storm winds made the house creak, and afterward we heard the thunder moving east. When the storm was gone we were strange with each other and tried too hard to recapture the way it had been while the storm was on.

At the Tarleson party the next day she got very drunk and very sick. I walked her for an endless time on the beach, and later she cried. The next day she went back north.

I felt there was a storm coming, and all the lights would go out, for all of us.

I went to bed and dreamed that I was at the drive-in and Niki, dressed as Lita had been, kept taking care of the customers in the other cars and would not look toward me, and I could not call to her because all the car windows were rolled tight and locked.

Chapter 8

Thursday morning at nine-thirty I drove to the plant. I drove into that section of the parking lot reserved for executive personnel and nosed into the space labeled K. Dean. By habit, I headed toward the entrance I had used in the old days.

A plant guard in gray uniform stepped out and blocked the doorway. "Have you got a pass, sir?"

"No, I haven't. I'm Gevan Dean, and Mr. Mottling is—"

"Sorry, if you got no pass, sir, you got to use the office entrance out on the street. I can't make any exceptions, Mr. Dean."

I went out the parking-lot gates and around and in the main entrance. Salesmen were waiting stolidly for the receptionist to give them the nod; and applicants for jobs were waiting nervously for their appointment with the personnel office.

The receptionist gave me a cool professional glance and then suddenly reognized me and rewarded me with a brilliant smile. "Good morning, Mr. Dean! Would you sign here, please? I'm afraid you'll have to wear this badge. Mr. Mottling said for you to come right up whenever you arrived."

I signed and pinned the badge on my lapel. It said: "Vistor—Offices Only."

"Shall I phone up and say you're on the way, Mr. Dean?"

"No thanks. I want to stop off and say hello to Mr. Granby first."

There was no need to give her that bit of information, but I did it consciously, knowing it was the sort of tidbit that would be transmitted by the office grapevine with the speed of light, and within a half hour I would be labeled a Granby supporter in the Granby-Mottling feud. I didn't know whose side I was on yet. But I wanted to give Mottling a bad moment, if at all possible.

Joan Perrit sat behind the big secretarial desk in Walter Granby's outer office. The desk was gray steel. The wall behind her was pale aqua. She wore a white blouse and, with her dark copper hair, the effect was that of an advertisement in color for office décor. She looked up quickly and smiled and said, "Good morning, Mr. Dean." Both the smile and the tone were professionally correct, and I knew her code would never permit the odd closeness of the previous evening to overlap the working day.

As I answered her I guess some of that speculation was readable in my expression, because she colored slightly.

"Is Walter in, Perry?"

"Colonel Dolson is in there with some vouchers right now, Mr. Dean." She reached toward the intercom on her desk. "But I think he'd like to know—"

"I'll wait, thanks. Last night was fun, Perry."

"Yes—it was."

"You go right ahead with whatever you're doing."

I sat and watched her. She was using an electric typewriter. As she did not have to take her fingers from the keys to return the carriage to the beginning of each new line, the soft clatter of the keys was continuous. I knew she was aware of being watched. Once she frowned and compressed her lips, snatched up an eraser and erased original and carbons. She finished, took the sheets out of the machine, and sorted them.

I said, "I'm seeing Walter before I see Mottling. How will the rumor factory handle that, Perry?"

"It might change the odds a little. I heard yesterday that in the mail room you can get seven to one if you want to bet on Mr. Granby."

The door of Walter's office opened suddenly and a man in uniform came out, stepping briskly. He was a wide man in his fifties. His cropped gray hair had not receded. His skin tone was a firm, warm, healthy pink. The uniform was beautifully tailored. The shoulder eagles were as bright as freshly minted dimes.

He was humming softly to himself. He smiled at Joan Perrit, gave me a quick sharp glance out of blue eyes that looked young and clear, and walked on for three sharp paces, setting his heels down firmly. He then stopped and made an about face with parade-ground precision. He gave me another of those sharp glances, and smiled broadly and came toward me, hand outstretched.

"You must be Gevan Dean! I can see the family resemblance. I'm Colonel Dolson."

I took his hand. His handshake was energetic. He exuded an aroma of barber shops, facials, rubdowns, manicures. He was a testimonial for prudent exercise, polished leather, a careful taste in brandy. His teeth gleamed.

I told him his guess was correct. "Damn glad to meet you, Dean. By God, Stanley promised me faithfully he'd get hold of me as soon as you arrived this morning."

"I haven't seen Mr. Mottling yet, Colonel."

He glanced toward the door to the inner office, and seemed to realize the implications of finding me here. He pursed his lips for a moment, and then the smile returned.

"Suppose I see you in Stanley's office as soon as you finish up here, Mr. Dean." It sounded enough like an order to annoy me. I made no response. "It was a damn shame about your brother, Dean. A shock to all of us. He was a sweet guy." Somehow the Colonel managed to say sweet in such a patronizing manner that it made it sound as though

Ken had been inane and ineffectual. I thanked him for his sympathy and he went off, his neat leather heels going clop-clop-clop on the composition floor, marching to the beat of unheard drums.

I glanced at Perry and saw that the expression on her face matched the way I felt.

I saluted the doorway and said, "Yes sir, sir!"

Perry laughed her good laugh. "I guess he can't help sounding like that, Mr. Dean."

"Is he a regular?"

"Oh, no. He's a reserve officer on active duty. I heard somebody say he owns a hardware store in Grand Rapids." She reached for the intercom switch again and I told her I'd walk in on him.

Walter Granby looked up at me and grunted with surprise. His slow smile spread the deep bloodhound folds of his cheeks like someone parting draperies with both hands.

"So you finally decided to come home, boy. Sit down. You've been missed around here."

I sat down and grinned at him. There was a stinging feeling in my eyes. Walter had gone to work for Grandfather Gevan at the age of seventeen. He was a link with a good past.

"I won't try to say anything about Ken, boy. You know how I feel, I imagine."

"I know, Walter. Somebody said something about you having a private war around here."

"I didn't enlist, boy. I was drafted." He looked older, wearier than I remembered, but he did not sound as though time had dulled the sharp edge of his mind.

"Do you want the job, Walter? Do you want to run the place?"

His eyes sharpened and his laugh was a deep rumble. "Egomania at my age? Not that way, boy. I'll try to take over just to make sure Mottling doesn't."

"No like?"

"You squirts don't seem to realize that on the inside a

man never thinks of himself as old. He never feels old. Mottling calls me 'sir' and acts like he wants to take my arm and help me up and down stairs. Some day he's going to ask for the inside story on how Lincoln got shot. By God, I may tell him, too."

"So you want him out because you don't like his approach?"

"Shouldn't you remember me a little better than that, boy? As a production man, except for certain tendencies I'd label fascist, he's pretty sharp. Of course, by the time he finishes driving away everybody with any brains in the production end, it may be a different story. I'd define him as a hell of a good man to come in on a trouble-shooting basis and get out again, and not so good for the long haul."

"What would you do, Walter, if it were all your baby?"

"Try to get back the production boys he's chased away. Hell, I'm a figure man. I'd need those boys back."

"How was Ken doing?"

He stared at me for a moment. "I think you could answer that yourself. Not good, Gev. Too soft for the job. Not enough iron in him. Not nasty like you used to be. Never came in to bang on my desk like you used to when you wanted to get your hot little hands on the reserves."

"My God, you'd think it was your money, Walter."

"I'm the watchdog, boy. That's my job. And we're in pretty fair shape right now. We haven't had to dig as deep as I thought we would. On plant expansion, on the fixed-price stuff, we get a percentage of the total contract price as soon as production facilities are set up. Sort of a percentage-of-completion deal. Almost like an advance payment."

"That," I said, "sounds as if one Walter Granby had done some operating."

"I pushed and pried a little. We've used short-term construction loans rather than dig down into the barrel."

I leaned back. It was much like old times to be in this office again. On his desk, mounted on a small walnut plaque, was the first piece of war production that had come through the old shop in World War I. It was subassembly, a portion of the bolt assembly of a machine gun, Browning patent. It used to be on my grandfather's desk over in the old office building. When my grandfather died, my father had given it to Walter. I guess the first time I ever noticed it was when I had gotten just tall enough to see over the edge of a desk.

"Finances are good, then," I said, "but we are having a top-level feud. What else is going on?"

"In C Building we're handling a cost-plus-fixed-fee contract with a price negotiation provision. Colonel Dolson is contracting officer and also a sort of free-lance purchasing agent for a lot of the stuff in the contract, as well as for the expansion of facilities here. And that gentleman can turn a voucher through before you can say, 'General Accounting Office.' I feel for the poor taxpayer, boy."

"I didn't know they were letting any cost-plus contracts these days."

"They don't, on standard items. Tanks, planes, guns, and so on. But there's no experience factor on the item we're making. So they're leaving it cost-plus until we've been in production for a while. Then it'll undoubtedly become fixed price, with a renegotiation clause. How about taking pity on an old man who saw Lincoln shot, boy?"

"What do you mean, Walter?"

"I've got all the work I can handle. Just say the word. Karch will put his weight behind you. You can vote yourself right in. Inside of a week you'll be as nasty as you ever were."

"It sounds as if you'd been conferring with your Miss Perrit."

He raised his shaggy white eyebrows. "Hmm! She feel that way too? Bright girl, Gev. Very intelligent. And it sounds to me as if *you'd* been conferring with her yourself. She wouldn't just up and say a thing like that."

I hoped the flush didn't show under my tan. Walter was as sharp as ever.

"Pretty, too," he said. "If I was thirty years younger I wouldn't have her around my office. Too distracting. Always had a soft spot for the reheaded gals." He put his big white paw on the phone. "Just say the word, Gev, and I'll have Karch on the line in three minutes. Don't give yourself time to think."

"I'm rusty, Walter. I've been out too long. Too much has happened."

He sighed and took his hand from the phone. "When I was a wet-eared kid your grandfather hired me. Later on I worked for your dad. I was glad to take orders from both of them. They had the Dean touch. When you first came in, I didn't think it was going to work out. You made it work. Now you're four years older and, I imagine, steadier and stronger. I want you back here. I'll sleep better nights."

I picked up the gun part from the walnut plaque. I bounced it gently in my hand. The silence grew. I replaced it on the desk.

"No, Walter."

He gave a heavy-shouldered shrug. "In the words of my granddaughter, you've turned chicken, boy. The job is so big it scares you."

"Don't try psychology, Walter."

He stared at me for a long moment, then picked up a paper on his desk. It was an obvious dismissal. He said, "Well, run along then, and dig around and then choose between Mottling and me." As I reached the office door he said, "I have a hunch you'll be wrong either way."

I walked out, angry at him. I went to my old office. Mottling's office now. His girl was a stranger, a lean blonde with a beaver-trap mouth and opaque blue eyes, and a pair of astonishing falsies. She gave me smile number seventeen and sent me in.

Mottling had a long leg hooked over the arm of his chair and he was smoking his pipe. Colonel Dolson about-faced from the window.

Mottling waved the pipe stem at me and said in a lazy voice, "Glad you could make it, Gevan. Curt Dolson here has something he wants to get off his chest. Go ahead, Colonel."

This time I received no dentifice smile. The Colonel locked his hands behind him and stood with polished brown shoes about eight inches apart. Parade rest, I imagined. He thrust his chin at me.

"Mr. Dean, I think I can save us all a lot of time if I make my position clear. I represent the Pentagon here, Mr. Dean. In fact, you can quite safely say that I *am* the Pentagon insofar as Dean Products, Incorporated, is concerned. I am not going to mince words. There is no time for the niceties. I feel it is my duty to present my point of view straight from the shoulder, with no beating about the bush."

His tone and manner made the back of my neck tingle. I took a step and a half and perched one haunch on the corner of Mottling's desk. "If you have something to say, Colonel, I suggest you get to it. So far you've told me you're the Pentagon." I kept my voice mild. Dolson looked shocked. I heard a soft snort of amusement from Mottling.

Dolson was a brighter shade of pink. "Very well, sir. Your brother was not capable of carrying the load. Backed up by Stanley here, he could manage. According to my orders, I am merely the Contracting Officer here. However, I have an unwritten responsibility to see everything is done to keep this company efficiently managed. I have every confidence in Mr. Mottling. And thus I do not intend to keep my mouth shut and watch a group of reactionary old fuds toss Stanley Mottling out and put in a has-been like Granby. A has-been, or perhaps I should say a never-was."

"An outrageously senile old man?" I asked him.

He paused for a moment and licked his lips. "Mr. Dean, it is your duty as a patriotic citizen of this country to put your vote solidly in back of Mottling at the Monday meeting. And if you are contemplating anything else, I should very much like to hear your reasons." He gave me the forward thrust of the chin again and stood there watching me with his clear blue warrior's eyes.

I sat swinging my leg. I looked at my shoe. I took out a cigarette and lit it and leaned over and tossed the match into Mottling's ash tray. "I'll be frank as you have been, Colonel."

"I expect that of you."

"You place your weight behind Mottling. In other words, you have taken a direct interest in the internal affairs of this organization."

"Because it relates directly to production of key items. I will gladly defend my stand on that."

"For the moment I'll assume you have both the right and the obligation to meddle in the internal affairs of this company."

"I do not consider it meddling."

"There is a gap in your reasoning, Colonel. You claim Mottling is the better man. In other words you are exercising judgment. But how do I know the quality of your judgment, Colonel? On the basis of what past experience do you consider yourself qualified to judge the caliber of executive personnel?"

"I consider myself an excellent judge of human nature, Dean."

"Have you ever heard anyone admit he was a poor judge? That little egotism seems to be a part of all of us. What experience do you have in industry that makes you a judge of executive ability?"

Dolson spluttered, "Young man, I have been here on the spot. I've watched Mottling and Granby at close range. I certainly am capable of judging—"

"Let's not get off the point, Colonel. I see you're not wearing a West Point ring. You must have *some* business background. What is it? How has it helped you judge these men?"

"I owned and managed my own business for a good many years."

"Oh. A manufacturing concern, perhaps?"

He began to look uneasy. "In—in a rather small way, I guess you might call it that."

"How many employees?"

"I don't see how that is pertinent."

"I intend to find out, Colonel, if you don't see fit to tell me."

He squared his shoulders. "Four. But I don't see—"

"Colonel, forgive me if I remind you that during World War II Dean Products employed over three thousand persons. The problems are quite different. I can see that you are fond of Mr. Mottling. He is a very likable man. Mr. Granby is not a likable man until you have known him for twenty years. You say you speak for the Pentagon. I imagine you know Major General McGay. He has employed tens of thousand of people in industrial operations, and he has lectured on industrial management at Harvard Graduate School of Business Administration. If you want to force an issue on this, Colonel, I would like to fly to Washington with you and listen to you tell General McGay exactly why you have taken sides in a question of the internal management of this company."

"Are you trying to threaten me, young man?"

"I am threatening you, Colonel. I am speaking as a stockholder in this corporation. As a stockholder, I expect complete impartiality from you. You are the Military. As a stockholder, I am interested in my dividends, and I am interested in my right to elect, or help elect, the officers and directors of this corporation. I resent being pushed, and I resent your pushing other stockholders. There's the phone. Tell me what you plan to do. I know I can get an appointment with General McGay for tomorrow." Throughout all this I had kept my voice calm and reasonable. I smiled at him. He looked shaken. I had turned out to be a very different item from what he had imagined.

"I think you should know, Dean, that I have been trying to follow my orders to the best of my ability."

"And I hope that I am making it clear you are stepping into an area where you don't belong, Colonel. I question your ability to function in that area. I question your experience. And I question your judgment when you insist on calling me Dean. I'm Mister Dean, Colonel. So step out of this, or we'll take it to Washington." The business about the name was childish, but I needed it as an additional jab to keep him off balance.

It took him a long and unhappy twenty seconds. Some of

the military starch wilted. He went over to Mottling and stuck out his hand. "Stanley, I did as much as I could. Good luck to you. And good day to you, *Mr. Dean*." He walked out without looking back, and closed the door gently behind him.

As soon as he was gone I felt the familiar weakness in my knees, the results of reaction. Mottling knocked his pipe out and started restuffing it. "When you were a kid," he asked, "did you pull the wings off flies?" He grinned at me.

"All the time."

"You were right, of course. Absolutely right. He was anxious to back me. I didn't think it would hurt to let him go ahead. Maybe it did, eh?"

"My reasoning doesn't run that way, Mr. Mottling. I just wanted him out of the picture."

"He's out and that was a thorough enough job to keep him out. Nice technique, Gevan. You didn't raise your voice once. By the way, who is this McGay? I can't remember hearing about him."

"I made him up."

He stared at me, lighted match poised over his pipe. Then he lowered the match and lit the pipe, making little pah-pah sounds with his lips. He shook the match out. "For God's sake, don't ever let Curt Dolson know that."

"I don't intend to."

"And don't let me ever play poker with you. By the way, are you for me or against me?"

I liked the way he asked that. "I really don't know yet."

"Once you make up your mind, I'd appreciate a little advance warning. That is, if you intend to back Granby. Let me know privately and I promise to keep it to myself. You see, if I'm going to be out, I want to get other irons into the fire as quickly as I can."

"I'll agree to that."

"Thanks. You know, I like the way you handled Dolson. I like the way your mind works, Gevan. I can understand better the difference between you and your brother. If I should be put in here as president, I'd like to have you stay around. You could be a big help."

"I don't plan to stay around."

"Going back to Florida?"

"That's the general idea."

"Niki told me she hopes you'll stay in Arland."

He was working on his pipe again. I couldn't read him. He seemed too amiable, too pleasant. It was the way perfectly good money seems to change in appearance the moment you begin to suspect it is counterfeit.

"You two are real chummy, I guess."

He glanced at me. His eye looked cold. "She's a good friend. Your brother was a good friend."

I was remembering his manner in the Lime Ridge house, his way of seeming completly familiar with the house, and at ease there. It seemed odd to me that I could handle Dolson in what could have been a most difficult situation, remembering the techniques of four years ago, yet if any personal equation contained the factor named Niki, confidence was gone. It was because the handling of men is a hypocritical operation. You must tailor your approach to the weakness you detect. Jolly some of them along, bully others, alternating fact with fancy. Appeal to fear, competence, loyalty, ambition. But when Niki became a factor, objectivity was lost. That, of all reasons, seemed the most valid one for my having left, four years ago. The loss of her had weakend my most valid function—that of getting the maximum return from the men I employed.

It was time for a neutral mask. I smiled at Mottling. "Niki needs her friends now," I said.

"Yes. I think she should take an interest in the company. I've tried to—well, indoctrinate seems to be the best word. She's intelligent. And, of course, she does have at least the secretarial slant to begin with."

"I think I'll take a look around."

"I guess you don't want a licensed guide," he said smiling.

I saw the cleverness of that. Had he tried to come along with me it would have implied that he was steering me toward what I should see, and away from what I shouldn't.

Letting me ramble around on my own was a good expression of self-confidence.

"You'll have to get a shop pass from Dolson's office," he said.

"In the old office building, I suppose?"

"Right. If you have any questions afterward, come on back."

We smiled at each other and I left. Among any group of chickens there is what the behavior specialists call "the pecking order." Put any batch of chickens together, and within a day or so, after considerable bickering, they will work it out. It is a rigid social system. Chicken number eight can peck chicken number nine without fear of retaliation. And chicken number seven can peck just as freely at chicken number eight. And, in the order, should any chicken develop an illness, an unexpected weakness, the formal caste system will be suspended just long enough for all the others to peck it to death.

You can watch the pecking order in operation among architects, plumbers, union officals, housewives, editors. It is fierce, formal, and ruthless. That clever book *Gamesmanship* describes a few of the more civilized methods of pecking. The tension between Mottling and me was based on our not having established precedence in the pecking order. It was necessary to us, as two highly competitive organisms, that it be established. And it would be. He was an able oppenent. And I was carrying Niki on my back.

Chapter 9

Colonel Dolson was out in the shop but a Captain Corning was there, a big, blond, lip-biting guy, guileless as a child. He told me the colonel had directed that I be given a pass to all areas. He filled it out carefully, rolled my right thumbprint onto it, and sent me over to a sink to wash. With the written pass went a gay red lapel button as big as a silver dollar, with "Special Pass" printed on it in black. He offered one of the guards or inspectors as a guide, but I told him I knew my way around.

There were many familiar faces out in the production areas—men who had been hired by my father, and some who had been hired by my grandfather. The older ones could remember, of course, when Kendall and I had been kids, and had been brought down there by Dad, and turned loose with warnings about not getting too close to the equipment. In those days the overhead shafts had whirred and rattled, and the big drive belts had slapped, and the shops had been dim and oily.

Now, in the production areas, each machine tool had its own power unit, and there were wide aisles, and light and air. It was a land of pale gray housings and Chinese red moving parts, and foremen in smocks, a place of panel-board controls. It was a place where the micro-exactitude of gauges was checked against the Johansson blocks in their temperature-controlled storage. But the oil-smell was the same, and the shriek of a high-speed cutting edge, and the reek of hot metal.

I could feel the hot, fast tempo of the work, and I could also sense the strain that always seems to permeate a plant when there is trouble upstairs. I caught the sidelong looks, the speculative glances. I could sense criticism. The deep Florida tan was something that spoke of indolence and fat living—and I suppose a great many of them who knew my name felt that the money for my four-year vacation had come from the value added to raw materials by them during their forty-hour weeks. "See that guy Dean roaming around today? Like he owned the place. He inherited a big chunk of the outfit and the son of a bitch has been sitting on his ass for four years. Pretty damn soft."

I could not forget my guilt as I acknowledged greetings from the men I knew. I had been trained to do a job as an executive. I had grown up with the knowledge of the responsibilities ahead of me. Then I had walked out, telling myself that if I didn't do the job somebody else would.

So I roamed through the old familiar places, and nodded at the ones I knew, and tried to come up with the right names. The regular commercial lines looked fat and happy. I saw new inroads automatiton had made, with whole banks of automatic equipment phased and scheduled on electronic tape and operated off master panel boards by men who never had to dirty their hands. I wondered if the very complexity of such a continuous production setup tended to freeze design to the extent of losing competitive standing in the marketplace. I saw some routine items for the military, made to the typical semi-obsolete designs, overspecified, asininely expensive to produce. I saw the hundred per cent inspection on those military items, required, yet both more expensive and less reliable than the statistical quality control methods I had installed long ago.

I was stopped at the door to C Building by guards who checked back with Captain Corning regarding the validity of my pass. They let me pass, and when I went in I found Miles Bennett in a small office just inside the door. He was a square blond man, a reliable, unimaginative production engineer. He shook hands warmly, and I saw new lines of strain in his face. I asked him about Molly and the kids, and he asked me if I could find him a job in Florida like washing cars. He was trying to appear calm, but he seemed jittery to me.

"Your security is really tight, Miles," I said.

"It's so tight, Gev, I don't even know what the hell I'm making here." When I stared at him, not comprehending what he meant, he took me down the widest aisle of the production floor to where a new wall had been built that cut off the final third of the huge room. Armed guards lounged by a massive door.

"Who can get through that door?" I asked.

"I can't. You can't. Mottling can. The Colonel and the Captain can. Your brother could, until they took away his clearance. You got to have something called a Special Q Clearance, Gev."

"What goes on back there?"

"We make this thing called a D4D. When we finish one, which isn't very damn often, believe me, it goes into that area. The guys in there all work for the government. Stuff is flown in from other sources. Some kind of final assembly goes on in there. Most of those guys have fancy degrees. Their testing equipment uses a lot of juice. When they have maybe a half dozen, which is just a guess based on my production here, they roll them out in a military truck, usually at night, with a convoy of jeeps with troops with automatic weapons."

I made a slow tour of the production layout, with Miles at my heels. No automation here. This was basic production equipment, every machine tended by a craftsman who kept his gauges handy. I looked at D4D that was about ready to go through the guarded door. It was an assembly of beautifully machined components, roughly the size and shape of those peck baskets I hadn't seen for years.

We went back to Miles Bennet's office. The closed door cut the noise level. He shrugged and shook his head.

"Close tolerances, it looks like," I said.

"There's one tapered hole we got to drill through about two inches of special alloy that's got to have the degree of taper dead nuts to a fifty thousandth, so we have to pour plugs and project them to check it out. Mirror finish. If you tried to use a trial plug the molecules would set up and you'd never get it out."

I whistled with genuine awe. "What has to be that close?"

He looked at me with haunted eyes that shifted quickly. "Make your own guesses, Gev."

I guessed out loud. "You've got a lot of parts machined out of light-weight alloys, so lightness is a factor. But there's good tough steel in there too, designed to give maximum crossbracing with minimum weight. And there's areas where you're using non-conductors. And some handy little pockets and casings and slots for one hell of a lot of electronic equipment. Damn it, Miles, if that stuff that goes in there is miniaturized, you'd have more than you'd need for one big fuse, and that's what it looks like, sort of, except for that hemispherical cavity and . . ."

I stopped suddenly. A fat, reinforced tube led to the cavity. A triggering device with explosive charge could slam a fat slug of rare material into the heart of its sister material affixed in the hemisphere, and achieve critical mass in the simplest possible fashion.

Bennet saw my expression and said, "I wish I never started to think about it, Gev."

"But you can't be sure."

He did not seem to hear me. He frowned down at the back of his fist. "Figure on a minimum of at least three safety devices and circuits prior to final arming, and figure a couple more after that, and then figure you'd have to have a couple of in-flight safety controls that couldn't be jammed. Then, once it's on course, ideally it would have a self-contained navigational circuit, not susceptible to any out-side influence, that could make final course correction."

"But you can't know it's the right guess, Miles."

"And the thing you'd really want is top security, because no matter what the ingenuity of man can devise, another man, knowing the precise design, can bitch up when it comes time to use it." He looked at me with an odd expression. "I keep dreaming about them, Gev. A hundred of them, all in flight at once, all arching down at sixteen thousand miles an hour. But they're never going the other way. They're all coming at us."

"Not if we can lob just as many back."

"And if everybody is sure they'll work."

Miles walked me out to the doorway to C Building. "It can wear you down," he said. We looked at each other and looked away. It was a feeling like a shared guilt, as though we had helped each other murder the innocent in some shameful way.

This had been going on while I was sunning myself on the Florida beaches. I got out of there. I got out fast, but I couldn't go quite fast enough to get away from myself. I didn't go back to Mottling's office. I turned in my passes and got into the car and drove away from the north end, away from smoke and sidings and chemical stinks. There was a man I should see. The only other Dean left in the direct blood line. Alfred, my father's brother.

I had a quick lunch in town, and walked to the Arland Athletic Club. After my Aunt Margaret died many years ago, Uncle Alfred sold the gray stone castle my grandfather had built. A grocery chain tore it down and put in a supermarket. Uncle Alfred moved into the Arland Athletic Club, a big downtown club in an ugly red-brick building.

They told me at the desk that they'd call Mr. Alfred Dean from the card room. I said I knew where it was and told the unfamiliar desk clerk that I had a nonresident membership. I bought cigarettes from him and went on through to the card room. There were six men playing a cut-in game of bridge. Uncle Alfred saw me at once. He held up three fingers and pointed to the lounge. He was playing a hand. I went into the lounge and took a magazine from the table. When he came through the door a few minutes later I tossed the magazine aside and stood up.

I remembered him as having a sharp, almost birdlike manner, startlingly young eyes and a zest for life. He had written me several times, urging me to go back into the firm. His letters contained a wry awareness of his own life of idleness. He said the business bored him and he was no good at it.

There was no jauntiness in his walk, none of the dapper briskness. He looked old, worn and aware of defeat. It hurt me to see that his head shook with a perpetual palsied tremble.

"Buy you a drink, Gevan," he said, steering me toward the bar. We took a table. We ordered. I saw his eyes suddenly fill with tears. It shocked me. He knuckled his eyes with a child's gesture and gave me an embarrassed smile. "I don't know what's wrong with me lately, boy. I get as silly as a girl."

"It's good to see you, Uncle Al."

The drinks came and he picked his up. "To Ken, God rest his soul."

We drank to that. He did not speak as distinctly as in the old days. "Cut to the same pattern, we were, Kenny and me. He never got up on his hind legs and quit. God knows he must have thought of it often enough. You quit, and you were the one shouldn't have. I remember the day I had to tell your grandfather I was walking out of the plant. But he had your dad. And that was enough. You could run it without Kenny. Kenny and me—too gentle or something. I don't know."

"What's going on at the plant, Uncle Al?"

"My God, he was mad at me that day. You should have heard him."

"What about Mottling, Uncle Al?"

"Mottling? Oh, him and that colonel fellow and Kenny's wife. Wrong group to be running the place, Karch says.

Says Mottling isn't sound. Walter Granby is the one we want. Mottling lives right here, you know. Right here in the club. Room on the top floor. He pats me on the head. Patronizing." For a moment there was a flash of the old Uncle Al, that dapper, spirited man.

It was as Walter had said. Maybe you never feel old on the inside. I remembered a trip, a long time ago, going to New York on the train with Uncle Al. I was about twelve. It was exciting, eating in the dining car and watching the world go by the windows and thinking about New York and what we would see. It was after Aunt Margaret died. We went to the club car after we ate, and Uncle Al had a drink that came out of a little bottle, and I had a ginger ale. When I finished it, he told me to go back to our seats while he stayed there. I thought I'd been bad or gotten on his nerves. An hour later I went back to look for him, and he was talking to a woman. She looked like the women on the posters in front of the movies, and she had a deep laugh, like a man's.

New York was so big and busy I didn't feel like twelve any more. I felt six years old. We had a suite in the hotel. It was an old-fashioned place where Uncle Al always stayed, and they all knew him.

We were there three days and it wasn't like I thought it would be. He would call the woman he met on the train, and then we would eat dinner and he would buy me something and tell me what time to go to bed and I would go back up to the room and he would go out. He'd sleep until nearly noon and I would go down early to the coffee shop and get breakfast. In the afternoon he would take me someplace. To the top of a building, or a museum. He acted tired and cross during the afternoons.

When we went home on the train he didn't talk much, and his hands were shaky and his eyes were red. Before we got to Arland he looked at me and said, like he was asking me for something, "You had a good time, Gevan boy. Remember that. You had a good time."

I said, "Yes, I had a good time, Uncle Al."

He leaned back and looked contented. I could remember that, the way he looked, and the way he always smelled of cigars and barber shops, and had a fresh flower in his lapel every day.

"Does Mr. Karch think he can vote Mottling out of there?"

Uncle Al seemed to come back from a distant place. I wondered how far his memory had ranged. "Oh, he says with my four thousand shares and what he had lined up among the old crowd, he can get Mottling out provided you don't vote, Gevan. You vote with us and it's a landslide. You vote with Mottling's crowd and we lose. I don't like that man. Guess that isn't much of a reason."

"Maybe it's as good as any other, Uncle Al."

His hand trembled visibly as he set his empty glass on the table. He said, indistinctly, "It hit me hard, Gevan, about Kenny. He was like me."

There was a resentment in me as he repeated that. When Ken and I had been kids, Uncle Al had been one of our favorite people. He had talked to us as though we were people, never talking down to us. I remember a time at the lake when Ken and I got sore at each other. Uncle Al was very grave about it. He got the gloves and laced them neatly and timed the rounds. I know it must have amused him to see us flailing away at each other with such deadly seriousness—and so little damage. We had to shake hands after it was over, and he announced it was a draw.

Later we began to see Uncle Al in a different focus. Though my father never spoke of it directly, we learned he resented the idleness of his brother, resented that Uncle Al got an income due to Dad's efforts. Ken and I began to see him as a sort of dapper and ridiculous grasshopper, a man of no true dignity whom we could no longer respect. He sensed the change in us, and we were never close to him again.

I sat and listened to his ramblings. I suddenly saw myself in a cruel, clear light. It often happens that way, I guess. A sudden analogy, a sudden and shocking increment of objectivity. I could no longer feel superior to Uncle Al. Though our reasons had been quite different, he and I had done precisely the same thing. Each of us had left our brother with the entire burden. There could be no dignity in us, and no self-respect. The world takes little cognizance of motivation. It is concerned with action. And what difference was there between an aimless and lonely old man and an aimless and lonely young man—both of them supported by the labor of others.

I had done to Ken precisely what Uncle Al had done to my father, and given Ken every reason for resentment. Yet I had no proof that he had resented my action in leaving him with the burden, a burden I was better qualified to handle. In that moment of realization I knew I had lost the chance to tell Ken this was the first time I had ever thought of myself in this way, ever seen exactly what I had done to him, and to myself. Someone had robbed me of my chance to tell Ken. I wanted whoever it was within reach of my hands, at that moment.

The old man talked on. I could no longer look at him with mild tolerance. He and I were one. He was what I could become once all sense of responsibility was deadened.

"I think of Kenny a lot," he was saying. "It's a damn shame, you know. He was a nice boy. Quiet. You were the noisy one. You were the one always getting the pair of you in scrapes. Always thought both of you would outlive me. I changed my will again yesterday, Gevan. I hadn't thought about my will for years, until Kenny died. Had Sam Higbee fix it up again. You get everything I've got, Gevan. The stock and some property and there'll be enough cash to take care of estate taxes. You were named after my dad, you know. Tough old man. Gevan Dean. You ought to go back, Gevan. You ought to go back to work, boy. You've taken four years off, I've—taken sixty."

I looked toward the bar to give him a chance to get himself under control.

After long seconds he spoke again and his voice was more brisk. "From a practical point of view it would work,

Gevan. Karch and Walter Granby would go along with it. I know there was trouble between you two boys, about that woman. With Kenny dead, that's over. You've got no reason to stay away now, Gevan."

"It's still a reason, Uncle Al."

"Nonsense! Good Lord, while you other Deans were running the business I got myself a liberal education in females. A woman like that is nothing to make a damn fool of yourself over. They had me to the house a lot of times. She's one of the greedy ones."

"What do you mean?"

"I shouldn't talk about Kenny's widow this way. But it's between you and me. She's one of those women who make the backs of your hands tingle. Like she wore a sandwich sign around with one word printed on it in big red letters. Sex. There are some like that who aren't after anything, and those are the best kind. But she uses it like a lever to pry loose what she wants, and those are the dangerous ones. I don't know what she wants. Money, security, position. She got all that when she married Kenny. But it didn't relax her. She's after more than that, and I don't know what it is. Don't think I'm just an old man rambling on and on and saying nothing. She isn't obvious about it. The clever ones never are. You and Kenny were overmatched with that one. Out of your league. She pried on Kenny until she finally broke his mainspring. I don't know how. Kenny gave up. He acted like there wasn't anything left to live for. You watch out for her, Gevan, because I don't know what she's after. . . ." His voice trailed off. He sat for a time, his lips moving in key with unspoken thoughts. He straightened up and looked at his watch.

"Gevan, it's nice to see you. Charles, give this boy another drink on my tab." He stood up and looked at his watch. "Got to get back into that game and get some of my money back." For a moment he looked troubled. "I never seem to win any more. Funny thing. Must be a bad run of cards. Come around for dinner here some night. Any night."

He went off, and it was a jaunty imitation of the brisk way he used to walk. The barman brought me another drink. The club was quiet, smelling of oiled wood, cigars, dust. Somebody was running a vacuum cleaner in one of the other rooms. The barman stood, heavy lidded, polishing a glass.

Kenny was the quiet one. The time mother went to California, Dad used to bring us here for dinner every night. It made us feel special to know women were never permitted in the club except once a year at a special party. We watched beefy men play handball, and we swam in the pool. Those were good years, in a safe world. I remembered we had played tag around the pool and Ken had fallen and cracked his head on the tile. The bump was on the back of his head and within minutes it was the size of an English walnut. Dad's friends had examined it with awe, and complimented Ken on not crying. I remembered standing aside and wishing it had been me, and wondering if I would have cried.

I finished the drink and walked into the April sunlight of Thursday afternoon. The day had grown much warmer. Seeing Uncle Al had depressed me. My mind operated on two levels. On the deeper level was the Granby-Mottling problem, the choice that had to be made. Uppermost in my mind was the problem of Ken. Who had killed him with such devious care? Who had fired a lead slug into the back of his head? The same head had gone crack on the tile, and he had stood there in the long ago, his mouth rigid with the effort of repressing the tears, for we were in a place where there were men, and men of course did not cry. Ever.

I knew I had to go back and see Niki. It would be childish to stay away from her when she was the one who was most likely to give me some small clue as to why he was killed.

I took my rented car out of the hotel garage and headed for the Lime Ridge house.

Chapter 10

The pretty little maid let me in and asked me to wait for a moment. She hurried off and came back and said, "If you would come with me, sir?"

She led me through the house and out to a small flagstone terrace built into an L of the house. There was a low wide wall around the other two sides. Niki, in a scanty, two-piece, terry-cloth sunsuit of bright yellow lay on a rustic chaise longue upholstered in quilted white plastic. She was in the glare of the afternoon sunlight, her body glistening with oil, and her ink-black hair piled high. She was propped up on one elbow and she had taken off her sun glasses to smile at me.

"How nice, Gevan!"

I looked up the slope of the back lawn toward aspen and birch. "It's nice here."

"That door opens into the master bedroom, and whenever we could, we'd have breakfast out here. But it doesn't catch the morning sun, so we couldn't really use it often. I'll show you the whole house sometime, Gevan."

I heard myself murmuring that it would be nice. She put her sun glasses on and lay back. They were the kind that are mirrors. You cannot see the eyes of the wearer. It gave her a blinded look. There was some pink in her skin tone. She lay drowsy in the sun, oiled and relaxed, and it was too easy to stare at the arching lines of her, at warm perfections.

"Sure you're not getting too much?" I asked, my voice harsh.

"Oh, I never burn."

I sat on the low wall and lit a cigarette. The mirrored glasses gave me the odd feeling that she couldn't see me. "Light two, dar—Gevan. How stupid! Almost calling you darling. The heat makes me feel so—very far away from myself."

"I know that feeling." I lit two cigarettes and took one to her. She lifted her chin a fraction of an inch and I put it between her lips. She inhaled deeply and took the cigarette from her lips. I sat on the wall again.

"Grief is such a funny thing, Gevan. It isn't constant, as you'd think. It goes and comes. You forget for a little minute, and then it all comes back smashing you down."

"I know."

"Of course you would know, wouldn't you. I can't seem to open my mouth without sounding inane. I wish—"

"What do you wish, Niki?"

"This will sound even worse. I wish we hadn't ever been—emotionally entangled. Then I could lean on you harder. The way it is, I feel—awkward and guilty." The mirrored eyes reflected the deep blue of April sky.

I did not answer. She sighed audibly. "You hate me, don't you, Gevan?"

I smiled at the blind lenses. "I was unique and irresistible. It never occurred to me that anybody *could* turn me down."

"That is a very bitter smile."

"Hurt pride."

She sat up and inspected her long, lithe, sun-reddened legs, poked experimentally at her thigh and watched the white finger-mark slowly disappear, then lay back again, snapping her cigarette out over the low wall into the grass.

"We won't get anywhere talking about it, I guess." The sun had moved. An edge of roof shadow touched her shoulder. "Would you roll me out from the wall a little bit, please?"

The chaise longue had two wooden wheels at the head part, and handles at the foot part. I lifted the handles and pulled her out a bit, and knew she watched me through the mirrored lenses as I did so.

"Why don't you take off your coat, Gevan? Your face is just dripping."

"Good idea." I took my coat off and rolled up the sleeves of my white shirt.

The lovely little amber-skinned maid came out onto the terrace, trim in a well-cut spring suit, demure in manner. "Excuse me, Mrs. Dean."

"Oh, you're ready to leave, Victoria?"

"Yes ma'am. I fixed a salad for you. It's in a yellow bowl on the second shelf in wax paper, ma'am, and the dressing is in the bottle next to it. If you don't need me earlier, I'll be back about midnight, I guess."

"Did your young man come for you? I didn't hear him drive in."

"He's parked out there on the road, ma'am."

"Please tell him again, Victoria, that when he comes to pick you up he's to feel free to drive in."

"I'll tell him again, ma'am. Good-by, Mrs. Dean. Good-by, sir."

After she left the terrace Niki said, "Victoria is a doll. She has two years of college, you know. She's working for me for a year to save enough to go back in the fall. She wants to be a teacher. The two of us rattle around in this house. It's so big. Yesterday I had her move from the servants' quarters to one of the guest suites. It makes the house seem less empty. People seem to be putting gentle pressure on me to move out of here, Gevan, after what happened. But this is my home. I feel safe here."

"It's a lot of overhead to house one person."

"The grounds? I share a gardener with the Delahays, my nearest neighbors. You can just see a bit of their roof through those poplars, Gevan, beyond that ridge. He's due here again tomorrow. I suppose it is quite a lot for just one person. But if you force me to be vulgar, there is quite a lot of money to go with it, you know. I don't think I'll stay here forever. But I won't leave for the sake of leaving. I'll have to know where I'm going."

"Don't you always?"

"Did you come here just to be nasty?"

"I actually came to ask you about that night Ken was killed, Niki. I've read the newspaper accounts. They don't say much."

She remained silent to the point of rudeness, then said, "I guess you have the right to ask. I'll have to give you some background on it, so you can understand just what that night was like."

"I know I'm asking a lot."

She stood up and adjusted a latch on the chaise so that the angled part folded down, turning it into a long cot. She picked up the bottle of sun oil from the floor and held it out to me and said, "It's a long story, so be a useful listener, dear."

I took the bottle of sun oil from her. She stretched out face down, her long legs angled toward the far side to make room for me to sit. She craned her hands back and unhooked the narrow strap of her halter. With one languid hand she put the mirrored sunglasses on the terrace stone, then sighed and snuggled into relaxation, her face turned away from me, her fingers laced above her head.

I tipped warm oil between her shoulder blades, and it ran down along the youthful indentation toward the small of her back. I caught it and began to spread it and work it into long brown silk of her, feeling the flat firm webs of muscle, the hidden ivory roundness of vertebrae, the clever flexing sheathing of scapula. She had piled her dark hair up out of the way, and the nape of her neck looked tender, girlish and vulnerable. There was a downy pattern of pale hair in the convexity of the small of her back, and the oil flattened it and darkened it.

"For the past six months or so, Gevan, we led the quiet

111

life. I couldn't say how much choice was involved. Yes, it was quiet. When you don't return invitations, people eventually stop asking you. Our evenings were all . . . very much alike. He would come in sometime after seven. I don't have to hide anything from you, Gevan. He would come home plastered. He was very owlish and solemn when he was drunk."

"I know."

"Completely proper, erect and dignified, pronouncing every syllable of every word, but completely blacked out. On . . . that night we had to eat sooner than usual after he got back because I'd promised Victoria she could leave early. She was going to Philadelphia to see a brother who was in the hospital. I served the dinner and she left before dessert. I read at the table while we ate. That's a little habit I picked up after we began to find out we didn't have anything left to say to each other."

She shifted her position slightly. "After dinner I cleared the table and loaded the dishwasher. By . . . by the time . . . by the time I . . ."

She had begun to lose the thread of her story. Her voice had begun to get deeper and rougher, and the precision of her diction had begun to blur. I knew what was happening. I should have long since capped the little bottle of scented oil and gone back to my seat on the low wall. I had told myself to do just that. I had told myself many times. Her back as amply protected against the sun of late afternoon. But instead of stopping, I was making longer, slower strokes, one stroke for each two beats of my heart.

"By the time I got back into the living-room, he . . . he had fallen . . . had fallen asleep on . . . asleep on . . . the couch. I . . . I covered . . . covered him . . . with a . . . covered him with a blanket . . . covered him . . ."

Her voice had become a sulky, whispering, rasping sound and her breathing had become long and deep. I had increased the firmness of my stroke, so that each long stroke, from waist to shoulder, moved her, back and forth, an insistent inch or two, face down on the quilted white plastic of the chaise.

She had begun to arch against each long pressure of my hand. Her back, I swear it, had flowered and luxuriated and changed under my touch, sleek, flexing, hypnotic. I had split into two Gevan Deans who could not communicate with each other. One watched it all, shamed by it, made wretched by this compulsion, wracked by the awareness of immediate guilt and the greater guilt yet to come, the way a child, in the midst of some private act it thinks evil, will yearn to stop and cannot. The other Gevan stroked the oiled, trembling, gasping woman, taking a hard joy in this way of reducing her, through her own need, into a savage helplessness. And throughout that time that could not be measured, after she had lost the ability to talk, there was the knowledge of the empty house, the empty sunny afternoon, bird sounds in the distant spring birches, the sliding sound of my hand upon her, the tearing sounds, like tiny snorings, that had begun to accompany her rough inhalations.

She eeled violently around with a great broken cry, two vowel sounds, as though she were trying to call out my name but could not fit the straining softnesses of her mouth to the consonants. The sun shrank the pupils of her eyes so that they were wide and blind and monstrously blue. She lunged upward, breasts aimed and tumid, to clasp me and pull me down, gasping and whining in her peak of need to accomplish the specifics of my defeat and depletion.

So I took my brother's widow, violent, oiled and naked, squirming and thrusting on quilted white plastic on a redwood chaise on a walled fieldstone terrace in April sunshine, out of the wind, protected by all the formal stature of the dead man's house. It was without grace, dignity, tenderness or affection. It was like trapping in some narrow place something hard to kill, then killing it clumsily, violently, in fear and hate, with dreadful weapons, killing it as quickly as you can.

When at last she stirred and made a small sound of irritable impatience, I moved to release her. She got up, scowling at the sun glare, stooped and picked the two scraps of yellow terry from the stone. In picking them up she lost her balance and had to take a quick step to catch herself. She walked heavily to the big glass door that opened into the bedroom. She pulled it open and walked on into the shadowy room without speaking or looking back, and the last I could see of her, fading like the smile of Alice's cat, was the almost luminous whiteness of the alternating clench of her buttocks.

I sat on the edge of the chaise. I bent over and retrieved my cigarettes and lighter from the tumble of my clothing, then swept it aside with the edge of my foot. I sat with my arms braced on my knees, staring down at the pattern of the stone between my bare feet. I felt dull, heavy, hairy and degraded, a fleshy animal who had reached the end of all its own precious pretention. I studied the brave beach-boy tan on my legs, and the slight continuous trembling of the fingers that held the cigarette. I heard a distant sound and identified it as the sound of a shower.

A man can acquire a false image of himself too easily. I sat numbed by the collapse of an image. I had sold myself a concept of a certain basic dignity and decency—call it a Gevan Dean ethic. But now I saw the inner sickness. It was a weakness. I repeated to myself that sad rationalization of all hollow trivial men: The libido has no conscience.

I sat in the listless carapace of my traitor flesh, spent, and sticky with Niki's sun oil and my drying sweat. I thought of Ken, and the vinegary tears of shame and self-pity began to squeeze out of my eyes, weak and stinging.

The shower sound had stopped. The sun began to touch the black tops of the poplars. I saw something out of the corner of my eye, a movement in the doorway. "Gevan?"

I turned my head slowly and looked at her. She held a big blue towel in front of her, covering her from throat to knee. Her mouth was pale without lipstick and she had the grace not to smile.

"You can use the shower now," she said in the tone she

would use with her maid. "Turn left through the bedroom." She backed away and disappeared.

A few minutes later I picked up my clothing and went inside. I dropped my things in a heap on the cherry-red carpeting and paused a moment to look at the luxurious room. It was big enough to accommodate two oversize double beds and shrink them to the proportion of twin beds. There was a special quietness about that room. At the far end was a couch, deep chair, low bookshelves, built-in television and music.

It was a bedroom for two people who loved each other. I thought of the tragic euphemism for what Niki and I had just done. It was called making love. Whatever it was we had made, it was not love. When she had ripped my back and bellowed her pain and completion, it was not love. Love has tenderness. What we had done was more suitable for the fetid cave of the Neanderthal after gorging on the steaming meat of one of the great carnivores.

Fluorescence turned the big bathroom into a brightness adequate for brain operations. The air was faintly steamy and elusively fragrant. The top corners of the mirrors were coated with a dwindling mist. She had laid out a big coral towel for me, precisely folded. Resting on the towel was one of those little kits luxury hotels provide the guest who stays over unexpectedly; aseptically packaged in a plastic bubble, shaving things, comb, toothbrush, nailfile, deodorant. The service was, I thought sourly, very complete in every shade of meaning of the word.

The shower, once I had learned the procedure on all the chrome dials and knobs, was superb. Such a shower inevitably makes some improvement in the morale. I was as low as I had ever been in my life. Improvement was the only possibility. I stayed in the shower a long time.

When I walked back into the bedroom with the coral towel knotted around my waist, she was curled in a deep chair by the window, her legs pulled up, a glass in her hand. She wore a pleated tailored white blouse, a narrow navy skirt. Her shining hair was pulled back tightly, and she had been very sparing with makeup. On a squat table beside her chair was a silver tray, a silver shaker frosted with moisture, a plump fragile cocktail glass like hers.

I realized the cleverness behind the effect she made, and had to appreciate it even though I knew it was contrived. This not only suggested her office costumes of long ago, reminding me of better times than these, but it had a clean and impersonal look that made things a little easier. Had she chosen a sensuous outfit, a revealing housecoat for example, and combed her hair long for me, she could possible have turned my stomach.

"Daiquiri here, if you want one, dear," she said. "Help yourself." She smiled at me in a shy, tentative way.

I went near her and poured the drink. It had a tart clean taste. "Good," I said.

"Your clothes were messy with that sun lotion."

"I'm a mad, impulsive creature."

"You wouldn't want to take them to the hotel. I've bundled them up. I know where I can drop them off myself and pick them up and keep them here until you can collect them. I . . . laid some things out on the bed."

I went over and looked. The things from my pockets were spread out. There were shorts, socks, a white shirt still in its retail cellophane, slacks that would look well enough with my jacket.

"You don't mind?" she asked in a meek voice.

"Somehow I can't get worked up about taking over his clothes. I've moved in on something more private than that."

"He wore those slacks twice. They're just back from their first trip to the cleaners. Everything else is brand new."

She had laid out my belt, tie and shoes. "I told you it isn't important. How could it be, now?"

"But you had me first!" she said with such despair I turned and looked across the room at her. Dusk had come into the room. Her face was a paleness against shadows,

116

just a little duskier than her blouse. "Long before him! You had me first!"

"That gives me special rights?" I said. I dropped the towel. She turned and looked out the window and sipped her drink. I dressed in my brother's clothing. The slacks were too big in the waist and too short, but not ludicrously so. The shirt sleeves were short. I dressed and put my jacket on and refilled my glass and sat on the couch, facing her.

"Gevan," she said softly, "we both knew it would happen sooner or . . ."

"You were saying that he had fallen asleep and you had covered him with a blanket."

"Gevan! Darling!"

"What happened after you covered him with the blanket?"

"But this is cruel! I want to talk about us."

"Baby, I thank you sincerely for the shower, the clothes, the rum and the roll in the hay, but don't make the mistake of thinking I am going to let you milk it for kicks by talking circles around it. You were telling me you covered him with a blanket."

She looked down into her drink for a long time. At last she shivered and straightened and lifted her chin and looked at me without expression. "I read until I finished my book. It was midnight. I went in and shook Ken awake and told him the time and told him I was going to bed. He said he had a headache and he was going to go out and see if the night air would help. I told him less liquor was the only thing that could help him. He didn't answer me. That was the last thing I ever said to him. It's a very loving farewell, isn't it?"

"You never know about such things in advance. How could you?"

"Thanks, darling. I came in here and went to bed. The bed on the right is mine. I left his bedlamp and the bathroom lights on. I was drifting off so quickly that when I heard the shot I thought it was part of a dream that had just begun. I began to wonder if he had fallen, or knocked something over. It's unbelievably quiet up here at night. I tried to go back to sleep, but I kept wondering what I had heard. I put on my robe and slippers and went through the house, calling him, but there wasn't any answer. I went outside and called. I knew I could be heard a long distance in the stillness. I walked around the whole house, and finally I was yelling so loudly I got hoarse the next day.

"I got a flashlight and went down the drive toward the gate. He was on the grass just inside the gate, near the lilacs. It isn't a gate really, just two posts with lights on top that you drive between. You saw it when you came here. The lights were out.

"When I found him I didn't think it was him. He looked so shrunken and little and flat against the ground, and his clothes looked too big for him. His face was bulging and horrible, and they say that happens because of the pressure of the bullet on the brain and . . ." She lost control for a few moments. She sat very still with her eyes shut, but when she opened them she continued in the same level voice.

"I can't really remember running to the house. The police came quickly. I had put a blanket over him. I knew he wouldn't want people looking at him the way he was. It was the same blanket I'd used to cover him after his drinks knocked him out. A lot of police came, and Lester and Stanley came. There were a lot of questions. I started to go to pieces. My doctor came and gave me a shot, and a nurse stayed here with me. I didn't wake up until late Saturday morning. I phoned you then but . . . I couldn't get you. You know the rest." She carefully refilled her glass.

"Yes," I said. "I know all the rest, including your mourning methods."

She stared at me. I wanted to smash her with my own guilt. But I had pushed it too far. She laughed at me, with derision and amusement. "*My* mourning methods! Oh, you are so blameless, Gevan Dean!" I knew, even in the dusk light, how the blue of her eyes had deepened. I saw the arched lines of her mouth, arrogant and sensuous. "Are you going to convince yourself you were raped, darling? It was a good trick, if you were, you know. My back was turned, wasn't it? Were you just trying to do the best job of oiling a lady's back that had ever been done? For God's sake, let's both try to be honest. It might be the only virtue we have left, you know. We'll call it *our* mourning procedure—for husband and brother. You see, darling, I have less to regret than you. I'm the one who didn't love him."

She rose to her feet and took two slow steps to stand tall over me, tall and mocking, sleek and resilient in her skin, smug in the aftermath of satisfactions. Long before, when we had known we would be married, we had found in each other an endless hunger for physical love. She had been marvelous to be with. She had demanded her pleasures with a boldness and a joy which had been a constant source of re-excitement to me. But the Niki I had known then was but an inquisitive emotional girl compared to the woman of riper body who stood before me, laughing at me. This one was in a full torrent of her maturity, aware of her strengths and their uses, her driving needs and just what would be most assuasive to them.

I lowered my face into my hands and felt her sit quickly beside me. She wrapped gentle fingers around my right wrist. "Let's not try to hurt each other," she whispered.

"You make it sound easy."

"Maybe we can do incredible things, darling. Like turning the calendar back a long way. It was all so good once upon a time. If we look for it, maybe we can find it again. Remember me? My name is Niki. I'm your girl."

The room was almost dark. She had created a special mood wherein I could find myself wanting to believe that somehow we could make the four lost years seem like an absurd mistake, and be together again.

I turned and looked at her. Her face was inches from mine. "I remember you very well," I said.

"And I remember you, Gevan. You are the man who had all the drive and all the energy, and one day you just . . . came to a stop."

"Because there wasn't anything worth working for."

"Do you feel guilty about that?"

"Why should I?"

"I had to ask. It's easier to ask things in the dark. Important things, darling. I don't want you all steamed up to get back into the rat race."

"What has that got . . ."

"Hush!" she said and touched my lips. "I have a crazy plan for us. It's no good here for us. Too much happened here. We'd have to live in a new way to catch up on all we've lost. We lost so much, darling. Let's go away together just as soon as we can. There's all the money we can ever use. We could get a boat, a motor-sailor we could crew ourselves, and . . . make a life out of following the sun."

She turned suddenly to put her head in my lap. She looked up at me. "Let's do that, Gevan. Let's really and truly do it, you and me. The hell with all of them."

She made it sound so good and so easy.

"And leave all this? Mottling says you've been taking a big interest in the company."

"Poo! He's been trying to bring me into the discussions. It's therapy, I guess. I can't contribute anything. He can run the company with my help or yours, dear. We wouldn't ever have to come back."

Yes indeed, off we would sail and in a couple of years we'd be able to speak fondly and tolerantly of good old Ken, and we'd be grateful to good old Stanley for keeping our dividends nice and fat. We'd just rove the blue seas and tie up at the fun places at the fashionable times, and make love, and drink too much, but always with adorable and enchanting people. And when the sex and sensation bit started to go a little dead, we could always give it a booster shot by taking exactly the right sort of couple on a little cruise, some adorable, enchanting pair too vulnerable to tell tales, and with some trading around and with some of the practices of the voyeur, we could put our romance right back on the up-beat, yes indeed, and we would push the good old machine until finally the parts wore out, at which time the medics could gut her like a trout and carve away portions of me, and we would then want a larger and more comfortable boat and somebody to run it for us while we sat in adjoining deck chairs astern, soft, fat, brown as saddles, and without one bloody word left to say to each other or one itching thing to do to each other, yes indeed. Bliss without end.

She must have anticipated what I was going to say, because she got up suddenly and said, "I'm restless, darling. Let's go for a walk."

We walked in darkness on the soft fresh grass. She found my hand in what seemed a most natural way. An airways beacon swept the south horizon. We walked past the garages and servant quarters, and down a tidied slope of lawn toward a pale caligraphy of young birches at the edge of the woodland. The first stars were out.

We stopped near the woods. "I'm ashamed," I said.

"So am I, darling! So am I! But we're the only ones who know about it, aren't we? Who have we hurt? A dead man? You see, we're not really ashamed of what we did. We broke a convention, dearest. We violated the code. We jumped the gun. We're ashamed because we didn't let what they call a decent interval elapse, that's all. The act wasn't shameful. Such a great need can't be shameful. It was just the timing, darling. Don't you see? We're going to be together anyway. Nothing can stop that, and we both know it. I've never stopped loving you and needing you, Gevan. So we have no reason to be ashamed."

"You make it sound reasonable, Niki. You've got that wonderful talent for making anything you want to do sound reasonable."

"You didn't use to be like this, Gevan. Why do you have to pick at things? Just enjoy, enjoy. You don't have to think so goddamn much, do you?"

I made a sound like a laugh. "Somebody else told me the same thing a little while ago."

"Who?"

"It doesn't matter. You don't know her."

She shrugged and turned away from me and looked up at the night sky. "I love the quiet out here. We're the only two people left in the world, darling."

"How dandy."

She spun back and put her hands on my shoulders. "You're still hostile toward me, darling. God knows I can't blame you, after the fool thing I did, and the way I almost lost you forever. But don't I deserve a chance to make it up to you? Isn't it worth it to you to give me a chance? Try to feel a little bit of kindness, dearest. This hostility is like a sickness, you know. It even carries over to Stanley."

"Mottling! What the hell has he got to do with this?"

"I'm trying to make you see your own confusion, Gevan," she said, sliding her hands down to my wrists. I sensed your immediate antagonism toward Stanley, and until I figured it out, it worried me. You see, you know I like and trust him. So now I believe that in some emotional irrational way, you have a compulsion to fight him just in order to spite me."

"For God's sake, Niki!"

"I'm trying to get you to be honest with yourself. That's the only way we can start off right, darling. A second chance is such a rare thing, it's worth every effort. I hurt you terribly. Yes. But I hurt myself too! Can't you see that? The four years were just as horrid for me as they were for you. You don't have to keep on trying to punish me now by . . . by doing hostile things like working against Stanley, who is really so terribly capable. You really have no real objection to him."

"He seems too damn plausible. He's driven too many good men away. I'm dubious about his management policies. What's that got to do with us?"

"Everything, because those are rationalizations to make your emotional hostility seem based on logic."

At my slight tug she released my wrists. I lit cigarettes. In the quick glow of flame I looked at the oval flatness and good high bones of her cheeks, and the shadowed eyes. It was getting cooler. We began to walk slowly back up the slope toward the home my brother had built for his bride.

"You'll have to give me a second reading on this," I told her. "We talk about us, and we get over into this Mottling running the company. Where is the connection? What the hell difference does it make to you whether Mottling or Granby or Joe Sandwich runs the outfit?"

She walked with her head bowed, scuffing the grass with her sandals. "I want to say it exactly right, because everything I say, you take the wrong way, you know."

"Take your time."

After a long silence she sighed, stopped and faced me. "Maybe it's all too involved and too female to explain. Reasons sort of overlap. In the first place, Ken wanted Stanley to be in charge. And, you can sneer at me if you want to, but I do feel obligation and loyalty toward your brother. It didn't work, and that wasn't entirely his fault, and he tried desperately hard to make it work. We both did. He was a good man. We both know that."

"I'm not sneering."

"Thank you for that, Gevan. Secondly, it's . . . it's like a test for us. You haven't been here long enough to learn anything pertinent about Stanley. So if you fight him, it's because you're fighting me. And what can we build on that kind of feeling? If you keep on trying to fight me, what will our life together be like? And there's the last thing, and maybe the most important, Gevan. I *do* know, more than most people, that grave sense of responsibility you have. So suppose you got Stanley out. You know Granby couldn't handle it. So you wouldn't go away with me. You'd stay here and back him up and help him and get more and more enmeshed. And I would have to stay here, because you would be here. But, Oh God, how I want to get away from here forever, with you. This is where I bitched up my life, Gevan. I don't think we can be happy here. And we need happiness. We need it so terribly."

I looked toward the dark house. Nothing in the world seemed safe and tangible. I thought of what Uncle Al had said about her motivations. The Lime Ridge house looked like a big, brooding trap. Ken had built it and it had caught him. Something had broken him in a shadowy merciless way, and something else had killed him too cleverly. Everything was shifting, implausible. This woman was someone I had never known and never would know.

"I don't know," I said, my voice loud and harsh and weary in the silence. "I have to sort things out. I've got to get back to town."

I expected protestations, pleadings, demands that we talk it all out here and now. But in a voice bright, casual and kindly, she said, as she patted my arm, "Too much is happening too fast, I know. Almost too much to take. And we have all the time there is, darling."

We walked toward my car. I opened the car door and turned toward her. She was closer than I had expected, and she swayed into me, parted my jacket, hooked the fingers of both hands around my belt and pulled and held us tightly together, her face in the hollow of my throat, her back arched in a way that laid the insistent firmness of her breasts against my chest. I could not stand like a fool with my arms at my sides. I put them around her, my hands light and meaningless on her back.

"It's a hell of a way to leave both of us," she murmured. Already there was a muzzy formlessness about her articulation, a roughening of her voice. Her breathing was slowing and deepening and I felt the faint ripening sag of her as her knees drowsed under her tumescent weight.

"Haven't we said . . ."

"I don't mean more talk. Can't you tell I don't mean more talk? I mean it could be so much better now the terrible edge is gone. Starving people gobble the food, honey. They don't take time for tasting. They fill their bellies, fast as they can. Too fast."

I could feel the heat of her slow exhalations against my throat. "We shouldn't have let that happen."

"I know, I know, I know," she said in a cross blurred voice. "But it did, and it's done, so what's wrong with getting all the good of it? Not starving now. Just a good hunger. Les' go in an be gourmets, darlin'. A slow slow sweet sweet feast. With all the tastes and flavors. No gobbling. All slow and long and sweet . . ."

She kept murmuring but the singsong words had become indistinct. It was a fuzzy droning, like a summer-sound of bees, and her body had begun its soft, inadvertent pulsings. In the ultimate second, just before I was forever lost, I pushed her slowly and firmly away from me. When I released her at arm's length I saw her waver in the starlight and catch her balance. She stood hunched for a time, her fists against her cheeks, and then straightened herself.

"You're right of course, darling," she said in the same tone she probably used for social telephoning.

"One guilt at a time."

"I suppose I should feel spurned and degraded. But somehow I don't. You *do* have a vast talent for turning me into . . . some unspeakable, panting *thing*, Gevan. Practically with no warning at all. Doesn't that stimulate your male ego?"

"Good night, Niki."

"With a friendship kiss," she said, and came close. With great wisdom, I kissed her cheek. She laughed at me and called me a coward.

When I was behind the wheel she bent down and looked through the window at me, her expression mischievous in the dashboard lights.

"You *do* realize you cheated us by being so conventional," she said. "Because next time we'll have to be all fierce and fast again before we can be the way we want to be. Do come back soon. You could be terribly weak and inconsistent and come back a little later, or get out of the car right now, and I wouldn't tease you about it, really."

She laughed at me and backed away. When I turned in the drive the lights swept across her and left her smiling in the darkness; that smile, caught in an instant of light, grooved forever into the brain's jelly—proud, strong and mocking.

I drove toward the pink glow of the city by night. I held

the wheel stiffly and drove slowly, and tried to keep her out
of my mind, tried to keep my mind blank and gray. When I
was a boy of ten I spent a summer on a farm my grandfather
owned. Ken and I were assigned chores. One sow showed
the ingenuity of a demon in escaping the pen. When she was
loose, we had to drop what we were doing, and herd her
back. She was a savage and knowing animal, and we armed
ourselves with stout sticks. It was a game of maneuver.
Ideally we would work her slowly back until the nearest one
of us could dart in and open the gate and the other would
stampede her through it before the rest of them could also
escape. But it never worked out that way. If we made the
slightest miscalculation, if we left too large a gap to right or
to left or between us, she would launch herself through it at
a dead run and we would have to begin all over again.

I had the same feeling of trying to herd something that
was endlessly alert to break loose.

And suddenly it did. All my desire for Niki came burning
and torrenting upon me, spewing into my mind all the
erotica of the solid, steady, metronomic surging of her hips
while her eyes rolled wild and all of her was supple in her
torment and her breasts were burning hardness, and her
arms grew awesomely strong, and her broken mouth was
lost in a demented babbling, keening and mewling between
the whistling gasps that measured, by their frequency, her
desperate climb to her peak of urgency. All the bright
hotness of her in my mind, coming so strongly and
suddenly, brought an icy sweat that soaked my body, and
brought a knotted aching tension to my loins, and made me
too sick and dizzy with my need to be able to drive. I pulled
over onto a wide shoulder, able to despise myself for noting
there was enough width for a U turn. I stopped and turned
off the motor and had the maniac idea that I should throw
the car key out into the darkness. I clenched the top of the
steering wheel, my fists close together, my forehead resting
on my fists. I rocked my head from side to side. In an
abandoned ballroom in my mind, countless naked images of

126

her danced to forgotten music, improvising obscene parodies I could not quite hear.

At one point I started the motor, I was that close to going back to her. But after a time the violence of my need began to fade. I had won, but I had no feeling of victory because I had won but one small skirmish. I had the sour wisdom of the addict who knows that the first episode of self-denial does not make future rejections easier. The need grows. All you can do is pray for increased strength with which to meet the next physiological assault.

I did not want to become the creature she could so easily turn me into. I did not want to release my grasp on pride and fall into the blind arena of sexual compulsion. Yet if there is no provable validity about any activity in which man indulges, if we are indeed but a ludicrous and self-important product of an accident of chemistry in the soupy sea of a brand-new planet . . .

I knew I could be too agile in such sly argumentation. Weak with emotional fatigue, I started the car and drove on into the city.

Chapter 11

As I walked through the hotel lobby, Joan Perrit got up from one of the lobby chairs and came toward me, earnest, pretty and worried.

"Mr. Dean, I've been waiting to—"

"You're not in the office now, Perry."

She flushed. "Gevan, then."

"You look all wound up. Buy you a drink?"

She lowered her voice. "There's someone who wants to talk to you, Gevan. I left her in the drugstore. If you're free, I'll bring her to your room in a few minutes. I tried to get you on the house phone and they said you were out."

I told her that would be fine and she smiled nervously and hurried off. I went up to my small suite. A few minutes later there was a tapping on my door. I let them in. I knew I had seen the other girl before, and then I remembered that when I had gotten my pass from Captain Corning, she had been at a typist's desk in the corner of his office.

She was a fluffy blonde in a cheap, bright outfit that emphasized her breasts and hips, She was the Hollywood ideal of the pretty starlet, her cheap, shallow beauty dependent upon the childishness of her features, the up-turned nose, pouting mouth, bland forehead, staring blue eyes. Though at the moment she looked frightened and rebellious, she was predictable as being, in other moods, a giggler, a snuggler, full of kittenish mannerisms and teasings.

"Mr. Dean, this is Alma Brady. She works in Colonel Dolson's office. She was hired by the Colonel as a clerk-bookkeeper. She has something to tell you."

"I waited for you," Alma said to Perry, "and I was about to go home. I was thinking about it. I guess I don't want to tell him anything after all." Her voice was thin and immature.

Perry took a step toward her, eyes hot. "You promised, Alma! You promised! You've got to tell him."

"Hold it," I said quickly. "Sit down, both of you. Behave."

Alma hesitated and then crossed over to a chair with a sulky strut, sat down, crossed her legs, patted her skirt smooth, hunted in her bag for cigarettes. I gave her a light. "How did you gals meet?"

Perry answered, "Alma rents a room near my house and we wait at the same bus stop, so we got friendly that way. She prepares the vouchers that Colonel Dolson handles through Mr. Granby's office as charges against the cost-plus contract."

"I don't want to get in any trouble," Alma said in her childish voice.

"I file our copies of the vouchers," Perry continued. "And I couldn't help noticing that there were certainly an awful lot of them coming from his office as charges against the D4D contract. So a couple of months ago I asked Alma if he was about through buying stuff. I wanted to know because I was going to have to set up new file folders and re-index them to keep them in order."

Alma had been staring stubbornly out the window. She turned sharply on Perry. "It wasn't any of your business what he bought."

"It wasn't," Perry said gently, "until we had that little chat today in the office. You made it my business, Alma."

"There's a lot of difference between telling you and

telling him. I don't want to get in any jam. I was just talking."

She turned stubbornly away and looked out the window. She exhaled smoke through her nose and it made her look like a petulant little dragon. Perry looked at me and shrugged. I edged my chair closer to Alma and said, "The last thing I want to do is get you in trouble, Miss Brady. I'd like to have you trust me."

"You say."

"I have no official connection with the firm. When I was president, Miss Perrit was my secretary. I have every confidence in her judgment. If she thinks you should tell me, then it is probably a good idea for you to tell me."

Alma looked at her cigarette and then obliquely at me. "She'll tell you anyway."

"She probably will. But I promise to keep you out of trouble if it's humanly possible."

The bland forehead wrinkled, and I could almost hear the wheels going around in her head. She sighed. "All right. Gee, I guess I've got to trust somebody in this thing. But the main thing is I want somebody to catch up with Curt Dolson and really clobber the hell out of him, but I don't want him knowing I had anything to do with it."

She looked at Perry. "Now I've started talking, I better cover some ground I didn't tell you today, Perry." She looked down at her crossed legs and tugged her skirt a bit forward where it had started to slip above her knee. She kept looking down. "He hired me in Washington and it was with the idea I'd be willing to be transferred here. I got here and it was a strange place to me, and you know, you get lonesome, especially around Christmas time. I got here just before Christmas. He was nice to me. I knew he was getting ideas. I mean that fatherly act is one you see through pretty easy, but I didn't brush him off because I was lonesome, and I figured if it ever came to an issue, I could handle it all right without making him sore. He got me a promotion right after Christmas and hinted about getting me another one. And he gave me a Christmas present and I thought that was sort of cute, you know. I guess he is a little smoother than I thought. He said we'd have our own private New Year's party. I took on so much champagne I thought I could even come up to his room here in the hotel and still handle him. Like a challenge, I guess. I don't know exactly how I ended up in bed with him, but I did. It wasn't going to happen again, believe me, but he was sweet about it, and sorry and all, and gave me presents, and I figured, oh, hell, the damage is done and who cares, so it got to be a regular thing. Now he's had enough. He's after the little broad that sings here. Hildy something. He's chasing her. He hasn't got time for me. Yesterday I tried to talk to him and he asked me what I was kicking about. I got my promotion, didn't I? That's why I want to see him get it in the neck. He's a stinker and I don't want to see him get away with doing that to me or anybody."

I said carefully, "It's unethical for a man in his position to get into that sort of situation, Miss Brady. But there isn't any basis there to—take any action against him."

She looked directly at me and her blue eyes narrowed. "All that, my friend, was telling you the why of it. I haven't gotten to the how yet." I sensed I had underestimated her intelligence. Those blue eyes in that moment were very knowing.

"I brought her here on account of the other part," Perry said.

"Mr. Dean, once it happened to me, I started thinking. I started wondering about something. When we were—going together, he was always in a sweat about money. He likes to live it up, you know. He borrowed money from Captain Corning a few times, near the end of the month. He had his pay and some income from that store of his. Then, while we were still—friendly, he started living better. That was back in late January and early February. He started carrying fat money around with him. And he gave me nicer things. This watch, for instance.

"It wasn't until after he broke if off that I began thinking about how he suddenly had a better income. When I got

131

here, Curt Dolson and Mr. Mottling weren't getting along at all. He used to yammer about Mottling to me. Then, in late January they kissed and made up or something. That was about the time Curt started having money.

"Then I remembered Perry asking me about those vouchers, and I thought some more and I wondered if Curt was pulling something. I began checking our purchase order file against shipping instructions and inventories. Curt was ordering a lot of things chargeable to the cost-plus contract. A lot of it was coming to the plant and a lot of it wasn't, even though the inventory reports checked against the total ordered. With Curt doing the ordering and also being responsible for inventories, he could order stuff and have it shipped someplace else. And I remembered that in January, about the time he and Mottling got friendly, he'd gotten permission to rent warehouse space in town because storage facilities at the plant weren't adequate. I kept checking the files every time I had a chance, and finally I spotted one purchase order that looked like a duplicate. It was made out to something called Acme Supply. That's right here in Arland, 56 River Street, and that's close to the warehouse space the Colonel rented. Letters from Acme are signed by some man named LeFay. I'm positive, Mr. Dean, that Curt is placing legitimate orders, then having the incoming stuff diverted to Acme, and then placing a duplicate order with Acme."

"Wait a minute," I said. "Let me get this straight. Say Dolson had to order typewriters. He'd order, say, three and divert two of them to that rented warehouse space?"

"Yes. Then he'd order two from Acme. Acme would get those two out of the rented space and deliver them to the plant. Dolson would see that Acme got paid. The records would show five typewriters ordered, three in use and two in storage, and because the Colonel keeps the warehouse inventory records, there isn't any way to check. Maybe he had the incoming stuff diverted to Acme somehow, so it never goes into storage, then places a duplicate order with Acme. That way, paying twice for the same stuff, he and this LaFay could split whatever they get for it."

"Are the amounts involved large?"

"I've found one for forty thousand. And smaller ones running five and ten and twenty and so on. They're for things that aren't bulky. Small machine tool items. Office equipment, office machines, and cutters and things I don't know anything about. Now you know as much as I do, and you can do anything with it you want to, just so you leave me out of it. I mean, I won't testify or anything. As far as I'm concerned, I haven't told you a thing."

She turned back toward the window, her childish mouth hard and set, and her eyes still narrow. I could see how Dolson's scheme could work. It would be a fast way to make money. But it could never be a safe way. It was a fool's game. There would be a day of reckoning and disgrace and prison. I could assume the girl wasn't lying. Her shrewdness enabled her to find out what was being done. But she did not have the creative intelligence to invent such a scheme just to embarrass Curt Dolson.

Perry said, "I spent an hour this afternoon checking our files. She's telling the truth, Mr. Dean."

Maybe it was the truth, but I mistrusted the way the girl tied it to Mottling. I decided it was coincidence that the two men should have started seeing eye to eye at the time Dolson devised his plan. I couldn't see Mottling implicating himself in a plan that could only have been devised by a very foolish and greedy little man. I couldn't see Mottling participating. His motivation was the hunger for power, not cash.

"Alma, thank you for telling me this," I said. "It's enormously important, and I'm grateful to you. Now suppose you run along and forget what you told us. Don't mention it to anybody else. Do you think the Colonel has any idea you suspect what he's doing?"

She stood up and said with dignity, "He wouldn't give me credit for being bright enough."

"Could you stay for a few minutes, Perry?" I asked her. She nodded. I let Alma out. I watched her walk toward the elevators, teetering along on too-high heels, her round hips swinging, her head high. I closed the door.

"What do you think, Gevan?" Perry asked.

"It sounds bad enough to be true, or true enough to be bad. I'm glad you brought her to me."

"I should have told Mr. Granby. The company is in the clear. We haven't the authority to disapprove any voucher presented by the Colonel in his capacity as contracting officer. Mr. Granby would know who to contact in Washington. But I knew she wouldn't talk to Mr. Granby. I wanted someone to hear it from her as soon as possible. She didn't tell me . . . about their relationship. It's—terribly sad, isn't it?"

"That's one word for it." She sat on the couch. Her wool suit was pale, of nubbly texture. I paced to the window.

"Perry, I think we've got to assume that at the least hint or suspicion, Dolson will try to cover himself. I think he's in so deep he can't cover himself completely, but he could make it a lot tougher to get the facts. You have a file of the dupes of al those vouchers?"

"Yes. I could dig out all the ones that went through for payment to Acme, and make a list of the items and the totals."

"Good! Do it inconspicuously. I'll see what I can find out about Acme. Then I know the next step. A phone call to Washington. On a thing like this they move fast. They'll have a bunch of people in here before Dolson can say General Accounting Office. And if they do it fast, all we can hope for is for some relationship between Dolson and Mottling showing up."

Perry's gray eyes were thoughtful. "I've wondered about that. I just can't see what Mr. Mottling would get out of any—relationship like that. It seems so—petty. And yet—"

"What are you thinking about?"

She shrugged. "I suppose it's meaningless. But you know the sort of man Colonel Dolson is. Self-important, sort of. Something happened a month ago. The Colonel and Mr. Mottling came out of Mr. Granby's office, through my office. Colonel Dolson was telling Mr. Mottling there were some drawings he'd have to have back immediately. Mr.

Mottling said he'd send those drawings back to Dolson when he was damn well ready to release them and not before. Colonel Dolson took it without a murmur, and he knew I heard it, and he didn't make any attempt to save face in front of me. It was as though Mr. Mottling had some special hold over him."

"That isn't much to go on."

"I realize that."

"Could you make a guess about the number of government checks that have cleared for Acme?"

"It doesn't work that way. Acme gets Dean Products' checks, out of the D4D account, and the government reimburses us. I'd guess, off-hand, Gevan, the total might be anywhere between one and two hundred thousand dollars."

Though I knew what a small percentage that would be of the multimillion-dollar government contracts in the shop, it was a figure that merited a soft whistle of awe. I had an important question to ask, and perhaps I asked it in too casual a voice. "Do you think Ken could have found out about this?" I couldn't see Dolson as a killer. But I didn't know LeFay.

She knew what I meant. "No, Gevan. Ever since Mr. Mottling came with the company, your brother stayed in his office. Nothing was routed to him, and he didn't take any interest in what was going on. I don't see how he could have found out."

I gave up that line of thought with regret. It would be such a perfect motive, and explain the clever detail surrounding the murder. It was after eight. I knew from the way she was dressed she had gone home before coming to the hotel.

"Have you eaten yet, Perry?"

"No. When you weren't here, I phoned Mother and told her I'd be home after dinner."

"Dinner with me, then?"

"Yes, thank you, Gevan." She smiled and I noticed a dimple in her right cheek. "It feels funny to call you Gevan out loud."

We went down and had a pleasant dinner in the grill. At one point she said, "I'm too honest, Gevan. Now I have to correct a half-truth."

"A half-truth is half a lie."

"I told you I came to you because I didn't think she'd talk to Mr. Granby. I had another reason, too. I'm trying to get you so involved in Dean Products you won't be able to get loose."

There was a candle on our table. She sat across from me, smiling, her face young and lovely in the flame's light. Too young and fresh and sweet. I was too involved with Niki to ever get loose. I thought of Niki in my arms, and in contrast to the gray-eyed girl across the table, the memory of Niki was smeared and shameful—but exciting.

After dinner I asked her if she'd like to try the Copper Lounge and listen to Hildy's show, but she said she should go home. I offered to get the car out and drive her back, but she said a cab would be fine. I walked her out to the sidewalk and hailed a taxi and watched her ride off, saw her turn and look through the back window of the cab at me.

I went to the Copper Lounge. Hildy Devereaux was standing at the bar, laughing and chattng with a young couple. She recognized me and gave me a quick smile. I gestured toward an empty table and raised one eyebrow in silent question. She nodded. I sat and ordered a drink and Hildy came over a few minutes later. I stood up and said, "Not purely social, Hildy, but I wish it was."

I pushed her chair in for her. She smiled up at me, saying, "I'm glad you came in. I think my curtain line last time was faintly nasty."

"Not noticeably." I sat down in the chair facing hers. "You set me off in a certain direction so you get a progress report before I spring a question."

"Progress?"

"In a negative way. I won't go into my reasoning. I just want to tell you that I'm personally convinced that Ken wasn't shot by Shennary. Shennary was cleverly framed. I don't know *why* Ken was killed. Or by whom. But it wasn't

Shennary and that means there was a good reason, premeditation, a lot of damn careful planning."

She thought it over. And shuddered. "The way it happened seemed too pat—but maybe I liked that answer better than the way this one makes me feel."

"I know. It makes the world a larger, darker place. I don't have to tell you not to repeat this, do I?"

"No. You don't have to, Gevan."

"Now this question may seem unrelated. It is—almost. The connection is tenuous. I want your reaction to Curt Dolson."

She gave a little start and her eyes widened. "What do I think of him? My God, that's a change of pace! He's in my hair, but so are a lot of others. He's just thicker-skinned than most. He's got an ego like nothing I ever saw before. He can't get it through his pointy head that I'm not on the verge of falling into his arms. He has propositions. Some of them include South-Sea cruises and emeralds. He gets pretty intent."

"That one with the emeralds is a pretty good offer for a chicken colonel to make, isn't it?"

"The boy is pretty well loaded. He owns a business that keeps him solvent enough. He's so damn smug. And so vain, too. He keeps sticking his chin out so the second chin won't show. He uses male perfume and goes around smelling like tweed and saddle leather and fire in the heather. Wears a corset, too, if I'm any judge. He's just a boy at heart."

"There's no chance of his hitting the right proposition?"

"That better be a joke, and you better start laughing like hell, or you're sitting here alone, Mr. D."

"It was a joke."

"There isn't exactly any halo above these flaxen locks, brother, but at least I can say all favors thus far distributed have been gratis."

"I said it was a joke."

"Okay, I forgive. Let me give you a briefing." She changed to an excellent imitation of Dolson's hearty baritone. " 'You can do your singing just for me, my dear.

137

This isn't the life for you.' I told him I loved this nasty life, and if I ever gave it up it wouldn't be for him or anybody remotely like him. Did that stop him? For about a tenth of a second. It took him that long to find my knee under the table. And it took me another tenth of a second to get my cigarette against the back of his hand."

I looked beyond her. "It seems you have been speaking of the devil."

She rolled her eyes ceilingward. "No. Oh, no! Give me strength."

Dolson came parade-grounding up, gave a Prussian bow from the waist, with a cool smile for me and a warm one for Hildy. "Evening, my dear. Hello, Mr. Dean." He pulled a chair out. "Hope this isn't taken."

"It is now," Hildy said glumly.

"Great little kidder," Dolson said fondly. He sat with back straight, shoulders squared, eagles shining.

"We were discussing you, Colonel," I said mildly.

It took him a moment to decide how to react. He showed us his white teeth and said, "Nothing good, I trust."

"We were wondering why a man of your means happens to be on active duty."

He shrugged his eagles. "Reserve, you know. Every man who has any training ought to put it at the service of his government. This is a critical era, Mr. Dean. We're all needed."

I sensed the criticism. He sat erect, smelling of Scotch and pine. His nails gleamed with some manicurist's dedication. His face glowed pink and healthy. It was as though Dolson had erected a facade to conceal the man behind it. Unlike Lester of the shifting masks, Dolson had only one acquired character: the brusque, hearty military man, with faint overtones of king and empire and the playing fields of Eton.

I wondered if he had been active in politics in his home town. I wondered how much affability, how much snap and sirring it had cost him to get that Legion of Merit ribbon. I wondered how he looked when he was alone and sat worrying about the money he was making and how he was making it. Was the pink face pouched and old and frightened? Did the plump pink shoulders sag?

I chose the opening instinctively, the opening he had just given me. "Colonel, I've been thinking along those lines myself. Patriotic duty and all that. Getting my shoulders to the wheel."

He beamed. "My boy, you'll feel better for it, believe me."

"Mr. Granby says he will withdraw in my favor, and Mr. Karch will back me. At the Monday meeting, I'll vote my holdings for myself, and take over where Ken left off." It took three long seconds for the toothy smile to fade away. He goggled at me. He slumped and the padded shoulders of the tunic rode up. He licked his lips. He was suddenly a very worried, very unmilitary, very nervous little man. He forced the smile back, but it had all the humor of a denture ad.

"Uh—commendable of course. I can understand any man wanting to do his bit." The heartiness was strained. "But let's not try to move too fast, Mr. Dean. That would be—uh—like my trying to take over an infantry division. A man should be—objective enough to know when a job is too big for him."

"Too big, Colonel? I'm afraid I don't understand, I've run the company before."

"I'm afraid this is a different proposition. That was mostly civilian production." He was getting over shock and warming to his argument. "Stanley Mottling has a national reputation and an astonishing record. It wouldn't be any service to the company to take over the position he fills so well. And if you don't mind my mentioning it, a four-year layoff doesn't sharpen a man's mind. Stanley Mottling's last four years have been full of accomplishment."

I pursed my lips and nodded. "Maybe there's something in that."

All the confidence was back. "Tell you what. Why don't you talk to Stanley about going to work under him? There are places where you could be very valuable. That would ease the load on Stanley."

"I guess I should reconsider, Colonel."

"That's using the old brain," he said. "Objectivity." He had brought his drink to the table and he lifted it and took a long drag with a shade too much relief.

"I agree I may be rusty," I said. "So I'll put my voting weight behind Walter Granby and let him take over."

He plunked his glass down. He stared at me. "Granby! Good God!"

"I'd rather back him. I know the man. I've got confidence in him. I don't agree with some of Mottling's policies."

"Good God!" he repeated in an empty voice.

I knew it was cruel to get him off balance with one idea and then slap him with the other one before he could get his feet planted. A cruel device—and effective when you need information that can only be given inadvertently.

He tried to use a tone of sweet reason. "Mr. Dean, you can't look at the world through a peashooter. Granby is *entirely* unsuitable, old boy."

I had been mild up to that point. So mild, I knew he had forgotten our chat in Mottling's office. So I discarded mildness and said, "It seems odd to me, Colonel, that you keep taking an interest in the internal affairs of the company. Didn't we cover that ground once?"

He murmured something about irreparable damage, critical contracts.

I turned to Hildy and said, "How long are you going to work here?"

"As long as the gross stays healthy in the lounge, I guess. Joe says I can sing here until I look like Whistler's mother, if the gross doesn't fade." She made her voice casual and winked meaningfully at me. I glanced at Dolson.

He seemed to have forgotten the two of us. He was staring down at the table top, motionless. Something about him made me think that perhaps this pseudo-hearty little man was not entirely ridiculous. Cornered creatures fight, and many have sharp teeth.

He looked at me, unsmiling, and said, "Just one thing. Is that your decision? Nothing can change it?"

It was not my decision. But it was so strong a hunch that I was able to state it too calmly for him to doubt it.

He smiled vaguely and got up. "It's your stock, I suppose. Too bad. I'll be back, Hildy."

"I'll try to conceal my impatience, Colonel."

"Great little kidder," he said, and patted her shoulder mechanically, taking no notice of her instinctive flinch. I watched him go. He went out the side door of the Copper Lounge, the one that opened onto the flight of wide stairs that led to the lobby.

Hildy ceremoniously offered her small hand. "You upset the Colonel. You made him very unhappy. It was very nice to watch. Does that make me a sadist?"

"I'll tell you all about that later. Right now I think the Colonel is off to make a phone call. If he makes it from a booth, we're sunk. But I think he may make it from his room. Are you chummy with the switchboard gals?"

"They love me," she said, and got up and hurried off, looking back just long enough for a conspiratorial wink. Her quick mind needed no blueprint. The soft brown hair bounced against honeyed shoulders, and her skirt swung with the quickness of her stride.

It took her five long minutes. She came back and slipped into the chair opposite me. "From the room like you thought. Here." She slid a slip of paper over to me, with a number written on it. Redwood 8-7171. It meant nothing to me.

"Now I sing again."

"Thanks for this, Hildy."

"Poo. Thank me by keeping me advised. Write it in invisible ink on the back of an old tennis player."

"It might not mean anything."

"Then come back when you know, Gev."

I listened to one good song, then went up to a lobby booth, inserted a dime and dialed the number. The line was busy. I lit a cigarette, waited a minute, and tried again. It rang twice and was answered. "Hello?"

I replaced the receiver on the hook and stepped out of the booth. The voice had been unmistakable, fruity, unctuous.

The resonant, noble voice of Lester Fitch. I checked the book and found that it was the number for his residence.

It was predictable. It was nothing that would be meaningful to Hildy. To me it meant a possible confirmation of Lester's larcenous instincts. I realized I should have taken steps to find out if the Colonel made other calls. Too late for that now.

I had convinced Dolson, and he had passed on the information, and I had the feeling that I had set something in motion. I didn't know what, or how big it was. But something had started to move.

I suddenly realized how very tired I was. The day had been full. It was incredible that this was only my third evening back in Arland.

The situation was becoming too complex. It was like one of those backlashes you sometimes get on a fishing reel. They look as if tugging one strand would free them. But you tug one strand and peel off some line and find another tangle farther down, and that one conceals two more.

I went to bed. I lay in darkness and watched a merry-go-round. All the gay horses with their noble wooden heads, surging up and down carrying the riders—carrying Mottling and Dolson and Fitch and Granby and Hildy and Perry and Niki and a faceless LeFay—with an empty saddle where Ken had ridden. They went around and around, and the music was a banjo jangle, but I didn't know the tune.

On this same evening, at dusk, the tarpon were in the big hole near the channel off Boca Grande, and the charter boats would be drift-fishing the hole. They would hit and the reels would sing. It was simple savagery more easy to comprehend and combat than the civilized variety which hides the teeth behind a smile.

I fell asleep wondering how Perry would react to a hundred and forty pounds of tarpon glinting high in the moonlight and falling back.

Chapter 12

Friday morning was rainy, blustery. Soggy papers whipped around River Street in tight spirals trying to paste themselves against your ankles. I stopped at a corner store and bought a plastic raincoat.

The night's sleep hadn't done me much good. Too much tension makes too many dreams. Niki, Perry, Hildy, Lita, Alma—all of them had twisted through my dreams in perfumed confusion, saying things I couldn't understand. At one point Mottling had been carefully explaining to me that a D4D was alive, and if you looked closely enough, you could see it breathe. He forced my head down against it, and under the metal skin I could hear the thud of a great slow heart. It felt oddly warm against my ear, and when I straightened up I saw it was a gigantic breast, and I had been listening to the womanheart. There was a second breast in the shadows off to the right, and beyond them a foreshortened sleeping face. My midget feet sank into the rubbery skin and Mottling was gone and I ran in terror and fell from the sleeping body into darkness. . . .

So when I awoke I felt tired and drained and odd, with sour mouth and aching joints.

River Street paralleled the river, but the warehouses blocked the view of it. Freighters off-loaded at the river docks into the warehouses for trans-shipment by rail and truck. Huge trucks were parked on the west side of the street, tailgates against the loading docks, cabs swiveled at right angles to the trailers to let traffic edge by. Men wheeled hand trucks into the trailers, and forklift trucks were hurrying with insect intentness. Wildcatters dickered for loads with warehouse agents, and assorted hangover victims huddled in doorways, watching the wan morning world, flinching at too much noise. The early bars were open, smelling of stale beer.

I found number 56 on the east side of the street, a narrow doorway with a flight of stairs leading up. The doorway was between a bar and a marine supply store. Just inside the door, fastened to the wall, was a series of small wooden signs. There was a studio of the dance, a Russian bath, a twine company, a watch repairman, a skin specialist, a Spanish teacher, and Acme Supply. The Acme Supply sign was newest. It indicated the fourth floor of the narrow building.

The wooden steps of the three flights were dished by fifty years of wear. Dun plaster had crumbled off the wall exposing small areas of naked lath. It was a strange location for a company that could be grossing as much as a quarter of a million a year. On the second floor landing I heard voices chanting, *"Yo tengo un lapiz."*

On the third floor a tired samba beat came through the door that announced the studio of the dance. A sailor stood in the hall talking in low tones to a miss in black velveteen slacks and a cerise blouse. Neither of them looked at me as I went by. She was shaking her head dully. His lips were an inch from her ear.

Acme shared the fourth floor with the skin specialist. On the opaque glass of the upper half of the aged oak door was painted, without caps: *acme—industrial supplies—c. armand lefay, president.*

There was a mail slot in the door. I knocked. No answer. I looked closely at the knob and saw dust on it. I tried the knob and found the door was locked.

The skin specialist's door was not locked. A sign said COME IN. I went in. A girl in white behind the desk looked up at me with visible annoyance. She was blonde and sallow and her eyes were set too close together. There was a book propped up in front of her, an historical novel with a mammary cover, and she had been filing her nails as she read.

"Do you have an appointment?" she asked. Her voice was colorless and nasal.

"I don't want to see the doctor. I was wondering how I could get in touch with your neighbor across the hall, Mr. LeFay. How often does he come in?"

"I couldn't say."

"Do you see him often?"

"I don't pay no attention."

"Have you ever seen him?"

"A couple times, sure."

"Could you tell me what he looks like?"

"What goes on? You a cop or a bill collector or what? Or you want to sell him something?"

"None of those. I just want to get in touch with him. I thought you might help me out. I'd appreciate it."

She smiled reluctantly. "You don't look like any of those things except maybe a salesman. He's a mousy little guy. I mean you wouldn't ever look at him close. He could be five-foot-four or five-foot-seven, and thirty-five or fifty-five. Just one of those people you don't look at."

"Does he have a secretary?"

"If he has, I've never seen her or heard her. I'm too busy to keep my nose in what goes on across the hall. Honest, I'm sorry I can't help you, but honest to God, I couldn't even tell you what it says on the door—and I couldn't care less."

I smiled, "I was going to ask you where he lives, but I guess that's no good."

She smiled, and again it looked as if it hurt her mouth. "I could maybe help a little bit. I got a hunch he lived right in that office for a while. It's against the rules, but who's going

145

to check? I figured that because I'd smell something cooking when I'd come in in the morning. But I haven't smelled anything lately."

"Have you ever seen an army officer in uniform on the stairs? Man in his fifties? Florid complexion?"

"I don't have time to keep going up and down the stairs and anyway, I keep my door shut all the time. That junky music from downstairs drives me nuts. The same records, over and over and over, and if all that's down there is a dance studio, I'll eat every record they got in the place. We've been here nine years and it gets worse and worse. The doctor talks about moving, but will he ever do anything? Not him. We'll be right here the day the goddamn place falls down."

I backed to the door. "Thanks a lot."

"For what?"

I went down the stairs. The sailor was gone. The girl in black slacks and cerise shirt was still there, cupping her elbow in her palm, shoulders against the wall, staring at the floor, smoking. She gave me an opaque look as I went by her, tramped on her cigarette, and went into the dance studio. Another record started to play.

I walked three blocks to my car. The rain had stopped. I tossed the raincoat onto the back seat. I put the car in a lot near the hotel and went to my room and called Mottling from there. I got him on the line and told him in as casual a voice as I could manage that I had decided to back Granby.

"I'm sorry, of course," he said smoothly, "but thanks for letting me know."

"That was the arrangement. Glad to do it."

"I guess you know I hate like the devil to give up this job. Thanks again for letting me know, fella. 'By now."

I hung up and frowned at the wall. The reaction had been too perfect, too casual. There was no doubt that he had known. Dolson had known, Lester had known, and Mottling had known. The phone rang, startling me. I picked it up.

"Gevan? Stanley Mottling again. Wondered if I have your permission to tell Mrs. Dean? She's anxious to know."

"I thought I'd go out there and tell her myself later on today."

"I think that's a good idea. See you at the meeting on Monday."

The moment I hung up, the phone rang again and the switchboard girl downstairs said, "I'm holding a call for you, Mr. Dean. Go ahead, miss."

"Gevan?" I recognized Perry's voice. She was upset.

"Yes, Perry."

"I'm across the street from the offices. This is the second time I tried to get you this morning, Gevan. I'm scared. Somebody got into my files last night, or before I got in this morning. The Acme folders are gone. I could still get totals from the books but they won't mean as much because they don't show the items."

"Was the file locked?"

"Yes. It's a combination safe file. But when Captain Corning came here, he got authority to change all the combinations on the safe files. He'd have a list in his office, of course. Colonel Dolson could have gotten hold of that list, wouldn't you think?"

After a few moments she asked in a small voice, "Are you still there, Gevan?"

"Sorry, I was thinking. There should be duplicates in the Army office files. Do you think Alma Brady could grab those, if they haven't already disappeared?"

"I thought of that when I couldn't get you on the phone. I made an excuse to go over there. She didn't come in this morning."

"Maybe she was too upset after last night. Do you have her address? I could go see her. You said a rooming house, didn't you?"

"Go by my house headed east and take the next right. It's in the middle of the block. A green and white house on the left. I think the number is 881. I've got to get back, Gevan.

147

I haven't told Mr. Granby about files being missing. Should I? He'll be wild."

"Keep it to yourself for a while. If there isn't a big furor, somebody is going to start wondering why. It may make them nervous."

It was just eleven o'clock when I parked in front of the only green and white house in the middle of the block. She had missed the number, but not by much. I went up onto the porch. The wind rocked a green wicker rocking chair. I pushed the bell and above the wind's sound I could hear it ring in the back of the house. I felt uneasy. Through the glass of the door, between lace curtains; I saw a vast woman waddling down the hallway toward the door, emerging from the gloom like something prehistoric.

She opened the door. She couldn't have been more than twenty pounds too light for a fat-lady job in any circus. Her eyes were pretty, and the rest of the huge face sagged in larded folds. She was a prisoner inside that flesh. Somewhere inside the half-barrel haunches, the ponderous, doughy breasts and belly, stood a woman who was not old and who had once been pretty. Her tiny pink mouth crouched warily back in the crevice between the slablike cheeks.

Her voice was thin and musical. "Good morning."

"I wonder if I could see Miss Alma Brady."

"You can find her over to Dean Products. She works civil service over there, for Colonel Dolson."

"She didn't report for work this morning."

"That's funny! If somebody's sick, the other girls, they tell me. I can't get upstairs and the girls, they all take care of their own rooms, so I wouldn't see her if she was sick in bed. Come to think of it, I didn't see her go out this morning." She moved to the foot of the stairs. The hall floor creaked under her weight.

"Alma! Alma, honey!" Her voice was thin, clear, and young. She was a yard across the hips.

We listened and she called again and there was no

148

answer. I said, "She might be asleep. If you could tell me which room I could go and check."

"Well—I don't like to break the rules and that's one of the rules, about no men on the second floor."

I had to try my Arland magic again. "My name is Dean. Gevan Dean. Dean Products. I can show you identification."

"I was wondering where I'd seen you and now I know it was in the papers, so I guess it's all right if *you* go on up, Mr. Dean. Golly, I didn't know Alma knew you. You go right on up and straight down the hall toward the back of the house to the last door on the left. You know, funny thing, that girl's been on my mind lately. She used to be so sunny, and lately she's been awful sour."

I went up two stairs at a time. The hall had a girl smell— perfume and lotions and astringents and wave set. And the echoes of night gigglings, and whispered confidences and man hunger and pillows salted with tears.

I knocked at Alma's door. There was no answer. I opened the door cautiously and saw that the room was empty. I went in. The bed had not been slept in. It looked as if our Alma had had a night on the tiles. I couldn't blame her. Not in her frame of mind. I remembered she had been carrying a red coat in my hotel room. I looked in her closet. No red coat. So the odds were she hadn't come back to her room last night. There was a picture on her maple dressing table. A tinted photograph of a young man in swim trunks. He looked stiffly into the camera, unsmiling, his arms held awkwardly so the muscles would bulge.

I went downstairs and gave the fat woman a reassuring smile. "I guess she just didn't come in at all last night."

"Oh, she came in, all right."

"You saw her?"

"No, but my room is off the kitchen, right under hers, and I heard her moving around, quiet like. It woke me up. I sleep light, and my clock has hands you can see in the dark. It was after three."

"I guess she came in and went out again, because the bed isn't slept in."

"You know, I remember thinking in the night it was good for her to be going out with a gentleman friend again. She used to keep real late hours, and come dragging in at dawn and sleep a little and go off to work bright as a dollar. I guess you can do that when you're young as she is. She was cheerful then, like I said, but since she's been spending the evenings in her room, she's been broody. No pleasant word for anybody, and she was one of my nicest girls. They don't go much for the late dates except on week ends, because some of them are studying a lot on their graduate work over to the college."

"Would it be too much trouble to check with your other girls and see if any of them saw her last night or this morning, Mrs. —"

"Colsinger. Martha Colsinger, Mr. Dean. Where should I phone you if I find out anything, or will you come back?"

"You can phone me at the Gardland. If I'm not in, please leave your name and I'll phone you back. I hope it isn't too much trouble."

"No, because I'd check anyway. I got a kind of uneasy feeling about all this. You don't think anything could have happened to her, do you?"

"I don't think so. I certainly hope not."

I thanked her and left. I told myself I was primarily interested in seeing Niki because I wanted to see what her reaction would be to my decision to back Walter Granby. Of course, it wasn't a final decision. It was a bluff. I had until the Monday meeting to make my actual decision.

But as I drove, a little too fast, toward the Lime Ridge house, I had enough fragmented decency to be conditionally honest with myself. I wanted to look at her. I wanted to see her because our sunlit orgy had become unreal and implausible. It was an episode I knew I should try to forget, yet, perversely, I wanted some confirmation from her that it had actually happened.

A time of sleep, even when it is as dream-torn as mine

had been, erects a curious barrier. The memory of that particular kind of frenzy becomes very like the memory of having been very drunk. It is difficult to credit yourself with the remembered things done and said. You say, "That could not have been me! I am not like that! There is some mistake. There is some significant thing I have forgotten which makes all the rest of it excusable."

Low, misty clouds were moving quickly, sometimes touching the tops of the rolling hills. The air was humid with spring, and warming rapidly.

Victoria greeted me, smiling, and told me to wait in the living-room. I watched her narrowly, alert for any subtle hint that she had learned, somehow, what had happened. Maids can make an entire construction from the smallest carelessness. I wondered if Niki had been properly careful with my stained clothing and with the toilet kit she had provided. Though usually I give less than a damn about what anybody thinks of how I live and what I do, I surprised myself with the extent of my concern for Victoria's good opinion. She struck me as being, in that only basic and pertinent way, a lady. And she would assess sudden and sweaty copulation between the new widow and the brother of the deceased as a unique vileness. Which it was.

There was no change in her remote, friendly politeness. As she walked away I suddenly knew that if Victoria guessed what had happened after she left, she would no longer be here. She was that sort of a person. So Niki, no matter what other motivations she might have, would be extraordinarily careful for fear of losing an exceptionally good servant.

I waited tensely in the rich silence of the big room. It was a handsome but sterile room. I saw it was a room without sign or stain that life had gone on in it. (This model home is in the hundred-and-fifty-thousand price range. Note the subtle yet effective use of color. The small placards show where each item may be purchased. Please do not touch anything.)

Niki came walking in quickly, brisk and smiling, coming

to me to put the quick light kiss at the corner of my mouth, then say with a housewife's glib affection, "Hello, my darling. I've missed you."

She wore a man's white shirt with the sleeves rolled up, and closely tailored pale blue denim ranch pants. Her hair was latched back with a twist of matching blue yarn. A scab of mud was drying on the right knee of the ranch pants. She carried work gloves and a muddy grubbing tool, shaped like a green steel claw. (And this model represents the lovely mistress of the $150,000 house who loves to work in her garden on warm spring mornings.)

"If you need props, you could wheel a wheelbarrow in."

She looked at the gloves and garden tool. "I didn't know I'd brought these in. I can be nervous too, you know. Give me that much credit, Gevan."

She walked over to place the tool and gloves on the raised hearth. As she did so, the pale crust of mud fell from her knee and broke on the rug. She squatted and carefully picked up every crumb, her back to me. The coarse denim was pulled as tight as her skin. There were no kidney pads of fat, no rope of softness above the stricture of the dark blue belt. There was a long and firm blending of line, from the reversed parentheses outlining the trimness of the waist, down into the reverse curve of the inverted, truncated, Valentine heart of solid buttocks. Even as she sat so effortlessly on her heels, she kept her back so straight, the small of her back was concave. Her figure was strangely deceptive. She was so basically sturdy as to be, in thigh, hip and breast, almost massive. Yet the total impression she gave was of actual slenderness. This was the product of her height, of the long oval of her face—designed for a more fragile woman—of the quick, light way she moved, of her short-waisted, leggy build, and of her lack of any sagging softnesses, any self-indulgent bulgings. She was styled for function, designed with the merciless economy men expend on the weapons with which they kill. There are never many of them in the world at any one time, and fewer who, like Niki, had peaked into such rich and awesome splendor.

Looking at her confirmed every memory of the previous day, and made me willing to partially—very partially—forgive myself. Hers was an earthiness and a primitive readiness that created a response so atavistic, all the intellectualizings and moralizings of a modern man were flung aside, like dust from a spinning disk.

She dropped the crumbs of mud into an ash tray, walked over and sat on the flat wooden arm of a handsome chair and seemed to study me with care. "I really thought you would come back last night. I thought of cute little ways of keeping you from feeling too awkward about coming back so soon."

"Would they have worked?"

"Probably not. But five minutes after you were here, it wouldn't have mattered, would it?"

"I almost came back."

"You were a stuffy fool not to." She carefully examined a fingernail. "You should know this isn't a good time, dear. If you want, I'll send her off on some errands, but I think it would be too obvious, don't you?"

"I didn't come here for . . ."

"Not so loud, darling!" She stood up. "I'll go change. Victoria will bring some ice. You make us some drinks and we'll have lunch."

"I can't stay that long, thanks."

With a waspish look, she said, "You make it pretty damn difficult for me to remember I'm spending the rest of my life with you."

"It's all decided?"

"Isn't it?"

"Yesterday you seemed to be setting up some conditions."

"Oh, that! Just get over all the hostility, sweet. But don't take too long, please. I want to be your girl, without all this . . . disputation."

I went over and sat on a low windowseat and looked at her across thirty feet of the room's silence. "We're trying to move too fast," I told her.

153

"I know it. I didn't mean it to be this way. I was going to be the muted widow, darling, with a carefully calculated sigh and snuffle from time to time, and I was going to be terribly proper about the whole routine. But that very first time I saw you, just before Stanley arrived, remember? My splendid intentions went all to hell. It was . . . like a spell. I guess I knew then I couldn't continue the act, but I told myself it was just one little slip that didn't count. Yesterday, darling, maybe you won't believe this, but I plotted that little sun-lotion routine just to prove to myself I was a girl of character. I was going to tease you, darling, that's all. I wanted you to want me and be able to do nothing about it. I thought you'd cap the bottle and scramble back to the wall and try to look as if it didn't matter, and I was going to be laughing at you, inside. But . . . all of a sudden there was no turning back for either of us. Yes, we're going too fast. I know that. I didn't plan it that way. But we are, and I don't think there's very much we can do about it."

"We can avoid opportunities like that."

"Don't be such a fool! We'll be creating opportunities like that. I will, certainly. Gevan, my darling, there is something you should know. I should have told you yesterday. It could make you feel better about us. For almost this whole past year he was totally impotent. I think it was a traumatic thing—that terrible scene. Maybe the knowledge that I've always belonged to you became so strong in his subconscious . . . When I tried to talk about it, and tried to get him to see a psychiatrist, he'd get almost violent. It . . . wasn't much of a marriage, Gevan. You should know that . . . and you should remember that Ken would want us to be happy. He did love us both."

Again I found myself resenting plausibility. It accounted for his drinking, weeping, and his loss of interest in his work. Maybe it explained why his interest in Hildy was so platonic. It was all so very neat—and so unlike the Ken I remembered.

"Pretty rough deal for a woman like you," I said. "Has Stanley been able to perform efficiently in that area too?"

After a momentary blankness of shock, she came striding toward me, her face contorted. "That is a goddamn filthy, vicious, stinking thing to say to . . ." She stopped six feet from me and closed her eyes. When her face was calm she opened her eyes and smiled and said, "I *must* make myself remember you are a very sensitive guy, my Gevan. You feel guilty about Ken, and you feel guilty about yesterday, and you want to punish yourself, so you keep striking out at me." She came close and made a soft thud as she dropped to her knees on the carpeting. She took my hand in both of hers, kissed the palm, and then held the palm of my hand against her cheek for a moment.

"Not Stanley, my friend. Not anybody, even though many men seem to have a sixth sense about such situations, and they make little hints about how discreet they could be. Hell, I'm not a hypocrite, Gevan. Certainly I was tempted. I was made to be loved a thousand times a year. There were some highly edgy times around here, believe me, when I'd stalk this house like a randy panther, fighting off that moment when I'd have to shame myself with some nasty, lonely little release or go completely out of my mind. I would ache for you, Gevan. So that's what happened to us yesterday, darling. So much saved up. Just before I lost the ability to think at all, I was wondering if I was frightening you or hurting you." She kissed my knuckles and sat back on her heels and smiled up at me. "When I woke up this morning I stretched and stretched. I felt all over silky and warm. I woke into a world full of roses and music and love talk. When I came out of my shower and brushed my teeth, I pretended I was going to crawl right back into bed with you and awaken you in some delicious way. I realized it wouldn't be long before I *could* do that, and it made me feel so good I laughed out loud. I guess you think we were dreadfully evil yesterday, Gevan. But today I feel like a bride. Nothing that can make me feel like this can be so horrible, can it?"

"I guess we'll have to talk this way," I said, "and I guess we will, if things are going to get the way you believe they'll be, but right now, Niki, I have to talk about what I came here to talk about."

"You look so earnest!"

"You made me believe this Mottling thing is important to you, so I decided the fair thing was to come and tell you what I decided. I do not believe Mottling is the man to run Dean Products. That is an objective decision. I'm not trying to spite you or hurt you or show hostility."

"But don't you understand that . . ."

"Let me finish. Walter Granby has certain weaknesses and limitations, but he has a lot of strengths too. I can stay around long enough to bring back the good men Mottling drove off, and get it all running smoothly and solidly, and headed in the right direction. That's my decision, and that's the way I vote my stock on Monday."

Niki came slowly and effortlessly to her feet, frowning. She walked to the coffee table, lit two cigarettes and came back to sit beside me on the windowseat and give me one of them.

"My first impulse is to go up in blue smoke," she said.

"I expected you to."

"But if I did you might not listen, and I want you to listen. Will you? This whole thing was botched, right from the beginning. Though our reasons are certainly as far apart as they could be, all of us put pressure on you, Gevan. Lester, Stanley, Colonel Dolson and me. We forgot how stubborn you are. We should have just spread the facts before you and let you make your own logical decision. We should have trusted your judgment. I know you would have backed Stanley."

"Maybe not, Niki. Maybe he isn't as sound as you people think."

She tapped her fist on my thigh. "But are you *competent* to sit in judgment of a man like Stanley Mottling, Gevan? Yes, you ran Dean Products and they all say you did well at it. But the world changes in four years. Stanley has intricate problems you never had to face. So he *did* get rid of some men you liked, and you resent it. Were they really as good as you thought they were? Or were they just very good at selling themselves to you? In all honesty, you must admit that possibility. Or maybe you made them feel so indispensable, they thought they could afford to ignore the new control methods Stanley introduced. Think about it, Gevan. I know you have a lot of self-confidence. But doesn't it get close to a sort of . . . egomania when you judge a man on the basis of rumor, gossip and one trip through the plant? How sound is that, darling?"

I got up from her side and began to pace through the big room. She had touched the source of my uneasiness. I had decided to come out for Granby as a bluff, but I had been getting closer to deciding that it was, indeed, the proper decision. Karch, Uncle Al and Granby didn't think much of Mottling, but how much of that was just an emotional resistance to change?

How badly had four years of idleness dulled the edge of my judgment? If I felt I had become too stale to take charge, could I not also be too stale to decide who should be in charge? Under Mottling the company was making a profit, a good one. Wasn't that the definitive index of excellence? Suppose I booted him out and things turned sour? A hell of a lot of people would be hurt.

Suddenly the easy answer became enormously desirable. I could switch to Mottling. I would look like a fool, but what could they expect from a beach bum? I could vote it the easy way and leave at once for Florida, and wait on the lazy beach for Niki to join me.

I sat in a big chair. She came over and sat on the arm of it and laid her arm across my shoulders. "Gevan, Gevan, my darling. Don't be so troubled. It's not a case of humoring me, actually. It's just the wisest decision you can make."

I looked up into her face, so close to mine. "I keep wondering why you can't just sit the hell back and collect your dividends?"

"I could have, if we hadn't gotten so involved in the whole thing, Gevan. I want to be proud of you. I want you to be wise and right."

"Have you made some kind of a deal with Mottling?"

"Don't be so damn childish and suspicious! You keep looking for things that aren't there."

"I have a hunch, a very strong hunch, I should vote Mottling out."

She sprang up and stared at me. "A hunch! Good God! You'd make a decision like that on a hunch? And they talk about female reasoning."

"But I can't ignore it."

"We're both being stubborn and we're both being silly. There's an easy way out, Gevan. Abstain from voting. Then whatever happens, neither of us will have any regrets."

It made sense. I remembered Uncle Al's estimate of their voting strength. Even my vote might not be quite enough to oust Mottling. It would save Niki's pride, and mine. I stood up. I was at the point of agreement when some perverse instinct, some final strand of resistance, made me say, "What would it cost me to vote for Granby, anyway?"

She gave me a long and level stare. Her mouth tightened. "Me," she said.

I stared at her. I was shocked and incredulous. "Do you really mean that?"

"I love you. I love you very much. But no love is worth spending your life in hell. And I suspect it would be hell, indeed, to live with a vain, silly man who is too stubborn and opinionated to compromise, a man who has your blind need to win all the marbles every time. Look at me, Gevan. Take a good long look. I know what I'm worth. I'm worth a lot more than you're willing to offer. I yearned for you for four years. I almost got used to it. I guess I can manage to get used to it sooner or later. If you decide I'm worth the price I put on myself, come back and tell me—before Monday."

Her eyes were somber and cool. She turned away and walked out of the room. I stood in the silence for a few minutes. She had given her ultimatum like a slap across the mouth. I could not pay that price for her, or for anything in the world. I let myself out, got into my car and left.

As I drove down Ridge Road I tried, without success, to make her determination to win the point fit with what I had learned about her during the months of our engagement. Then she had seemed to be a balanced person, free of this obsessive bull-headedness.

I tried some conjectures, just for size. Ken needs help with the firm. Niki recommends Mottling, an old friend or flame. Mottling arrives. They have an affair. Ken learns of it somehow. That is what was tearing him in half. He loves Niki too much to bring it to a showdown, for fear of losing her entirely. At that point the theory began to fall apart. Why should she make Mottling's keeping his job a condition for our getting together again, unless there was still something between her and Mottling? Yet what could still exist between them if she wanted to go away from Arland and never come back?

I was doing thirty-five on the two-lane road, that slow driving pace you maintain when you are thinking hard. The long hill was about a seven-degree grade down to the valley floor. I heard something coming behind me, coming fast. I looked in the rear-vision mirror and saw the front end of a truck, alarmingly close, too close to give him a chance to swing out around me, too close for me to avoid him by tramping on the gas. Time was measured in micro-seconds. There was no time to examine the shoulder of the road. I turned hard right, rocking the car up onto the left wheels. It seemed to hang there, poised and vulnerable before it lunged down into the wide, shallow ditch. I was tensed for the smashing blow of the truck against the back of the car. But the truck roared by, the engine sound fading to a minor key as my car bounced high over the far side of a shallow ditch, plunged head-on toward a thick utility pole. I fought the wheel, hauling it back so, for a second or two, it rode down the center of the wide ditch before momentum was lost, the wheels sank deep into the rain-drenched earth and the motor stalled.

Silence was sudden and intense. Rain dripped from overhead leaves onto the metal car top. I listened. The truck was out of sight down the slope. I was listening for the brake-scream and long shattering crash as it went into the heavy traffic by the stop lights on the valley floor. I listened for a long time and heard no sound.

I lit a cigarette with the solemn care and formality of a drunk. I opened the car door and got out. It was difficult to keep my legs braced under me. I guessed that the truck had been doing better than eighty. And it had been big. At that speed it would have bunted me end over end. The driver had been asleep—or drunk—or criminally careless—or—

It was like the moment in the hotel suite with that feeling that someone had just left. That same creeping chill along the back of my neck. For a few moments I believed it had been a cold-blooded attempt to kill me in an exceptionally messy way. I felt very alone. It was an instinctive fear. Then I began to reason it out. It had to be an accidental thing. To presuppose intent meant giving the unknown assailant credit for an incredible piece of timing. I was once again giving myself the lead in a melodrama. The part was beginning to feel familiar.

To get back to sanity, I walked around the car, looking at the situation. My shoes sank into the mud. The car was unmarked, but very probably the wheels had been knocked out of line, or the frame wrenched. There was no traffic on the Ridge Road hill. It had been a big, fast gray truck. That was all I knew. I had but one glimpse of it, lasting not over half a second, through the constricted field of the rear-vision mirror. Not much information to give the traffic patrol.

My knees began to feel better. I flipped the cigarette away and got behind the wheel and started the motor. I tried to rock the car out of the mud. I gained about a foot and then it settled in, deeper than before. A pickup truck stopped beside me. It belonged to a farm equipment dealer.

I told the heavy-set driver what had happened. He cursed the local traffic in general and fast trucks in particular. He had a chain and we hooked it to the front left corner of the frame. On the first try it came up out of the ditch and diagonally across the shoulder and onto the pavement, the rear wheels slapping mud up into the fender wells. I tried to pay him, but he refused belligerently, tossed his chain in the back of the pickup, and drove off.

I drove down the hill at a sedate pace. There was no front-end shimmy, but I knew that didn't mean too much. I took it back to the rental agency and explained what had happened. I borrowed a rag and wiped my shoes off. I had lunch at a diner across the street while the agency checked the alignment. When I went back, they said the castor, chamber, and toe-in were way out of line, and they had a new sedan ready to go, and a new form for my signature.

The near-accident had made me feel washed-out, dulled. I parked in a lot in town, wandered into a movie. I sat there in the semi-gloom for an hour. Over the soundtrack I could hear thunder moving down the valley. I looked at the movie and did not see it. I was seeing Niki and Uncle Al, seeing Ken, fusty with after-dinner napping, taking a cool walk at midnight toward something that stood waiting for him by the entrance posts. I wondered if it would all make sense if I could see it from a different angle, if I could step out of myself, if I could climb up on some hypothetical box and look at all of them in some new way. . . .

It was Friday again. One week ago my brother had been alive in Arland, not knowing it was his last day of life, not knowing there were so few breaths and steps and heartbeats left to him. From Sergeant Portugal's point of view it had been a random and accidental death, as meaningless as most crimes of violence. Yet everything I had found out had pointed to its having been carefully planned. The motive, once discovered, might be that ingredient which would make Niki's obsession and preoccupation understandable.

My hunch grew stronger. A hunch that Ken, somehow, on his last day of life, had done some one thing, had performed one action that had triggered all the rest of it, so that, in the night, the firing pin had fallen inevitably against the primer of the thirty-eight cartridge.

I left the movie. Rain was a streaming curtain, fringed with silver where it danced high off the asphalt in the false dusk of mid-afternoon. I knew that I must turn the calendar back. I would become Ken on that Friday of a week ago, and I would try to do what he had done, go where he had gone, try to feel what he had felt. The plant was the place to catch up with him on that day, to catch up with my death-marked brother moving inevitably toward his appointment by the gateposts of the Lime Ridge house.

Chapter 13

The lights were on in the Dean Products' offices. The reception girl gave me my pass when I signed the register. Dulled by the heavy rain, the sound of the production areas filtered into the offices like the thick slow beatings of a hundred dozen giant hearts.

Perry gave me a startled look when I walked into her office. "Oh! Did you see Alma?"

Niki and the near-accident had driven Alma Brady completely out of my mind I looked blankly at Perry for a moment and said, "She didn't sleep at her place last night. She was back there for a few minutes around three and then apparently went out again."

"Do you think she—could have been with the Colonel, Gevan?"

"Not considering how she felt about him last night." I had moved close to her desk and we kept our voices low. I saw an object on her desk that looked vaguely familiar, and, without thinking, I picked it up. It was a small comic figure, a gay-colored plaster figure of a golfer in the middle of a grotesque swing, and I remembered I had been given it at the Arland Golf Club as a consolation prize one day long ago. It had been on my desk the day I cleared out my personal belongings, and I remembered tossing it into the wastebasket with a lot of other junk, because on that day I had no appreciation for the comic.

I replaced it and looked at her and saw she was blushing furiously. "I always sort of liked him," she said. "I rescued him. You chipped his nose when you threw him in the basket, but I found the chip and glued it back on. He's a mascot, sort of."

"He didn't do me much good."

She went abruptly back to the Dolson-Brady problem. "I know it doesn't seem logical that she'd go back to Colonel Dolson, Mr. Dean, but on the other hand, the files *are* missing, and that might be what would happen if she told him about telling us. I mean maybe she regretted it later."

"After you left in the cab, Perry, I went to the Copper Lounge. I ran into Dolson. I had the idea of needling him into taking some action. I scared him thoroughly by telling him I was backing Granby. With Walter running the whole show, it wouldn't be very damn long before he'd start checking Dolson's purchases more thoroughly. So that may be what made him get hold of the files—or get somebody to take them out of this office. I moved too fast, if that's the case. I should have waited."

She reached out and moved the figurine to a place where her typewriter carriage wouldn't knock him over.

"Perry, which office was Ken using?"

"When Mr. Mottling arrived, Ken moved out of your office and gave it to him. Your brother took over the office where Mr. Mirrian used to be."

"I know the one. Has anybody else moved in?"

"No. It's empty. I don't believe anybody has even been in there since—last Friday. There wouldn't have been anything in there that had to be processed."

I saw the faint bluish shadows under her eyes. "You look tired, Perry. What did you do—have a late date after you left me?"

"No. I just—couldn't sleep. There seem to be so many things that don't make any sense. It's like there's something we don't know. Something big and important, and if we knew it, or could guess it, then everything else would be—understandable. Maybe when you go to that Acme office . . ."

"I went there this morning. Nobody there. It's just a mailing address, a cubbyhole. Perry, word will get around that I'm in the plant. They may check with you. Call me and tell me who's looking for me. I'll be in my brother's office."

"Yes, sir," she said, and I realized I had dropped back into the habit of giving her orders. She looked amused.

I got to the office where Ken had been without encountering anyone in the hall who looked even vaguely familiar. The outer office door was closed. I went in and shut it behind me. It was designed like the other executive offices, with the windowless outer office for the secretary. There was dust on the secretarial desk—more dust than could accumulate in one week, and it gave me a wry appraisal of my brother's importance in the firm. I opened the second door and went into his office. It was small, with pale paneling, pale green plaster walls above the paneling, a gray steel desk. The room was as gray as the rain outside.

I sat in Ken's chair and pushed the black button of the fluorescent desk lamp. The tube flickered, then glowed with a steady white light. The light slanted across the bottom half of a framed picture of Niki, bold against her mouth, shadowing her eyes.

I sat there and tried to pretend I was Ken, tried to think as he had thought. Perhaps he had merely sat there, waiting for the long hours to pass until he could leave without being too obvious, and go to the Copper Lounge, to Hildy and stingers and a sedate alcoholic haze. I needed clues to what had been troubling him. I began looking through the desk.

There were pencils in the top drawer, and paper clips, and scratch pads. The other drawers were equally devoid of any hint of the personality of the man who had sat at this desk—a few cigars, some antique copies of *Business Week*, some engineering journals, a few competitors' catalogues with their prices penciled in. Ken never wanted to be a big wheel. He lacked drive. He had been useful to me. He was content to let me make the decisions, and when I asked him to do something, he did it doggedly, thoroughly, and well. He was slow, methodical, and performed best when not under pressure, when there was no deadline.

I had left him perched on a high, vulnerable place. With complete objectivity, I knew that he was an employee type. Responsibility made him uneasy.

His appointment pad was on the right corner of the desk. It was that brand which has a clock embedded in the middle, the dial showing through the circular hole in the cover, each page divided into wedge-shaped sections to correspond with the hours of the day as shown on the clock.

All the sheets had been torn off down to the previous Monday. And that sheet was blank. I began to wonder why the Monday sheet would be on top rather than the sheet for the previous Saturday. Saturday was a working day. Assuming he tore off the Friday sheet before he left the office that last time, there was no reason for him to remove the Saturday sheet. I checked blank pages and found the pad included sheets for Sundays also. So two sheets had been removed.

I picked up the pad and tilted it so that any indentations of previous notations would show up. The Monday sheet was unmarked. I looked at the pencils in the drawer again. All had very soft lead.

I knew I had to operate on assumption, with the knowledge that if one assumption was illogical, all the rest in the chain would be meaningless. Assume that Kendall had made a notation on the pad for either Friday or Saturday. Perhaps it had been a memo of an appointment someone did not want him to keep. Then the removal of that incriminating or indicative sheet was in direct relation to his death. And the death, of course, was in a cause-and-effect relationship to the appointment.

This was dangerously vague, yet I could take that assumption another step. If Joe Gardland and Hildy Deveraux had given me the picture of a man facing a tremendous problem, was, then, the missing notation an indication that he had at last made up his mind? And, having made a decision, could he be permitted to live?

The tremendous and almost insoluble problem involved some facet of Niki.

Uncle Al sensed something odd about her, about her motivations.

I sensed the same oddness.

Niki knew why Ken's life had become unbearable only when a conflict became too great. What conflict? Love for Niki versus—what? Versus, perhaps, an old-fashioned word? Honor, decency, dignity, self-respect?

Niki had walked into our lives out of a December rain, and over a candle-dark table she had shown me the shape of her mouth, the bright slant of blue eyes. Niki Webb from Cleveland, indignant, yet with a flavor of being amused at her own indignation, at her boldness in stopping me in the rain to protest. I'd bullied Hilderman into taking her on, even though, at that time, the office staff was being cut.

She had appeared and changed our lives—changed mine, and Ken's was ended. I tried to think of the things she had told me about herself, about he past, during the months of our engagement. I reached for the phone and then pulled my hand back. It would be a ghoulish shock for an unsuspecting switchboard girl to have that particular light blink on her board, and hear my voice, so like Ken's, asking for Hilderman.

I went to Hilderman's office. He was out in the shop someplace. His girl was new, a young girl with chunky hips and a self-important manner. I asked for the Personnel card on a Miss N. Webb who had been hired four and a half years ago, and who had resigned several months later.

"That would be in the storage file."

"Obviously."

"I'm not supposed to give out cards without Mr. Hilderman's okay. And only authorized peole can look at them."

She irritated me. She was full of petty authority. And I

could see that, as I had hoped, the name meant nothing to her and she did not know me.

Petty authority wilts under a show of force. "Young lady, I am Gevan Dean, and unless I have that card in my hand within two minutes, Mr. Hilderman is going to have a change in his staff as of now."

Her mouth sagged and her high color faded. "I'm—I'm terribly sorry, Mr. Dean. I didn't know—I mean, I—"

"I'm glad to see you take your job so seriously, miss."

"Yes, I—I'll get it right away. Webb did you say? W-e-b-b?"

She trotted off. She was back quickly, huffing the dust from the card. "Here you are, sir." As she handed it over, I could sense a rebirth of reluctance. She was beginning to wonder if Hilderman would give her hell for disobeying his office rule. I could guess she would try to get the card back into the file without Hilderman ever realizing it had been gone.

I took the card to Ken's office, sat at his desk and placed it squarely in front of me under the blue-white fluorescence. The small picture was not good. It gaunted her face and hardened her mouth. The information on the card confirmed the little she had told me of her past. Parents dead. No brothers or sisters. A business school. Job in a Cleveland office. Palmer Mutual Life Insurance Company, Inc. Position—Secretary to the Chief Adjustor. She had given that firm as a reference, and the information on the card indicated that the reference had checked her out as satisfactory.

I saw a smudge near the name of the company. I looked at it closely and saw that someone had penciled a small question mark there, and had partially erased it. There was a routing card stapled to the Personnel card. I looked at the routing card and saw that this Personnel card had been taken out of the storage file a year ago. I saw my brother's initials scrawled beside the date.

I sat very still. It was the first clue I had found. Ken had examined this card. Perhaps he had made that question mark. It could only mean that Ken had become interested in her past. I could almost assume he had found some inconsistency in her history, and had taken the card out to check. If he had made the question mark, the inconsistency involved the office where she had worked.

I was no longer eager to try to spend the rest of the day as Ken had spent his last day of life. Through luck and logic I had found a loose piece. I intended to give it a good hard tug and see what happened. The girl in Personnel seemed pleased to get the card back so quickly. She was too anxious to get it back into the storage file to ask for my initials on the routing card. I hesitated in the hall, wondering if I should tell Perry I was leaving. There seemed little point in it. The rain had turned into a steady downpour. It got under the collar of the plastic raincoat and trickled down my back. I drove to the hotel. Traffic moved cautiously, dimmers on. I went to my suite and placed the Cleveland call, then took off my raincoat as I was waiting for it to come through. I had asked for anyone at Palmer Mutual Life in Cleveland.

The phone rang. "Ready with your call, sir. Go ahead."

"Palmer Mutual," a girl said.

"My name is Dean. I'm calling from Arland. I think I want to speak to your Chief Adjustor."

"Are you reporting the death of a policyholder, sir?"

"No. How long has your Chief Adjustor held that job there?"

"Mr. Wilther has been Chief Adjustor for a long time, sir. Twelve years."

"Could you connect me with him, please?"

"One moment, sir."

I waited perhaps a full minute and then a man spoke with a heavy, friendly voice. "Hello again, Mr. Dean. What's on your mind this time?"

"This time? Oh, I see. My brother must have phoned you."

"I thought it was the same Mr. Dean phoning from Arland again."

"When was that?"

"Maybe a year ago."

"Would you mind telling me what he phoned you about?"

"I guess there's no harm in that, Mr. Dean. He phoned about a girl who used to work here. Before she went with Dean Products. The name escapes me at the moment."

"Miss Webb. Miss Niki Webb."

"Yes, that's the girl. He called up to ask me if I'd dig our copy of the letter of recommendation out of the files. He held the line and I had a girl get it out. It said she was satisfactory. Honest, energetic, and likable. We were sorry to see her go. She said it was some personal trouble. We never did learn the details."

"Is that all my brother wanted to know?"

"That time, yes. But he called back the next day and asked a funny thing. He asked me to describe her. Getting the phone call had sort of refreshed my memory. I hadn't seen the girl in over three years, you understand. So I described her. Tall, dark, very pretty, and so on. Gray eyes."

"Gray?"

"Your brother picked that up too. I was sure because that was what I remembered the best about her. Bug-luminous gray eyes. To make sure I checked with the other people around here, the ones who remember her. They all insist her eyes were gray, not blue as your brother seemed to think. I was curious and he promised he'd call me back and tell me the story, or write me. He never did. That business about the eyes being gray sort of rattled him. You know what I mean? His voice got shaky. What's up, Mr. Dean?"

"I don't know yet, Mr. Wilther."

"You sound as shaky as your brother did."

"It's—a shock to me. It isn't what I was thinking of. I can see how it might have been even more of a shock to my brother."

"Maybe it's none of my business, and tell me so if that's the way you feel about it, but I would like to know what goes on."

I had a sudden idea and I said quickly, "Mr. Wilther, do

you have some sort of an organization there that investigates insurance frauds?"

"In a very small way, Mr. Dean. For bigger stuff we use a national organization. But I don't see how we could justify doing any work where there's no insurance interest involved in—"

"Suppose I pay all costs with a bonus for speed."

"We're in the insurance business, Mr. Dean."

"Then could you call it a favor to a potential policy-holder?"

"How big a policy?" he asked quickly.

"Say a hundred thousand straight life. You can check up on me very easily."

"I don't have to—if you're one of the Deans. I checked on your brother after that phone call. I shouldn't do anything, even as a favor to a policyholder, but I'm a man who gets curious about things. Too curious, maybe. What do you want done?"

"Check on that girl who worked for you. The gray-eyed one. Niki Webb. There are second cousins in Cleveland, I believe. Get pictures and fingerprints if you can. Find out what happened when she left Cleveland. The one who calls herself Niki Webb, a blue-eyed one, showed up here the following December. She resigned there a few months earlier, I believe."

"In September, Mr. Dean."

"Let me know as soon as you find out anything. You can phone me here at the Hotel Gardland. I'm Gevan Dean." I gave him the suite number.

"Right. I'll mail you a bill for services after we've finished. It might help if I knew the reason for the impersonation."

"I wish I knew. It doesn't make sense yet."

"I'll try to give it a priority handling. Are you too busy to go take a physical for that policy?"

"At the moment, yes. Next week sometime."

I hung up. My hands felt sticky. I washed them. I had found a new way to put myself in Ken's shoes. Suppose you are married to a lovely woman, and deeply in love with her, and you learn she is not who she pretends to be; you find out she is wearing a mask. By unmasking her, you may lose her. Your marriage is a fiction, yet you can't face a life without her.

I was going to carry a lot of tension around with me until I heard from Wilther. I wondered if Ken had found out why she was hiding under some other name. Who had she been? What had she been? Why do people change their identity? To escape from something. From the consequence of some criminal act. Or they are running out on some responsibility. Or, as in the traditional con game, there is a mark to be fleeced. I knew the history of the girl whose identity she had assumed. But what of Niki's own history? I began to imagine strange and terrible things. Yes, oddly, discovering the flaw in identity made Niki, as a person, more believable. From the beginning there had been just too much sophistication, too much poise for a girl who had no more experience of the world than the genuine Niki Webb. I realized it had bothered me four years ago without my putting my finger on the exact reason. It had not been the sly wanton pretending to be a lady. It had been more subtle.

After useless conjecture, I went to the phone and made a call which I knew I should have made right after meeting Stanley Mottling. It took the long-distance operator a half-hour to locate Mort Brice. He had been one of the young assistant deans when I was at the Business School. Since that time he had formed a company in New York that was partly devoted to handling industrial management problems on contract, but was mainly a clearinghouse for executive personnel all over the country and over most of the world, finding the right man available for the right job as soon as it opened up.

I got him on the line and Mort said, "My God, it's the beachcomber! What in the world are you doing? Going back to work?" His voice changed suddenly and I knew he had remembered Ken's death. It was the sort of news his office would pick up quickly. "Say, I didn't mean to sound so flip,

Gev. I forgot for a minute about your brother. That was a hell of a thing, Gev. Shocking."

"A bad thing, Mort. I'm trying to get things straightened out."

"Hope you'll keep us in mind if you need a couple of shrewd boys to fill out the roster. Production men are in damn short supply, but I think I could round up a couple for you. I understand you people have a lot of government work. Loaded you down, haven't they?"

"Pretty heavily. But that isn't what I called about. I'm being pressured to put a man named Stanley Mottling in as president, now that Ken is gone. I thought you might have an opinion, if you know him."

"Oh, I know him. But I don't like to give any opinions."

"Isn't that your business?"

"It is when I can stay cool and calm and objective. But that is one gent I don't like. He's shrewd, able, maybe brilliant. All the adjectives. But I don't like him."

"He's driven away some of the men I had a lot of confidence in when I was here."

"Then they needed driving, Gev. One thing I *do* know about Mottling, his strong point is that he can recognize ability and then delegate authority and responsibility."

"The hell you say! That's the last thing he's done here. And he drove away good men. Hell, you know one of them. He came through your office. Poulson."

"He resigned for a better offer."

"No. Mottling drove him out, and drove out other men just as good."

There was a silence on the line. "Were they undercutting him, maybe?"

"I think you know Poulson better than that."

I heard an odd sound over the line and then I remembered Mort Brice's little habit of snapping his front teeth with his thumbnail when he was thinking hard. "It sounds funny," he said.

"I'm paying a phone bill to have you tell me something I knew already."

"I can tell you one thing, Gev. If Mottling has done what you say he has done—and I'll buy that—don't for one minute think that it was done out of stupidity or carelessness or anything like that. He had a good reason. He's the type who would have a special reason. So try thinking along these lines: What can he gain by fumbling production? You say he drove production men away. Would it depress market values of your stock so he could buy in somehow? Could he get a whack at ownership and control by driving down dividends to the point where he could pick up shares here and there on the side?"

"Not the way the stock is held, and we're better than seventy per cent cost plus, so a production fumble wouldn't change the dividend picture too much."

"Then that won't wash. But whether you know it or not, Mottling is pretty heavy in the pocket. His father was one hell of a smart engineer. His father built steel and tractor plants and even got into hydroelectric stuff for the Russians during the twenties. He got them started on air frame production in the Ural area, too. They paid him very well, very *damn* well, for services rendered. There was some sort of tax dodge, so that Internal Revenue got no slice of what Mottling Senior was paid. He was over there quite a while, and then his wife got involved with some colonel-general or something, and got one of those fast divorces they had in those days. Mottling Senior brought Stanley home. The boy might have been about fourteen then. He got his training at Cal Tech and later at the Stanford Business."

"I don't want to sound weird about this, Mort, but look at it this way. What other reason is there for fumbling government production?"

I heard Mort whistle softly. "You mean the sympathies are with his mother's adopted country? I'm afraid that won't go, Gev. He's been investigated nine ways from Sunday. Hell, I happen to know he had better than a full year at Oak Ridge before he left there to go with National Electronics. I don't think we can twist this into a B movie plot. I think you ought to worry about that bundle of money. He's been around. Maybe Dean Products is what he wanted all along, and he just found it. That money hasn't shrunk any since his father died. Would ten million bucks at the right place at the right time buy control of Dean? Think along those lines."

"Thanks, Mort. I'll do that."

"Watch him closely."

"Mort, if he has that much, he wouldn't have any reason to get tangled up in any crooked financial deals, would he?"

"He's too smart for that. If it wasn't for my instinctive dislike for the guy, I'd tell you to try to get him out of there. But I'm just prejudiced enough so that my advice may stink. Maybe he's the right man for the job."

I thanked him again and told him I didn't know when I might be coming to New York, and parried his questions about my own future plans.

I hung up. Dusk had come and the rain had stopped, but I could hear yet another storm coming down the valley out of the north, like a black bowling ball rolling down an echoing valley. I stretched out on the bed with an ash tray beside me.

When a storm is on the way it does something to the animal part of you, to that very deep, dark place where all reasoning is based on instinct. I've heard and read the neat little explanations for that. All about variations in barometric pressure, and the charge of negative electricity that travels in advance of the thunderheads. But there's something else too, something all tied up with our caves of long ago, and the wet rock, and trees crashing.

I remembered the feel of the air, the look of the sky, on that Sunday past when I had headed the "Vunderbar" back toward Indian Rocks.

Now there was the same storm feeling in Arland, in the air and among the people. Currents of personal emotional electricity. There had been Niki, the bereaved wife, and Dolson, the brusque colonel, and Mottling, the quiet executive. But I had seen a few gestures that didn't seem quite right, heard a few words that seemed oddly timed, heard with the third ear the words that were not said, felt the tingle of unknown currents. And I had done a few small things that had turned two of them into imposter and thief. What would Mottling become? Imposter, thief—and what was needed to round out the circle: Murderer?

Not with his own hands. Not Mottling. Not when authority could be delegated. But that was one field where you were not permitted to delegate responsibility.

He might want me killed if I—

I punched my cigarette out in the ash tray beside me. It had been a big gray truck. It had been a new-looking truck. Trucks have horns. They bray like great monsters to clear the road ahead. And the truck had come barreling down the hill at me, had come silently, except for the roar of the straining motor. Instinct had been right. Logic had been wrong. It had been a miracle of timing, because it had been the apex of very careful planning. A truck far up the hill. A driver watching the house, seeing Niki's signal that the victim had proved stubborn. Then the cigarette end slipped away, and the man climbing into the high cab, and idling the motor and waiting for the glint of my car as I turned out of the drive.

Instinct had been right. And it had probably been right when it had warned me that someone had been in my room, someone with motivations more devious than any hotel maid.

Perhaps Ken's death had been the first hint of thunder beyond the horizon—or that first wind that riffles the water, dies into a weighted stillness. The hidden animal dreads the storm. I could feel the pricklings of warning pulling at my skin. It had been an area of suspicion, and now suspicion was confirmed as the gale warnings went up, as the cyclical winds gathered force.

My decision had placed the burden of action on Mottling. It was his move. He had made one move. He would make another. Something was up, and whatever it might be, he had too much at stake to withdraw tamely, defeated.

I listened to the thunder, and my thoughts were long, slow and tormented. Who was the blue-eyed woman who had taken the place of Niki Webb? Perhaps she too was lying down, listening to the storm sounds, and perhaps her thoughts were as twisted as my own. I could be there, with her. It would be easy to tell myself it would be in the interest of furthering my investigation. The need for scruple was gone. If she was not Niki Webb, there had been no legal marriage. If she had signaled for the attempt on my life, this could be a special sort of revenge—to take her, to dull the new edge of lust, and then tell her what filth she was.

The phone rang three times, insistently, before I could get to it. The sound brushed away the erotic images of Niki.

Chapter 14

It was Sergeant Portugal, calling from the lobby. He wanted to come up and I told him to come right ahead.

I splashed cold water on my face. He knocked and I let him in. He half-smiled and nodded at me, walked over to the chair by the windows and sat down heavily, dropped his hat on the floor beside the chair. I asked him if I could order a drink sent up. He said a beer would go pretty good. I phoned the order. I sat on the couch, conscious of his unhealthy look, his heavy breathing. He offered me a cigar which I refused. He slid the cellophane from one, bit off the end, spat it into his palm, and dropped it in the ash tray. He took his time getting the cigar to burn smoothly and evenly in the match flame.

"This," he said quietly, "is just between you and me. Not the department. Just the two of us." He acted ill at ease.

"How do you mean?"

"It all went too easy. I kept telling myself that sometimes the worst ones are easy. But I didn't tell myself loud enough or something. I've been in this game a long time. I know any cop is a damn fool if he tries to keep looking around after the district attorney's office is satisfied with the file. I should have stayed the hell out. I thought I'd take one more

178

little look. Now I'm stuck with it. You didn't buy Shennary, did you?"

"I wondered about him."

"How about after you saw the girl?"

"After I saw her, I was sure he didn't do it. She made sense."

"You could have phoned me and told me about the gun. Would that have hurt anything?"

"You seemed sure it was Shennary. I didn't think it would change anything, Sergeant."

"After I cuffed it out of her, she showed me and told me she showed you, too. I leaned on everybody in that fleabag motel, one at a time. Finally I found a girl, another one of those car hoppers. She lives a few doors down from Shennary's girl and she was walking home late that night your brother got it. She saw a trucker stop after midnight and walk up to the Genelli girl's door and stand there and then go away. She remembered the name of the van line. I figured if I could get the guy to tell me nobody was at home a little after midnight in the Genelli girl's place, then I could feel better about Shennary. The name of the line was Gobart Brothers. I find the home office is in Philly. They cooperate and look up the name of the fellow who would be tooling one of their rigs through here about that time Friday night. Turns out it is a guy named Joe Russo. I got him up here this morning. He said he used to run around with Lita. He told me he was going to knock and then he heard a guy inside yelling at Lita and she was yelling back. A hell of a scrap. He said he went away. I made him wait in an office. I brought in six guys, on the other side of a door, and made them talk loud. He picked out Shennary as the guy he heard. I mixed up the order and made him do it three times. He was right every time.

"It sounds like a smart thing to do, Sergeant."

"I wish to hell I hadn't done it."

"Why have you told me?"

"To fill you in. So long as I got work ahead of me that I'll have to do on my own time because the Shennary case is officially closed out of our files, I want to save time. I figure if you weren't satisfied with Shennary, you've been lookin' around. If it wasn't Shennary, the gun was planted in his room and that spells premeditation, and that means motive, and you've been in a better position to think up a good motive for anybody killing your brother than I have. If you can't tip me to anything, I've got to start digging on my own. The place I start is with the widow. She is a handsome chunk of stuff and she inherits a nice piece of money from your brother. The tipster was a man, so I start thinking in terms of her playing around on the side. That is, unless you can give me something."

"Why do you start with that motive, Sergeant?"

"Because I have got experience in police work. When you are green in this work, everything is strange. But after a while you see the patterns and how they work. This is an upper-bracket murder. That means one thing to me. It has to be money, sex, or blackmail. In an upper-bracket murder the victim is knocked off for what he's worth, or to get him out of somebody's bed, or to shut his mouth up about something he might say or threatens to say to the wrong people. They all come out that way, when you have premeditation. Sometimes the upper-brackets get drunk and kill somebody because they don't like the part in their hair, but this wasn't any spur-of-the-moment thing. Something was nibbling on your brother. We know it wasn't money. He was getting along fine, the way salary and dividends add up. So he was worried about sex or blackmail. He seems clean. I can't figure any blackmail aimed at him. So it all smells like sex to me, like somebody got next to that sister-in-law of yours and your brother found out."

"I don't think that's a good guess."

He looked blandly at me. "You have a better guess?"

"Not necessarily."

"Mr. Dean, kindly don't try to kid me. I know you're hiding something. Maybe four or five times in your life you try to conceal essential information. But twenty times a day I am prying information out of people. No amateur does good bucking a pro."

It was dangerous to underrate this man. His mind was

quicker and keener than I had suspected. "All right. I'll be honest with you at least this far, Sergeant. Something big is going on. I think Ken found out what it is. I think it concerns the company and I think it concerns his wife. I don't know what that big thing is. I just think I know the general area where I have to look. I think Ken made up his mind to let some cats out of some bags, and that's why he was killed. I'm not ready to say anymore than that. It would be guesswork, and it would sound silly as hell. I want to look around. I promise I'll come to you just as soon as I have something definite."

For long minutes he looked as if he were falling asleep. Then he got clumsily to his feet, brushed ashes from the front of his coat. "Okay, I can't push you if you don't want to be pushed. I'll keep looking around in my own way on my own time. But if it *is* big, like you hint, do me one favor."

"Yes?"

"Write down all these crazy guesses of yours and put them in the hotel safe, addressed to me. Amateurs always seem to have accidents."

He waited for my promise and then left. I stood at the door after he had closed it softly behind him. There was a prickling at the nape of my neck.

I sat down at once and wrote out what I had learned, and a batch of guesses. They sounded melodramatic and absurd. I was tempted to tear up the sheets of hotel stationery. But I sealed them in an envelope and wrote his name on the outside of the envelope.

The phone rang at that moment. A thin, musical voice said, "Mr. Dean? This is Martha Colsinger."

I remembered the huge woman from the boarding house. Over the phone her voice had a young shy sound.

"Yes. Have you found out anything?"

"Well, a couple of my girls are home now. I've been talking to them, you know, about Alma. She didn't come home yet."

"Did the girls tell you anything?"

"These two, they live together in a front room, the

biggest one, that used to be the living-room. They had the lights out last night and they were sitting in the windowseat that goes across the front of the big bay window. They were talking late because one of them has some kind of love trouble and she is pretty depressed about it, you know, and her friend was trying to cheer her up. They are both nice girls that go to the graduate school over to the college. Miriam, she comes from Albany, and she is the one that—"

"Did they see Alma Brady?"

"I was coming to that. No, they didn't. They didn't see anybody come in, but around three they heard the front door close and a man went off the porch real quiet and walked away. I've told the city people we got to have more lights on this street. If I've told them once, I've told them a hundred times. It can give you a creepy feeling thinking about a man prowling around in here last night. I feel responsible for my girls, and with a lot of low-class people in town, and with those sailors all over the place from the Naval Training Station, you never know what—"

"Could the girls describe the man?"

"Like I was saying, the lights aren't strong enough on this street, so they couldn't see him good. They said he was a smallish man dressed dark, walking quick and soft. Now I've been thinking maybe it was him I heard walking around up there in Alma's room. It makes me terrible nervous and I can't understand her never coming home since Thursday morning when she went to work. Do you think I ought to phone the police and report her missing?"

"That might be the wise thing to do."

"The girls didn't say anything to me until I started asking, because they thought it was somebody sneaked a boy friend in after I got to bed and he was sneaking out again. But I told them about Alma and now they're nervous like I am. The man is here changing the lock. It's a big expense whenever a girl loses her front-door key because I don't feel right if there's a key around that just about anybody could have. There's one key for each girl, and one for me, and if that man got in with a key, he had to use Alma's key. I'll phone the police right now."

AREA OF SUSPICION

"Mrs. Colsinger, I'd consider it a favor if you didn't mention my visit."

"Well," she said dubiously, "if they ask me if somebody was around asking about her, I don't feel awful much like telling lies about it."

"If they ask you directly, tell them. Just don't volunteer the information. I'd like to tell you the reason, but I can't right now. I assure you it's a good reason."

She seemed to accept that. "Maybe, Mr. Dean, I ought to go ahead and wire her people, too. They live in Junction City, Kansas."

"I wouldn't do that yet, Mrs. Colsinger. It might only worry them when there's nothing they can do. Maybe she'll come in later tonight."

"I certainly hope so. I certainly hope nothing happened to Alma."

She sighed and hung up. I put my jacket on and took the letter for Portugal to the hotel desk and asked the clerk to put it in the safe. He glanced curiously at the addressee.

"If I should—check out of the hotel, I'd like to have you send that over to Sergeant Portugal by messenger. Could you do that?"

"Yes, sir. Of course."

As I turned away from the desk Lester Fitch came toward me, his polished lenses reflecting the lobby lights.

"Gevan! So nice to run into you."

"Hello, Lester."

He was beaming, cordial. "How about a cocktail, old boy? Heard you've been on the move."

"I'm busy, Lester."

"I'll be frank. Niki phoned me. She asked me to talk to you. It won't take long."

I permitted myself to be steered to the Copper Lounge. We took stools at the bar. The place was beginning to fill up with the five o'clockers.

We ordered and he said, "This climate must be repulsive after Florida, Gevan. Aren't you anxious to get back?"

"Are you anxious to have me go back, Lester?"

He pursed his lips. "You *are* on the defensive, aren't you? Would you mind if I do a little diagnosing?"

The mask was easy to identify. Fitch, the family lawyer. Just like a family doctor. This medicine may taste bad, old boy, but in the long run it will help you. Drink it down. His expression was just right. Serious, concerned, noble.

I sipped my drink. "Go on, Doctor. Diagnose."

"Gevan, your pride is hurt. Your viewpoint of this whole Dean Products situation is irrational, just because of hurt pride. Certainly, deep down, you must realize that Stanley Mottling is more qualified than you are to run a firm like Dean Products has become. Once you admit that, old boy, you can give up this dog-in-the-manger attitude that has us all so worried."

"Don't forget poor, decrepit, old, broken-down Granby."

"That's not far off the mark. Six months of the job would kill him. By then Stanley would be settled in some other job and where would we be?"

"Up the creek, all on account of my stupid pride."

"Gevan, I know you're being sarcastic. Actually, I'm trying to help. I've always liked you. I don't like to see—so many things thrown away."

The inference did not please me. I did not like what he was hinting at.

"Many things, Lester."

He leaned closer, twisting his empty glass on the bar top, making wet smears. "You'd be hurting more than the company, Gevan. You'd be hurting Niki too. Hurting her terribly. You must see that. She's in love with you. And this attitude of yours—it's sabotaging her."

Just a good old friend of the family. Sabotage. A lovely word. It gives you quite a mental picture: greasy little men scuttling through warehouses and tossing incendiary pencils into dark corners and molding gelignite to bridge trusses. But there are other kinds. Who can do the best job of sabotaging a school system? One grimy little boy—or the superintendent of schools?

"*Are* you listening to me, Gevan?"

"Sure. What were you saying?"

But I kept thinking while he rambled on. Suppose our grimy little boy wanted to do a thorough job of sabotage. If he was bright enough, he would lead such an exemplary life that he could become superintendent of schools without anyone every suspecting that his sole motivation was to eventually kick down all the school buildings.

". . . Niki has her pride too, Gevan. She wants Ken's plans to be carried out. And Ken's plans included Stanley Mottling. Ken was able to forget his pride and hand the reins over to Stanley. You can prove that you're just as big a man as Ken was."

"That's what's spoiling our lives, Lester. All my foolish, stubborn pride."

He edged closer. "I know you're trying to make fun of me, Gevan. But remember, it was Niki who asked me to try to talk sense into you." He lowered his voice and there was a thin coating of slime on his words. "But I'll bet you if you do things her way at the Monday meeting, it shouldn't be too hard to arrange to join her on a trip she's taking. It could be handled in a discreet way. Join up in some other city, you know. I'm almost positive it could be worked." He underlined the thought by giving me a little nudge with his elbow. A sly and lascivious little nudge.

I was suddenly very, very tired of Lester. I wondered what I was doing, sitting at the bar listening to him. I didn't want him offering me the delights of Niki in return for being an obedient boy. There is a limit to the number of handsprings you can turn for the bonus of a fair white body.

I closed my fingers around his wrist. My hand and wrist are toughened by a lot of big tarpon, by makos and tuna in season off Bimini, by water skis behind fast boats. It was childish, schoolyard competition. I clenched my hand on his wrist, on the soft office-flesh, until my knuckles popped and I felt the strain in my shoulder—until his mouth twisted and loosened and I had turned him back to that Lester Fitch of Arland High School, fair game for kids half his size, loping along, blubbering with fear. I took all his masks from him and for a moment enjoyed just that, then felt self-disgust and released him quickly.

I made my voice flat, calm. "Now I'll diagnose, Lester. Now I'll tell you something. You've gotten into something that's way over your head. You're scared witless. Your nerves are shot. You're in a mess you'd like to get out of and know damn well you can't."

He made a weak effort to put on a standard mask. Indignation. "I don't know what you're talking about!"

"I'm talking about you. I know you, Lester. The world hasn't appreciated you. You haven't been able to move fast enough. You'll use any method. You'll be crooked if you have to be, to get that power and appreciation faster. You're mixed up with Dolson. Both of you are thieves. Neither of you are worth a damn. I don't know how you were angled into it, but it's too late for you to get out, Lester. You know it and I know it and Dolson knows it."

He could not look at me. Perhaps any human being has a right to personal dignity. I had stripped Lester naked, yet it was not done in idle cruelty. It was an application of sudden, unexpected pressure—the kind that opens up a hidden fracture-line.

He sat for what seemed like a long time, with his pale hands motionless on the edge of the bar. He turned toward me. I've never seen so much hate.

His voice was barely audible. "You've always had every damn thing, haven't you? All the things I've wanted. All right. Keep prying. Keep shoving people around. Keep acting smarter and bigger than everybody, because that's what I want you to do. I want you to keep your goddamn nose in business that doesn't concern you, because if you get too annoying, they'll smash you the way they'd smash a bug on a wall. Without even thinking about it. And I want that to happen to you, Mr. Gevan Dean."

"The way they smashed Ken?" I asked softly.

Hate and pressure had opened the fracture-line. He realized he had said too much. The fracture closed slowly. His eyes became remote again behind optical lenses. He got up from the stool, moving carefully, like a man ill or drunk.

He walked away and he did not look like the brisk young man on his way up, the young man to watch. He looked like a toy with a spring that had almost run down.

I had another drink. Perry was right. There was something big and formless in the darkness. I could almost make out the shape of it. Almost.

I paid and left. I went to the lobby and picked up a newspaper. The headlines reflected a world in a tension of conflicting ideologies so familiar to us, we accept it with a glance, yet do not dare think deeply about it. I scanned the front page and saw a box near the bottom of the page. I stopped so quickly on my way to the elevators that the man behind me ran into me, grunted, showed his teeth, and hurried on.

The body of a young girl, recovered from the river eleven miles south of the city at noon had been identified at press time as Alma Brady, civil-service employee at Dean Products. Death was caused by drowning, and the penciled suicide note in the pocket of her red coat confirmed the police theory that she had jumped from one of the Arland bridges some time Thursday night. The note indicated she had been depressed over a love affair.

Poor little chippy, tumbling down the river in her red coat. I could not see her as a suicide type. She was too much on the make, too hungry for life, too tough-minded. With Dolson out of the picture she had started thinking about the next man, not about the river.

There had been a vulnerability about her, but not of the sort that causes suicides. I was making a snap judgment, based on being with her for a half-hour, yet I felt certain she had not killed herself.

Ken had taken his gamble and lost. I mourned him, yet, since I had learned his death had perhaps not been as pointless as I had first thought, I had lost that feeling of resentment a needless death creates. Alma's death was different. I was positive the fluffy blonde had been murdered. And my anger was strong—stronger than the anger I felt at Ken's death, because it was more impersonal. There was a callousness about her death. Smashed, Lester had said, like a bug on a wall. Smashed in a professional way which I knew Fitch and Dolson were incapable of.

I turned away from the elevators and hurried to a phone booth in the lobby, found Perry's home phone number, and dialed. Her mother told me Joan had called earlier to say she was working late and would get her dinner across the street from the offices. I thanked her hurriedly and phoned the plant. The switchboard was closed. The night plug on the number I dialed was into a line to the engineering offices. A man with a weary voice gave me the night number for Granby's office.

I did not completely realize the extent of my own tension until the sound of Perry's voice came over the line. I sighed from my heels.

"This is Gevan, Perry. Did you hear about it?"

"I'm sick over it. I wish I'd known it hit her so hard. I thought she was mad at him but not hurt that bad. If I'd known, I could have—stayed with her or something."

"*Did* it hit her that hard?"

"What do you mean?"

"Perry, I don't want to go into it, not over the phone, but I don't believe it was suicide."

She made a thin attempt at laughter. "But, good Lord, Colonel Dolson couldn't possible have—"

"It's more than Dolson. Have you eaten?"

"I just got back five minutes ago."

"What time will you be through?"

"Eight-thirty, Gevan."

"I'll be parked as close to the main entrance as I can get. I'll feel better if you lock your office door."

"You're frightening me, Gevan."

"I think it's time to be frightened."

It was seven by the clock in the lobby. The storm-lull was over. All the phony words had been said, all the untimed gestures made. Lester had talked his hate, and he would report that no persuasion would work on me. Now the storm could ride down the line of the wind, while the sky changed from brass to ink.

Chapter 15

The hotel made me restless. I wished I had asked her to quit. My raincoat was in my room. I went to the elevators. One came up from the basement level, the Copper Lounge level. The starter motioned me toward it. The door opened and I got in. Colonel Dolson was in there. A husky bellhop and a waiter were supporting him, one holding each arm. His cropped gray hair still had an authoritative bristle, but the face was sagging and lost, the eyes dull. The front of his beautifully tailored uniform jacket was smeared, and his smell was nauseous.

"You shouldn't have stopped for anybody," the waiter said to the operator.

"You shoulda took him up in the freight cage," the operator said.

"Just run your elevator, sonny," the waiter said.

Dolson stared at the elevator floor. He mumbled and breathed wetly through his mouth. He didn't recognize me, and I couldn't understand what he was saying.

They got off at six. When the door slid shut, I asked the operator if they had to take him very far.

"Just to six-eleven, around the first corner. Imagine a guy like that! He wants to get stinking, he ought to wear civvies. He don't have to wear the uniform all the time."

"Does it happen often?"

"I never see him that bad before. Now they got to strip him and drop him in the sack. Special service. Courtesy of the hotel."

I got off at my floor and got my coat. The telephone rang. When I answered it, there was no one there. I smoked a cigarette, wondering about the call, feeling uneasy about it, and then heard the cautious rattle of fingernails against my door. I opened it. Hildy was standing there, brown eyes wide. She came in quickly and closed the door and leaned against it. She was wearing a yellow dress, one obviously styled for the lounge. Over it she wore a polo coat, too large for her, unbuttoned, the sleeves turned up above her wrists.

"Something," she said, "depth-bombed the good Colonel."

"I saw him in the elevator."

"Then you know the condition. Messy, wasn't he? You've been interested in him, so I thought you ought to know this. Tonight was the night. He leaned pretty hard on me. Just pack a little bag, dear. We'll start in my car. Acapulco, Rio, the Argentine. He couldn't believe my *no* was final. He offered one other inducement, Gevan. A sheaf of bills—of large, coarse, crude money. Honest to God, I never saw so much money all at one time since I was a little kid and my daddy took me through the Mint with all the other tourists. Maybe there's larceny in my heart. For five seconds I was thinking about going along for the ride and the off-chance of rolling him."

"Do you think he actually intends to take off, Hildy?"

"Yes. He can't act that good. When the money didn't work, he started drinking too fast and he told me that somebody had told him everything was set, whatever that means. And he said that, by God, he was no fool and he wasn't going to wait around and be a clay pigeon for anybody, by God. He knew when the sign said the end of the road, and this was it."

"Now he's too drunk to go any place," I said.

"Maybe some of that load is my fault. He kept insisting I

give him some reason why I wouldn't go with him. I finally gave him the reason. I told him every time he put his hand on me it made me feel like the time I was a little kid and Buddy Higgins from across the street put an angleworm in my bathing suit."

"God!"

"I know. Maybe it was too rough. Something was fracturing him and that finished him. He wasn't lucid very long after I told him that. I guess it's best that he got so he couldn't talk at all. I think he could spout some stuff that would make his little pal sore at him."

"What little pal?"

She gave me a quick glance and pulled the folded-back sleeve up so she could look at her watch. "I've got to go sing. Could you take a look at the Colonel, Gevan, just to make sure he doesn't fly out any windows?"

"How do I get into his room?"

She handed me a key. "With this. He forced it on me during one of his relatively sober moments. Be a good guy, Gevan. I've got to run."

"Do you want a report?"

"Please."

After she left for the elevators, I went in the opposite direction, toward the stairs. I went down to the sixth and found six-eleven. I knocked and listened with my ear against the door panel, then let myself in. They'd taken off his jacket, tie, and shoes and put him on the bed. He didn't stir when I turned the lights on. I made a careful search. I found a .45 Colt in the bureau, complete with web belt holster, and extra clips. I thumbed his eyelid up. He was too far gone to twitch. He blew bubbles in the corner of his mouth. The Colonel was a careful man. There was nothing in the room to incriminate him. So I took a look through his pockets. All Army officers come equipped with little black notebooks for their shirt pockets. I stood over him and thumbed through his little black notebook.

Most of the pages were full of unimportant stuff. Memos about appointments. Shopping lists. There were two pages of names in the back. Josie, Annabelle, Alma, Judy, Moira, and so on. The names had one, two, or three stars. Alma had four stars. The colonel's code. I replaced this notebook, pulled the blanket down, and levered him over onto his stomach. I pried his wallet out of his hip pocket. He had sixty-three dollars, and enough membership cards to prove he was a joiner. I put the wallet back. I had just covered him up again when I heard a key in the door. Joe Gardland came in. The husky bellhop was behind him. Joe registered acute surprise.

"What the hell are you doing in here, Gevvy?"

"A friend of the Colonel's asked me to take a look at him and see if he was all right."

"How did you get in?"

"The friend gave me a key. Here. You want it?"

Joe took it and handed it to the bellhop. "Here you go, Willy. Leave it off at the desk." The bellhop looked nervous. He took the key and nodded and left.

Joe shut the door. "Is he okay?"

"Except for the head he's going to have."

Joe stared at the unconscious officer. He took a handkerchief out of his pocket and wiped his forehead. "Once in a long while," he said, "a hotel owner gets a break. Not often. Just once in a while. Willy is a good boy. He decided the Colonel would like his jacket cleaned. On the way down, Willy finds a fat envelope in the inside pocket. He takes a look in the envelope and sees money. So he does the right thing. He brings it to me. Thank God he didn't count it. If he had, I'd never have seen him again. Even a nice boy like Willy has a price. I take the envelope into my office. I start counting. Pretty soon I start sweating. I can't get it into the safe fast enough, and I don't even like having it there. I come to wake him up and tell him the dough is safe. What are they paying colonels lately, anyway?"

"Not that much, Joe."

He walked over and took a close look at the body. "This bird-colonel is really a bird, Gevvy. He has a built-in wolf call. Around four o'clock he had to come back from the plant and have a chat with the police. They tied him in with the little girl who took a leap off the bridge. You know about that?"

"Yes. I knew her. Was Dolson mentioned in her suicide note?"

"No. The way I understand it, they'd been seen around. Not lately, though. They were seen in clubs and so on."

"How did Dolson make out with the police?"

"I got a report. I have to keep in touch when there's a chance I might get some bad publicity for the hotel. He was very manly with them. Straight-from-the-shoulder stuff. 'Yes, men, I knew the little girl. Yes, indeed. Like a daughter to me. Lonely, you know. Took her around a bit until she got better acquainted here. Helped her morale.'"

"Did they buy that?"

"I guess they had to. Anyway, even if they figured he'd been jumping her, they wouldn't want to smear up his career. I don't like the son of a bitch, but he is decorative around here. Until tonight. It doesn't look like he'll wake up in a hurry, does it?"

"Not for hours."

"I usually get along good with the military, Gevvy. Most of the brass is okay. Once in a while you get one of these. Eagles on his shoulders, and he thinks he's the Second Coming. I'll bet you in his home town they'd blackball him at the Lion's Club. Then all of a sudden he's back in uniform and he's a social lion. Knows every headwaiter in town."

"Will you do me a favor, Joe? He's going to wake up and find the money missing and come yelling to you. I want you to stall him."

"How, for God's sake? He'll run to the cops."

"He might not. He might be very easy to stall. Think up some excuse. Maybe you took it to the bank for safe-keeping."

Joe was quick. "Could be the money is not the Colonel's?"

"Could be."

"I want to ask questions, but I can tell by that look in

193

your eye you're not going to answer them. Okay, I'll do it. I'm getting soft in the head anyway. Let's get out of here.''

We rode down in the elevator. Joe got off at the lobby. I went down the next level and into the Copper Lounge. I stood just inside the door. Hildy was singing "All of Me." When I caught her eye, I held up a circle of thumb and finger. She nodded.

I went through the tunnel to the hotel garage and waited by the ramp until my rented car was brought down. I was too early at the plant. There were lights on in the offices. A second shift was going full blast in C and B buildings. I turned off the car lights and slouched in the seat and lit a cigarette. I was parked directly across from the main entrance. I wondered if the time had come when I should stop nosing around independently. It might be wise, first thing in the morning, to go to the regional office of the FBI and speak to the Special Agent in Charge, and give him what I knew about Acme Supply. If it didn't fall within their jurisdiction, they could put me in touch with the right organization. Men from the General Accounting Office would come to the plant and make a complete audit of all vouchers and payments on the D4D contract. The money in Joe's safe could be impounded, and they could ask the Colonel how he happened to have that much money in cash. Alma was dead, but Perry and I could swear to what she had told us. Perry could inform them of the missing files. And the Colonel would be soon drawing a set of coveralls from the supply counter at Leavenworth.

I was on my third cigarette when Perry came out, slim against the lights behind her, pausing at the top of the steps. I turned on the lights and beeped the horn. She came hurrying across the street, and in the slant of street lights I saw her smiling.

With Perry beside me, and the April rain dotting the windshield between slow strokes of the wipers, I drove through the center of town and out South River Boulevard. Perry sat half-facing me, her knees pulled up on the seat, and listened without interruption as I told her what had happened and what I suspected. When I stopped for a light I looked over at her. She wore no hat and her hair looked burnished and lovely.

"What do you mean, Gevan, when you talk about the whole thing dissolving?"

"I feel that the Colonel's racket is only a part of it. Files disappear, Alma dies, the Colonel takes off. That leaves only a mail drop, and one unidentified, obscure little man. So the Colonel is caught and disgraced and imprisoned. The Army replaces him and cleans up the mess. Maybe they catch one C. Armand LeFay, and maybe they don't. But it's like giving the getaway car in a bank robbery a parking ticket. Lester Fitch is implicated. Niki is implicated. Mottling is implicated. I can't see Dolson in any position of knowledge where he could drag them all in, even to save his own hide."

"What do they get out of all this, Gevan?"

"It's becoming obvious. They get access to the most carefully guarded secret of all—the production rate of the D4D. It gives them the chance to foul up the production program, and sabotage what we produce."

I took a quick glance at her as we passed the glaring lights of a shopping center. Her head was tilted and she was giving me an odd, puzzled, almost pitying smile.

"What's the matter?" I asked.

"Gevan, really! I mean isn't that a little too much?"

"It's been a cold war so long, Perry, too many people have forgotten it's a war. We're leery of dramatics. Too many commy hunts have made the whole bit unfashionable. Warring ideologies are in stasis, Perry. Tell me why?"

"Well . . . I suppose it's because if anybody starts anything, we'll destroy each other."

"Okay so far. Now assume that in spite of Cuba and the Congo and all the rest of it, they get the idea they're losing ground in the cold war. Would they give up?"

"I don't know what you want me to say."

"Just suppose, Perry, that a year and a half or two years, the Kremlin decided they have to take the risk of turning it into a hot war. What would they do? They would intensify all espionage activities. We know they've done that. They would yell about peace, about the impossibility of nuclear war, and their earnest desire to compete economically. They're doing that. And let's try to take a shrewd guess about their third step. I think they would commit their most valuable agents, the ones who've never been given an assignment, the ones who've worked themselves carefully and deeply into our industrial, scientific and military structure. When they've pulled enough of our teeth, and gently loosened the rest of them, they can take the most horrible gamble the world has ever seen, and convince those historians who survive that we started it. How many Mottlings, after all the years of waiting, have suddenly been put to work?"

"But what can he . . ."

"The D4D is part of the guidance and control system for an ICBM which we can assume operational. They're doubtless being made elsewhere too. Maybe there are even alternate designs. But they stuck Stanley Mottling on this one."

"What . . . how could he . . ."

"First he rides the top production brains out of the picture. Poulson, Fitz, Garroway and the others. He replaces them with fools, stooges and conspirators. Next he corrupts the Colonel, and that is easy because the Colonel is a vain, stupid, greedy little man. On his own I doubt he could figure out how to ream the government. So Mottling maybe made the plausible suggestion of renting outside storage space, then adjusted procedures to give Dolson a freer hand with purchase orders, then had LeFay contact him on the outside and show him the way to wealth and plenty. And one day Dolson found out Mottling owned him, the way a man owns a dog, and Mottling started to use him. Remember, Dolson is contracting officer, inspection officer and shipping officer. Change a few specs, bitch a few dimensions, and you're in the business of manufacturing intercontinental duds. Dolson could divert the few good ones to Canaveral, or wherever they test them by seeing how they fly."

"It sounds as if . . . you really know."

"When the big guess is right, Perry, all the little mysteries make sense. Ken was a wooden executive, but he was a damn fine engineer. I think he finally caught on. And they had to shut him up quickly."

"Horrible!" she whispered.

"If they could keep twenty Mottlings busy for one year, they could afford to pull the string, Perry. They'd bang us twenty to one. They'd have some wounds to lick, but we'd be stone cold dead."

I'd been driving so automatically I had to check landmarks to find out where I was. I recognized a country road that turned off to the right, and remembered it as the way we used to get to the river long ago, the place to take a gal who gave the slightest promise of co-operation, a place of beer and blankets and clumsy ecstasies.

As I turned into the road, I said, "Know this place?"

"If you hadn't depressed me so much, I'd try to make jokes, like asking you what kind of girl you think I am anyhow. But this doesn't seem to be the night for jolly patter, Gevan."

We rode the four miles to the riverbank in silence. There were three other cars parked there, widely spaced, lights out, facing the dark oiled flow of the river. I lighted two cigarettes and gave one to Perry, pleased to find she had the gift of silence and the wisdom to know when it was necessary.

I had been thinking aloud when I had talked to her. It was like the old days. Ideas had always flowed more freely when I had been dictating to her.

It was ironic that it had been Lester who had triggered my conjecture with his innocent use of the word sabotage. It had embarrassed me to bring that idea up when talking to Mort Brice about Mottling. We're all too afraid of being thought dramatic. We're terrified of being thought ridiculous.

It all made sense when I began to think of Mottling as a man who had lived a life that was a triumph of misdirection. They would commit such a man only when the gamble became important enough, the same way, long ago, they had finally committed Klaus Fuchs. I could not waste my energy fretting about Mottling's motives. If I was right, something had twisted him, irreparably, too many years ago. The pipe and shaggy tweed hid an incurable sickness of the soul.

Obviously, Mottling would be provided with all the highly trained people he could use. Others, like Fitch and Dolson, could be corrupted and enlisted and forced to serve. And, because he was of the utmost importance, every effort would be made to keep him well in the clear, above suspicion.

Suddenly I had a frightening appreciation of how careful their planning was. It had to go back at least five years, to a decision made to infiltrate a big heavy-industry corporation being run by a pair of bachelor brothers. A woman was an obvious wedge. A special woman, clever, dedicated, merciless and superbly trained. She needed an identity, so they searched until they found a friendless girl without family, in Cleveland, who matched closely enough in age and size. The real Niki Webb gave up her name and her life, and I succumbed to the wiles of an expert, masterful as a grub worm in a hen run.

Ken and I, at that time, made a hell of a good team. She had a long and intimate chance to appraise me, and perhaps she decided I was too strong and too able. So she arranged her surprise party, after giving Ken the treatment that had been so effective with me. She couldn't know how it would come out. I might have killed one of them or both of them. The result would have been the same—to make Dean Products more vulnerable by destroying able management. I destroyed it when I walked out. So she married Ken and slowly gutted him, and made room for Mottling to come in when it was time.

But Ken fooled them. He figured it out, and they had to

kill him. And it was disconcerting to learn I was no beach bum. They had thrown everything at me, including Niki, and nothing had worked, so they had tried with the truck, and that hadn't worked.

Now, maybe, they were sweating. I'd stirred up too much. I'd caused them to fold the Dolson swindle, empty the files and kill Dolson's blonde playmate. They would have to protect all the apparatus they had left. I shuddered.

"Somebody walked over your grave," Perry said. My eyes had become accustomed to that faint light cast by the reflection of the distant city on the overcast. The rain had stopped again. She sat facing me, her back against the far door, her legs curled on the seat. When she raised her cigarette to her lips, the red glow of inhalation exposed the pleasant girlish structure of her face.

"Wherever the grave is," I said, "I hope it's a long time waiting for me."

"The good die young," she said with a throaty amusement. "Feel safe."

In the new silence I was aware of how comfortable I was with her. I felt no need to strut, protest, strike attitudes, invent gambits. She knew me well, so well I could afford the rare luxury of being entirely myself. In the warmth and relaxation of that relationship I grew pleasantly aware of her in a physical way. She was girl-in-the-dark, nubile, fragrant—a slender, quick-minded copper-blonde who had become dear to me long before there was any of this awareness. I felt a special stir of tenderness toward her.

"It was so unreal to me when you were talking, Gevan," she said. "It all sounded wild and mad. That business of gray eyes and blue eyes, and Niki being somebody else—I wondered if you were losing your mind. But . . . every minute it seems more real and true. I remember something. I think it fits."

"In what way?"

"I told you the other night how much I hated her after you started to date her. I used to yearn for ugly, terrible things to happen to her. She seemed so . . . invulnerable.

We used to talk about her. She was polite and friendly to all the other girls, but nobody could get an inch closer to her. She seemed to be laughing at all of us, somehow. There was a lot of gossip . . . on account of the way she got her job. She made us all feel inadequate. There was a strangeness about her we all sensed. She didn't seem entirely real. One of the girls was from Cleveland too, and about the same age. She kept trying to pump Niki, to find out more about her, and we kept egging the girl on. Niki was polite and evasive. One day the girl cornered her, alone, in the second floor stock room, determined to pin Niki down. We never found out what actually happened. When the girl came back to her desk she acted frightened out of her wits. She was chalky and shaking, and she moved strangely, as if she'd been hurt somehow. In the middle of the afternoon she suddenly had hysterics and went home. Two days later she gave notice. She wouldn't tell us what happened. She wouldn't even talk about it. It made Niki seem more eerie than ever. When I found out you were going to marry her, I knew with all my heart that it was a dreadful mistake. I didn't know why. I just knew it. It seems to fit, doesn't it?"

"Yes."

"I'm so glad you didn't marry her, Gevan. I'm so glad you didn't have that kind of relationship with her. She's like . . . some kind of animal, different from all the rest of us."

I thought of white quilted plastic, the black line of poplars watching us, the sliding scent of the sun oil, the narrow scabs on my back. The vividness of my total recall seemed as inexcusable at this time and place as if I had shouted an obscenity into the silence. Yet so complete was my reappraisal of the dark, compelling magic of Niki that I had the feeling of being convalescent. I had gone under a strange knife. A rotten place had been cleaned and drained. With proper care and caution, I could live a long life.

"I never knew her at all," I said.

"I don't think your brother did, either."

"Would you sneer at an act of total cowardice, Perry?

Excuse me, dammit, but that Perry name doesn't set quite right. Joan fits so much better."

"Joan is family. Perry is kind of a public name. It sounds better to me for you to call me Joan. What am I supposed to sneer at?"

"I've brought you to an old-timey necking spot, and now I think I'll take you to a motel."

"This is terribly sudden. I can't imagine such a thing. What kind of a girl do you think I am? Pick a nice pretty motel, huh?"

"No joke. We're out of town and we'll keep going. I'm not the hero type. The conspiracy is too big and too tough and too ruthless. We'll make some miles, and then you can phone your mother and tell some feeble lies, and then we'll make more miles, and we'll hole up, in two widely separated rooms, if you say so. In the morning we start making long-distance phone calls from wherever we are, some of them to people who will remember me and listen to me. We'll come back after the Feds have the situation in hand."

I was barely able to see her nod before she spoke. "I've always thought heroes would be very dull people, Gevan. I got over wanting one when I was eleven. If, in all your guesses, you're only twenty per cent right, it is still a very good time to go hide. And afterward, Gevan, there is another thing you are going to do. I took a lot of orders from you in bygone days. Now you take one from me, sir. You haven't been proud of yourself for a long time. You haven't been pleased with yourself. You haven't had any basic, important satisfactions. So I'm ordering you to go back to work where you belong, and do the job you were meant to do, and stop being a forlorn, dramatic, bored guy."

I sat waiting for my own anger, annoyance and indignation. Enough people had been prodding me. But I thought of going back, and I felt a hollow fluttering of excitement and anticipation in my belly.

"You are a marvel, Miss Joan. As long as it's an order, ma'am, I'll obey it, ma'am."

She laughed with her gladness. I reached on impulse and took hold of her wrist. I had wanted to pull her toward me, with some vague idea of sealing this vow with a kiss that would be light and quick and gay. Her laughter stopped. Her wrist was warm and fine and delicate. There was a tremulous resistance in her, an audible catch of her breath.

How fine, I thought. How very fine that it should be this way, so that I can be permitted a feeling of protective tenderness, rather than to have my slightest touch bring the woman surging and bulging against me, all blurred, gasping, softening, with blinded hungry gropings, digging at me with breasts and groin, usurping the aggressive function of the male, using me with a need so animal, so unselective, that were she to be interrupted on her dogged way to her completion, it would take her long moments to remember my name.

Joan knew who I was, every moment. She said my name after the first tentative kissing, made sweet by the shy-bold curling and shift of her lips, and again, with small and breathless laughter after kneeling in the seat, her palms flat against my cheeks to hold me for the rain of kisses in quick, prodigal, random diffusion, and again, with a note of wonder, after a long and bruising time, a bittersweet ferocity, an adult hunger.

I held her then, tightly, marveling at a sweet fit of her against me, so perfect as to seem habitual, like coming home, with the silk of her hair against the angle of my jaw, our fast hearts and breathing mingled. This closeness was not enough, and I thought that perhaps the sweet and complete coupling of our bodies—which would come in our good time at some other place—might also have this same flavor of not being the ultimate closeness for us, because this time, and forever, it was the celebration of the joining of the spirit in which we were involved. Our bodies would be good with each other. We could sense that. But they, no matter how hot and keen their pleasures, would be merely symbolizing the more valid union of the souls of Gevan and

Joan, rather than performing an ancient act complete in itself.

I whispered to her, "You said the big crush ended. You said you got over it."

"Of course it ended, dear. I just didn't tell you what it turned into. Just hold me tight, like this, for a long, long time."

I looked beyond her, through the car window. I saw the silhouette of a faceless man. As I lunged to trip the lock on the door on her side, the door behind me was ripped open and a hard arm clamped around my throat, dragging me out from behind the wheel as Joan screamed.

I tried to grab the wheel but my hand slipped. I went back and down, the concealed running board scraping against the small of my back, my shoulders thudding against wet grass. In the endless moment of the fall, I thought of my stupidity in making no effort to find out if we were followed, no attempt to see the car that had probably hung back, lights off, following the rented sedan. And I also thought of the truck that had come barreling down on the hill when I left Niki's house. Mottling had told her I was coming. The penalty for stupidity was high. Too high, because Joan was in it too, and the Brady girl had talked before they killed her.

The fall released the pressure on my throat. I braced my feet against the side of the car and thrust myself over in a backward somersault, swinging my legs high as I came over. My right shoe thudded against something and I heard a gasp of pain. I landed on my hands and knees, facing the car. I swung and dived forward, arms spread wide. A knee glanced off my cheek, making my eyes water, but I grabbed one leg and drove ahead hard, like a linesman.

I could hear the other cars starting up, racing motors as they left hastily, and one set of headlights swept across us just as my man went down. They had heard the screams and this was trouble and the people in the other cars wanted no part of it. Joan screamed again, and this time there was a flat quality to it, and I guessed she had been dragged out of the car on the other side. I clambered over the man as he fell and hammered down with my fist where his face should have been. My fist hit wet earth. He was like an eel. On the next try I hit him squarely and felt something give under my knuckles, felt the frightening eel-like vitality slow into thick movements. I had to get to her and stop whatever it was they were doing to her. I scrambled away from the man on the ground, felt his fingers grasp weakly at my ankle as I stumbled toward the hood of the car. I went around the hood and saw a churning shadow, heard Joan whimpering with effort and fear as I grabbed at the shadows and felt her slimness under my hands. I released her, trying to shove her out of danger, and turned to take a blow above the eye that felt as though it cracked my skull. I yelled thickly to Joan, "Run! Run!" I lunged toward the shadow which had struck me. My arms were dead and, as I grasped him, I took another blow in the dead center of my forehead. I went down onto my knees, trying to hold onto him. He struck down at the nape of my neck and I slid my face into the wet grass. My slack fingers had slid to his ankle. I groaned and yanked the ankle toward me and bit it as hard as I could, the wool of the sock in my teeth. He yelled and kicked free and I rolled toward the bigger shadow of the car and, like a bruised animal hunting a hole, I wormed under the car. I took two deep, gasping breaths and wiggled on out the other side, my shoulder banging something on the underside of the car.

There was a silence. The rain came again, whispering along the river. I crouched, my knuckles against the wet grass, wetness soaking through one knee. I came silently to my feet, my head clearing. The river made wet, sucking sounds against the bank. A boat hooted, far away. I listened for some sound from Joan. Suddenly I heard a gasp and quick running footsteps in the grass. A flashlight clicked on and the beam swept toward the rear of the car, swept on out and pinned Perry as she ran across the rutted grass. She ran fleetly, like a slim boy.

There was an odd sound. A sort of whistling chunk.

Joan's scissoring legs made one more stride and she pitched forward onto her face in the grass, falling in a boneless, nightmare way.

The light went off.

I went around the car, my shoes skidding and slipping on the grass, half-hearing the noise I was making in my throat as I strained toward a shadow, reaching for it, feeling my finger tips brush fabric. The tears of rage were running out of my eyes. I ran slam into the front end of a black locomotive. It thundered over me and ground me down into darkness, rolled me into something small and black that bounded along the ties between the roaring steel wheels.

The train rumbled off into an echoing distance. I was in a car. I slumped sideways in the back seat. Something pressed warm and heavy against my thigh. I crawled my hand along and touched it, traced a smooth cheek, brushed hair of silk. The car moved, uneasily. It seemed to waddle like something fat and tired and old. I squinted toward the front seat. It was an old joke. Nobody was driving, mister. We were all sitting in the back seat. The car bumped and moved again. Somebody expelled breath in a sharp whistle of effort. The hood tipped down suddenly, pitching me forward toward the back of the driver's seat. I could look down the gleam of the hood and I saw it glide down into the black mirror of the river surface, and I saw the black mirror, swirled and broken, slide up and cover the windshield and the world. The car tilted slow, unsupported, and it glided down in slow motion, like a trick movie shot of a car going off a cliff.

It nudged bottom gently and swayed, and swayed some more, and folded softly over onto its weary side, down in the darkness, down in the river, where death was a hard, thin hissing as the water gushed in through a dozen places, spattering my face, rising up my side. It had been a slow dream, mildly amusing, and I had been a spectator, watching it all in entranced numbness. But the cold hard jet of water from the window nearest me smashed into my face and brought me back to alertness—and panic.

There was some air trapped in the car, but it was going quickly. My mind started to work. I ripped off the constricting jacket, reached down and pulled my shoes off underwater. I remembered it was a two-door sedan. I got hold of her and shoved her toward the vertical dashboard. I took a deep breath of the precious air and shoved myself forward in the car. I braced my feet against the door, reached up and got the door handle of the door on the driver's side, the one uppermost. The girl was under water. I couldn't force the door. I risked one more breath, knowing that when the last of the air was gone the pressure would be equalized and the door would open if it was not sprung. I found the window crank and turned it. The air bubbled up and the black water closed around me, the pressure humming in my ears. I thrust against the door. It opened. I got girl around the waist.

I bulled up against the door and worked through it, pulling on the girl. She got caught somehow. I tugged hard, and she came free. As we went upward through the door, it tried to close on my feet like something alive, trying to bite. I tore free. I clawed upward through chill layers of water that pressed hard in my ears. I kept kicking, holding her, pulling at the water with my free hand, and it was a nightmare of climbing up a ladder with rubber rungs.

My lungs were straining against my locked throat and I knew soon there would be no more will to keep my throat locked and the black water would come in.

My head broke through into the cold moist air of the rainy night. I gasped out the staleness and sucked the good air deep. The light was faint. The current was taking us, and the shore trees moved slowly by against the glow of the distant city. I found I was holding her wrong, holding her with her head under water. I turned her around, with her face in the air. I cupped one hand under her chin and towed her on her back, angling toward shore. The bank was too steep. I couldn't get any hold on it. She slipped away from me and I reached and caught her just as she was slipping under the surface. I floated with her, straining for the bank.

My feet touched. I stood in waist-deep water. I pushed her ahead of me, forcing her upward against the bank. I used roots to claw my way up. I shoved her over the crest and dragged her to a level space and straightened out her body and rolled her over onto her face, adjusting her arms and legs the way the book says. I put my finger in her slack mouth and hooked her tongue forward so she wouldn't swallow it.

I knelt with one knee between her legs. I pressed down and forward against the rib cage just above the small of her back, slowly increasing the pressure, then slid my hands back quickly, hooked my fingers on the ridges of hip bone and lifted her pelvis and diaphragm on the reverse count, to suck fresh air back into slack lungs. At first I was trembling so badly from effort, the rhythm was uncertain. Then I began to steady into it. Press—one, two, three. Lift—one, two, three. Press—one, two, three. Lift—one, two, three. I did not let myself think I was working on a body that was dead when it went into the river. I had a vision of the back of her head smashed under the soft copper hair, smashed by the thing that had whistled and thudded and tumbled her like a rag doll. But there was no light and I could not see, and I was doing the only thing I could do, and it was better not to think about it.

There was no time, no clocks, no night. Existence was divided into two motions: press-lift. I worked over her. My arms were clumsy, bloated things. The small of my back was like a tooth broken down to the nerves. I had no thought of stopping. It became a mania. I could not remember why I was doing this. I worked with my eyes squeezed against the pain, my jaw sagging.

She made a choking, coughing sound, and she whispered and stirred under my hands. I rested my hands on her, lightly, and felt the swell and fall of her breathing. I found her pulse. It was slow and steady. I crawled away from her and pitched forward, my cheek against the mud. Nausea curled inside me and faded. I wept with weakness. After a time I crawled back to her. I fingered the back of her head, and felt the stickiness.

I stood up weakly and saw, far off, golden rectangles of lighted windows. They were home, and fireside. I gathered her up. She seemed very heavy. She was unconscious. I fumbled over two fences, carrying her. I dropped her once and told her aloud that I was sorry about being so clumsy. I picked her up again.

Chickens made querulous sounds in their sleep. A dog came charging out, yapping in valiant hysteria. See me, the brave dog, defending my land. Hear my bold voice.

A hard, white yard light went on and there was a big barn shape near me, with a smell of tractors. I tripped and caught myself.

"Who's that? Who's out there?" a man yelled.

"Accident!" I croaked. "River."

I came into the cone of light. A gaunt man peered at me. He took two long strides and caught Perry as she started to slip away from me again.

I followed him into the kitchen. The house was full of kids. The television was on. The kitchen tilted slowly and the linoleum hammered the side of my head. I tried slowly and laboriously to get up and somebody helped me, saying, "Easy does it! Easy does it!"

I smiled to show I was just fine. I leaned on him and said carefully, "Please . . . get a doctor. Phone Arland Police. Get hold of Portugal . . . Sergeant Portugal. Nobody else, please. Tell him . . . Dean wants him. Tell him . . . how to get here."

Chapter 16

I knew the calls had been made. I wanted to sleep. But the man knew I was badly chilled and shocked and he got me into a hot tub. It had the right effect. I felt life and strength coming back into drained muscles. He left me when he was sure I wouldn't pass out in the tub. He left fresh underwear, a wool shirt, and blue jeans. I soaked for a long time. I could hear heavy voices in the house, and people walking around. I got out and used the big rough towel. I looked in the mirror. There was a knot in the middle of my forehead. My left cheek was puffed and purple, the eye swollen to a slit.

I dressed in the clothes left there for me and walked out of the steamy bathroom. Kids peered at me and darted into other bedrooms. I went into the living-room. Sergeant Portugal stood there, looking solid and safe and comforting. He was talking to a tired-looking young man with an unkempt mustache.

"How is she?" I asked.

"By God, you look rough, Dean," Portugal said. "Meet the doctor." He was bouncing a small object in his hand. He held it up between thumb and forefinger. "The doc took this out of her head."

"She'll be all right, Mr. Dean," the doctor said.

"I figure it was an air gun," Portugal said.

"A powerful one. It hit at an angle right at the crown of her head, and traveled between scalp and skull all the way around and came to rest just above her left eyebrow. If it hadn't hit at an angle, I'd judge it could very easily have perforated the skull."

"Can I see her?"

"No. I removed the pellet, treated her for shock, and gave her a shot that will keep her out for eight hours. She's okay to be moved. There's an ambulance on the way out."

"She'll go into Arland General under another name, Mr. Dean," Portugal said. "And you and I are going into town too, so let's thank these people and arrange about clothes and see if your wallet is dry, and you can start talking on the way in."

I rode with Portugal in his sedan. As we turned onto the highway, the ambulance turned in. I talked. I kept nothing back. I was so weary, I would begin to ramble until Portugal would haul me back onto the subject with a terse question. He stopped near a drugstore and made a phone call. I sat in the darkness. I felt uneasy. The river had done something to my nerves. Every time I thought of Joan I felt gladness.

Portugal came back. He got in and didn't start the motor. "I got to make another call in ten minutes. We'll wait right here."

"What call?"

"I got to know where to take you. I got to know where they want you."

"They?"

He turned. There was enough light on his heavy face so that I could see his weary smile. "It's out of my league. You're going to be in good hands. Just relax and ride with it, Mr. Dean."

Suddenly he was shaking me awake. I came to, bleared with sleep. "Did you make your call?" I mumbled.

"Made it and drove three miles. You're to go with them."

I saw two men standing by the sedan. We were parked in

an alley. I sensed that we were in downtown Arland. I got out and turned to thank Portugal, but the sedan was already in motion.

"Please follow me, Mr. Dean," one of the men said. We went through a door and down steps and through a boiler room to a waiting basement elevator. The elevator took us up to a high floor, to an empty, echoing corridor, to lighted offices.

There was a man waiting, sitting at a table. There were three empty chairs. There was a small microphone on the table, a large tape recorder with oversized reels on a stand. The two men who brought me up looked young and competent. The seated man was older. I was conscious of the poor fit of the wool shirt and the jeans, of my bruised face and soggy shoes.

"Please sit down, Mr. Dean. My name is Tancey. I'm with the FBI." He did not introduce the other two. We all sat down. Tancey was one of those curiously professorial-looking men who, on closer examination, suffer a subtle alteration. You see the hard-knuckled hands then, and the steady eyes, and the breadth of chest, and the clean, compact physical movements, and you wonder what gave you the original impression of the subdued scholar.

Tancey turned on the tape recorder, checked the gain, gave the date and hour and my name, and began asking questions. They took me through it, right from the beginning. Facts and conjectures. And when I did not give enough detail to satisfy them, they made me back up and go over the incident again. They asked questions that seemed to me to be immaterial, and when I asked a question, it was ignored. They were not rude. They were businesslike. It was a strain. I kept yawning. At last Tancey was satisfied. He turned off the recorder, rewound the tape, checked it for sound, using the monitor speaker. I heard my own voice, scratchy with fatigue.

During the last half-hour of it, I had begun to get annoyed. They were undoubtedly fine, capable men, but their attitude was as though they were dealing with a rather stupid, naughty child.

Tancey lit a cigarette and gave me a weary smile. "We may have to go over some of it again tomorrow, Mr. Dean."

"Can I go back to the hotel now?"

"I'm afraid not. You and Miss Perrit were murdered tonight. We'll keep it that way."

"How about her people? You can't keep them in the dark."

"They've been contacted. They'll co-operate. They know she's all right. We had them report her missing."

"There's something about this cloak-and-dagger atmosphere that doesn't set too well with me, Mr. Tancey. Why don't you sweat it out of Colonel Dolson and wrap it up?"

"You'll be taken to a place where you can sleep and we'll see you in the morning."

"Mr. Tancey, I got myself and Miss Perrit off the bottom of the river. I've opened up for you. I'm tired. But I'm not going to accept being brushed off. I want to know the score, and I think I've earned the right to know the score."

Tancey looked at me. It was the first time he had looked at me as a human being rather than a source of information. I sensed the extent of his dedication.

"I'm tired too, Mr. Dean. I haven't meant to brush you off. Colonel Dolson died tonight. It was arranged to look like a suicide, with note and all. The note was in the form of a confession, so it could have been written by him in exchange for a promise to get him out of the country."

Weariness had so dulled my reaction time that it took long minutes to understand what had happened, and the implications of it. With Dolson dead, Stanley Mottling might be in the clear. Not beyond suspicion, but beyond proof.

"There is something else you should understand, Mr. Dean," he continued in his grave voice. "Your will names your brother without any alternate heir. If you had died tonight, his estate would inherit, and that means his widow would inherit your holdings, giving her a solid sixteen thousand voting shares."

I hadn't thought of that. Tancey said, "There is more we can talk about. Believe me, Mr. Dean, I'm willing to talk to you, but right now I think you'd better go to bed."

I could not resist. The brisk young men took me down in the elevator and out through the basement to a car waiting in the alley. I managed to stay awake while they drove me to an old Georgian brick house in an old and no longer fashionable residential section of the city. I was taken to a bedroom. The bed opened like a cave and gobbled me up . . .

They were efficient. When I woke up I could tell by the sun that it was at least mid-morning. My wrist watch had stopped. The river had gotten into it. Someone had visited my hotel suite. My toilet kit was there, and the rest of my clothing. There was a morning paper just inside the door. I felt astonishingly good. I wondered about Joan. I wondered if the doctor had been lying to me. That thought shadowed the sunshine. My face was not swollen, but I had a black eye that looked like a comedy effect. Deep blue and purple, and I knew it would fade to bilious saffron before bleaching out. I showered and shaved and sat on the side of the bed and looked through the paper.

Dolson's suicide got less of a play than I had expected. It got one column on page three, with a picture of a thinner, younger Dolson in uniform with leaves on his shoulders instead of eagles. There was an indirect hint about his speculations. There was no attempt to link his death to the Brady suicide or my brother's murder. As any alert legman might easily sense some connection, I guessed Tancey's people had put a partial lid on the whole thing.

There was some blah about Dean Products being a key plant in the defense program, and some more about officials of the space program arriving today by plane from Washington.

I found myself in the last paragraph:

Mr. Gevan Dean, a resident of Florida, arrived this past week to attend a meeting of the Board of Directors of Dean Products, Inc. He resigned from the presidency of the firm four years ago, relinquishing that position to his brother, who was recently slain. It is not expected that Mr. Gevan Dean will resume active participation in the management of the firm. As yet Mr. Gevan Dean has not been reached for comment on the Dolson suicide.

Also I found that somebody had whipped out a quick editorial. It spoke of all the loyal, efficient men who take leaves of absence from their firms to serve their country as reserve officers on active duty, aiding the military by donating skilled services for lower pay than they could command in industry, and it went on to say how it was a shame that the dishonesty of one man could bring down unfavorable publicity on all those others who do such a splendid job.

I dressed and went downstairs. It seemed very quiet. I found a dining room with small tables, each set for four places. A stone-faced woman asked me if I wanted breakfast, and how I wanted my eggs. She served me with ruthless efficiency. The coffee was superb. Kids were having a noisy Saturday morning somewhere nearby. I could hear them yelling. There was no sound in the big house. There was something institutional in the way the house was furnished, in the plates and utensils.

A stocky nurse in rustling white came in and smiled at me and said, "Mr. Dean? Mind if I join you for some coffee?"

"Please do." She had a broad, pleasant Irish face.

"I'm Ellen McCarthy, Mr. Dean."

"Do you happen to know anything about Joan Perrit?"

"Oh, yes. She was brought here from the hospital about an hour ago. She's sleeping right now."

"How is she?"

"Fine. Or they wouldn't have moved her. She had a headache and a slight cold. No fever."

"Can I see her?"

"Later. Perhaps this afternoon, Mr. Dean. She'll be sitting up by then, and back on her feet tomorrow."

The apprehension in the back of my mind faded away, and I grinned so broadly at Nurse McCarthy that she looked startled. After she left me, I wandered toward the front of the house. A young man stepped out of a room and said, courteously, "Please stay away from the front of the house, Mr. Dean. Mr. Tancey's orders."

"When will he be here?"

"I'm sorry, I couldn't say."

I looked around the rest of the house. There were books and magazines in the study, and I was permitted to go out into the small walled garden.

It was noon when Tancey arrived. He came alone. He found me in the study and sat down. It was obvious that he hadn't been to bed. He had a gray stubble of beard. It made him look more human.

"Sorry we had to give you such a going over last night, Mr. Dean."

"I understand."

"Some people wanted that tape in a hurry. This is just one part of a picture that's been developing for some time."

I stared at him. "They knew about this? Who?"

"Just whom you'd imagine, Mr. Dean. When a pattern began to show, a coordinated team was set up. CIA people, and service counterintelligence people, some of us, and some from other specialized agencies. The most effective part of the job has been done by working from the other end, triple-checking operational readiness of complete missile assemblies, reworking the dogs at base installations. Some essential stuff from Dean Products was carefully bitched, so Dean was on the list. Some people have been planted on you, but reports have been negative and we weren't slated to move in strong until some other deals were cleaned up."

"How was our stuff defective?" I asked him.

He gave me an almost pitying smile. "I'm no technician,

Mr. Dean. But they gave me a crash course. I think I can lose you with one question. When you change the conductivity of one of the ferride plastics, what effect could that have on the reliability of adjacent transistors, diodes, cryotons, masers, parametric amplifiers and so on? Give up?"

"You lost me in the first ten words."

"Don't look so troubled. The more sophisticated the birds you build, the more craftily they can be bitched. Take even a sturdy bird like the Polaris—it can and has been jiggered in such a way that the guidance system poops out after six months in the stockpile. That's among the first ones that were caught. At Dean we'd been thinking in terms of employees, not management, until you started thumping around. Now it's being reappraised."

"Can you tell me the status?"

"Some of it. A limited security clearance came through for you this morning. We know of at least four operating outside the plant, and we can assume a few more. LeFay is one of those. We expect to locate him soon. Another one of them rooms in the same place Shennary lived, which makes a neat fit for a murder weapon plant. We're checking out your brother's widow."

"Who is she?"

"All we have so far is proof she's not Niki Webb. Your Mr. Wilther in Cleveland did a nice job. The photographer who takes the graduation pictures at the high school she went to keeps a file of negatives going way back, for no good reason. We got a blowup of her. There's a fair resemblance, until the experts start measuring and comparing facial dimensions—placement of the ears, interpupilary gap, etc."

"Where did she come from?"

He shrugged. "We'll find out. It's been narrowed down. The one that looks best so far is Mary Gerrity, code name Charlotte. Slum kid from Chicago. When she was fifteen, tough as hemp and alley-cat smart, a pinko professor bedded her down, sold her his version of social paradise and steered her into the YCL. That was in 1941. He sensed when he was about to be picked up and took off with her for Mexico City. Three years later he got killed down there. We got the word it was a party discipline thing. She disappeared. In 1947 when our people were trying to plug some bad leaks in Berlin it turned out she was servicing a BG who should have known better. She was netted and while they were still trying to crack her open, indignant consular types showed up with papers all in order proving she was a Polish citizen and pried her loose. In the next few years we made her a couple of times in group photos out of Moscow, big party fetes and banquets. I'm telling you all this because I'm sure this is the right one, and we'll know for certain when that maid, Victoria, turns over something with some good prints on it. Next time we picked up her trail was, for God's sake, in Cambodia, but it was a old trail and the damage was done, and she'd gone the bedroom route to do it. Five years ago we knew she was back in Mexico. It was a good guess she was coming in, and it was our hunch she was all set up for some kind of permanent cover, but we lost her, and we've been looking for her ever since, because we know she's been given top training and she's one of the very best they've got. Five years ago any fool could guess that Dean Products would get some critical space contracts. So they sent the Dean brothers a special package."

"And it blew us to hell," I said in a sick voice.

"Because the package was tailored for bachelor brothers, Mr. Dean. The laymen who sneer at the Mata Hari angle and think it's corny are damn fools. One shrewd broad who despises men so much she adores every minute of banging them because it cuts them down to animal level, and who can accept party discipline out of a tough, genuine dedication, and is such a package it dries out your mouth to look at the walk on her, a broad like that is worth, at the very least, one pair of nuclear subs. Don't call yourself a fool. You swing an amateur bat against big league pitching, and you should average out zero zero zero. But you've batted about zero two five, which is exceptional. She chased you off and swung the door open for Mottling when the time was ripe. Now you're helping us close it a lot sooner than we would have."

"Can you pick up Mottling too?"

"Wish we could. We'd have to have solid proof, and there won't be any of that laying around, or anybody who'll talk. But I hope from here on we can keep him away from critical areas. That's the most we could expect, and we'll be happy with that."

"How about Lester Fitch? He'll break easy."

"But give us nothing. He's a fringe operator. He cut himself into Dolson's take. Blackmail based on something he found out by accident, I'd say. It's made him anxious to have things keep going exactly as they were. If you or Granby took over, Dolson might get moved away from the trough, so it made him a hot Mottling man. Perhaps your brother said just enough to him so that Fitch felt there was more to your brother's death than met the eye. I think he's been highly nervous lately."

"You said Joan and I are going to stay murdered for a while. How long?"

"Until the Monday meeting, and then we'll see if shock has any effect on those people. Probably it won't. Think this over, Mr. Dean. If they *had* killed you two, and if we had fumbled the ball when we got around to looking into Dean Products, Mottling would be in, and, because your will still leaves everything to your brother, his estate would pick up the marbles, and that shifty broad would be sitting on sixteen thousand shares of voting stock. If our shock doesn't work, you can at least vote Mottling out."

"And put Granby in?"

"That's your problem."

"No little lecture about where my duty lies?"

He stood up. "I've got to have some sleep. About duty, so-called, you have to live with yourself, and I have to live with myself, and that's the one trap nobody ever gets out of." He walked out.

I went to the window overlooking the walled garden.

May is a good month in Florida. The tarpon are moving north. The mosquitoes aren't out in force yet. It's a good month to go to Marathon and stalk bonefish across the flats.

The size of the alternative frightened me. I would be mouldering a tremendous responsibility. It would ride my back, day and night. But at the same time the thought of it gave me a crawling holiday-feeling of anticipation.

Chapter 17

I was in the small walled garden at three o'clock when Nurse McCarthy came walking slowly out into the sunlight, with a wan Joan leaning on her arm. I stood up quickly, went over to her and took her other arm.

"Joan! God, should you be walking around?"

"It was either this or tie her to the bed," McCarthy said.

"How do you feel, honey?"

"Want to race?" Joan said. Her head bandage was bright white against the coppery hair.

She stood with McCarthy holding her while I unfolded a deck chair for her. We put her in the chair. She shut her eyes. "Whooo! Now go away, McCarthy, because when the world stops going around I'm going to get kissed."

"Don't tax your strength, dearie," the nurse said, and beamed, and rustled off.

Joan opened her eyes. "Now?"

"Now," I said. And did. Her lips were sweet.

"Better than that," she said. "I'm not *that* fragile."

So we made it a little better, and it was very fine indeed. She sat back, looking smug. "Now you've got my cold too, probably."

"Indubitably."

"Now tell me about it. I ran. I was going to get away and

get help and something hit me on the back of the head and I fell clunk into a hospital bed, with a headache like a brass band and a case of sniffles and my back feeling like somebody had worked it over with a ball bat."

I told her. In detail. I tried to keep it calm, but I heard my own voice getting a nervous edge to it. She listened and became more pale. I saw what I was doing to her and exerted more control. I tried to make light comedy out of dropping her, and fumbling over those fences and falling on my face in the kitchen. Her color became better. But she was very grave.

"Thank you, Gevan," she said in a small voice.

"For what?"

"For all the days of my life from now on. Thank you very much because they are going to be good days."

"You don't mind my taking an ownership interest in them?"

"Try to get out of it. Just try. I'll follow you on the street, beating on a pan and waving a sign: 'This man ruined me!'"

"Ruined you?"

"That's just a suggestion—for after I get my strength back. My God, Gevan, that's a delicious black eye!"

"And that's a delectable bandage."

"They shaved the top of my head. It's hideous. They let me look with a hand mirror when they changed the dressing. I look like one of those monastery types. You're looking at me funny."

"I'm making up for all the time of having you around and *not* looking at you."

"What's the verdict?"

"You are lovely, Joan Perrit. You have good bones."

"Thick ones, apparently."

"Mind if I keep staring?"

"If you keep staring in just that way, I'm going to clutch at you. That's bad technique. I'm supposed to be shy and girlish and reserved. Mother said never clutch. It makes men nervous."

"Make me nervous."

It was a fine Saturday and a fine Sunday. We spent every possible moment together. We had talking to do, but I haven't the faintest idea of what we talked about. We were memorizing each other. If it happens to somebody else, it is just a standard moon-June case of love. When it happens to you, it changes the world.

It had never been this way before. Not with anybody. She was alive and gay, and there was no question about what we would do with our lives. She was Joan and I wanted her for keeps. I wanted her complete with her sudden fits of shyness, and faint awkwardnesses of posture, and the clean, soft texture of her skin, and the good bones, and the structural miracle of wrist and ankle, and the surprising richness of the curve of her waist. I looked at her body and I wanted it ripe with our child. I had never felt that way before. I told her about that and she said it was a good thing. She said it could probably be arranged, that she'd seen a diagram somewhere about how you went about it. There was a lustiness about her sense of humor that I had never suspected, and it delighted me. She told me gravely that she needed to know nothing about other women in my life, because given the opportunity, she felt confident that she could induce in me considerable amnesia on that point. By the look of her eyes and lips when she said it, I had no doubt it was true. Each moment with her made the narrowness of her escape more terrifying. . . .

The meeting was scheduled for ten o'clock on Monday morning. I was smuggled into the offices ahead of the early birds, and had a long wait in a storeroom full of office supplies. On the way to the offices Tancey told me that LeFay had been picked up in Baltimore and brought back to Arland, and there was no file on him.

At the proper moment one of Tancey's young men unlocked the door and nodded to me. It was quarter after ten. I followed him to the paneled board room. I felt ridiculous as I walked toward the room, as though I were a female entertainer about to leap up out of a big pasteboard pie.

I erased a wide, idiotic smile from my lips as I walked in. I came very close to yelling. "Surprise!"

At first the room was a smear of smoke and faces. Uncle Al spoiled my electric moment by saying, "Thought you'd forgotten about this, Gevan."

Tancey was in the room. I looked at Mottling and saw that look of a professional gambler who had learned not to tear up the cards when he loses. There is always another hand coming up. Niki may have gone pallid when she saw me, but I could not be certain. Her eyes were like Mottling's. Cool, aware, speculative.

Then I saw Lester Fitch. The flesh of his face had sagged loose from the bone. His complexion was yellow. He mumbled something to Karch, the Chairman of the Board, and left the room, wavering so that his shoulder struck against the door-jamb as he left. One of Tancey's young men followed him.

The proceedings were brief. The books confirmed my holdings and voting privilege. Walter Granby requested permission to speak. He stated that he hoped I would resume active management of the firm, pleading that he could be more valuable if he could continue to devote his entire attention to financial matters. Karch made an objection that seemed too routine. Uncle Al backed Granby's suggestion. They all stared at me. I cleared my throat and heard myself saying that under the circumstances I would be glad to take over if it could be confirmed by a vote. Granby declined the nomination Karch made. The voting was between me and Mottling. I saw why Niki had wanted me to abstain from voting. One sizeable shareholder had been won over by Mottling, and I saw from the expression on Karch's face that it was an unpleasant surprise. Had I not voted, Mottling would have been in.

With my block of voting shares, it was no contest. I was in. And I knew I had to show I could handle it, show that previous success had not been a fluke. I saw Tancey watching me with something like amusement in his eyes. There was a polite spatter of applause. I was renamed to the Board. I blocked Lester's appointment to the Board.

Karch closed the meeting and people moved slowly out of the smoky room into the wide hallway. Niki came up to me in the hall and put her hand in mine and looked into my eyes. "I guess I was a stubborn, officious fool, darling. I should have realized this is where you belong. Where you have always belonged."

"How do you mean that?"

"I don't know anything about all this company business. I thought I was doing what Ken wanted. I guess he would have wanted you to come back more than anything. I just didn't see it that way. I do, now."

"Thank you, Niki."

"Come on out to the house about five, will you darling? We'll have a drink to you. Just the two of us. Please?"

"I'll let you know." Stanley Mottling came up to us, smiling.

He congratulated me and then said, "I'll stick around and help out as long as you need me, Gevan."

"I appreciate that."

They both smiled at me. Their smiles were warm. It seemed incredible they were acting a part. They hadn't given up. They would never give up. Blocked in one direction, they were instinctively seeking another.

My arrival was bad news, but Dolson was gone and LeFay was gone, and they were safe. They could concentrate on taking over Gevan Dean. The woman could marry him. Mottling could stick close to him at the plant. Maybe it could be managed just as well this way. I returned their smiles. I wanted to tell Mottling to be out of the plant in ten minutes, but I didn't know how Tancey wanted me to handle it. I thanked them for their good wishes and watched them walk down the corridor together, and I heard Niki's warm, calm laugh.

I found out which office was Lester's. I went there and opened the door and walked in without knocking. It was an trusion. Lester sat behind his desk. Tancey and the young man who had followed Lester Fitch flanked him, facing him. Tancey gave me an annoyed glance.

Lester said dully, "I tell you I don't know what you're talking about." His face was still yellow.

"Mr. Fitch," Tancey said calmly, "You're being stupid. Sit down, Mr. Dean, and listen to this."

"I don't know what you're talking about. I felt sick and I had to leave. Something I ate, I think."

"Who told you Mr. Dean was dead?"

"His wife called me right after he was shot."

"Not that Mr. Dean. This one."

"I didn't think Gevan was dead. I don't know what you mean."

"If I ever saw a man seeing a ghost, it was you, Fitch. We've got your playmate, LeFay. He's told us how it was worked, with you and Dolson. We can prove every bit of it. You're a lawyer. You must know criminal law. This isn't a case of nailing you for getting your hands on government money. I want you for murder, too. For being an accessory to the murder of the Brady girl."

"But I didn't even know they were going to—" He stopped abruptly.

"How did you get in with Dolson?"

"I found out how he was doing it. Nobody else knew. He had to let me in. I set Acme up on a better basis than they had it. Safer."

"Who told you Gevan Dean was dead? Was it Mottling?"

His eyes went wide. His shock was evident. "Mottling! He hasn't got anything to do with—" I saw the shock fade and his eyes get wary as he began to figure out some of the things that had evidently bothered him because they hadn't added up.

"Come now, Fitch. Mottling and LeFay corrupted Dolson, then used the knowledge of his thefts to blackmail him into sabotaging production. Don't look so innocent."

Lester looked bewildered. "Sabotage? It was only the

money. LeFay said Ken had found out about it, and he would fix it. I didn't know until afterwards he was going to have him killed."

I butted in. "Why did you want me to back Mottling if you didn't know he was in on it?"

"I didn't. LeFay was afraid of what Granby might find out, if he was in charge, being a financial man and all. He thought Granby might change the office procedure on purchases and that would spoil it."

Tancey sighed. "It hangs together, Mr. Dean. I don't think Fitch knew about the other. As it is, we can give him a few years in a federal prison." He talked as if Lester wasn't in the room. That, more than anything else, seemed to crack Lester Fitch.

He said, in a quick, thin voice, "Look, I'll cooperate in any way. I'll pay back every nickel. I'll testify to everything. Please, Mr. Tancey. Please. If you want me to, I'll testify that Mr. Mottling helped set up the Acme swindle and even got some of the money. I know I did wrong, and you've got to give me a break."

Tancey didn't even look at him. As far as Tancey was concerned, Lester had not spoken. The young man with Tancey gave Lester a contemptuous glance.

"Take him in," Tancey said.

The lunch bells were sounding out in the production areas. Lester stood up slowly, pushing the chair out of his way. Then he whirled and moved with a speed that caught us off balance. He plunged through the ground-floor window, protecting his face with his arms. I saw him roll and bound to his feet and start running toward the lunch crowd thronging toward the gates.

Tancey shoved me out of the way. He had a short-barreled revolver in his hand. He aimed at the running man and fired once. Lester went down hard, with a long, shrill scream. His thigh was curiously shortened and twisted and he grasped at it with his hands as he worked himself in a slow circle on the ground, like a crippled insect.

People ran over, formed a circle around him. He screamed again and again. It reminded me of another scene long ago, when the kids at recess had gathered around Lester in that same way. A boy who came up to Lester's shoulder had belted him solidly on the nose. And Lester had screamed in that same way, and the crowd standing around him had looked just the same. Awed, and ashamed.

Tancey said quietly, holstering the gun, "We need him for the LeFay testimony."

"Nice shooting, sir."

"Thank you, Larkin. Make the necessary arrangements, please."

Larkin left. The gate guards were dispersing the curious. I saw the shards of Lester's broken glasses glinting in the noon sun.

I said to Tancey, "Niki—Mary Gerrity, or whatever I'm supposed to call her—asked me to stop out at her house at five."

"We'll be picking her up before then."

"Let me go out there at five. Pick her up after that. Give me some time with her first. Just ten minutes. I owe Ken that much."

"I don't like it. I don't want to lose her."

"You can cover the place, can't you?"

"Yes, but—"

"I've earned it, haven't I?"

He shrugged. "All right. It's not smart. But all right."

We talked some more. "I don't think we can tag Mottling. We'd have to have a good reliable witness who saw Mottling and LeFay together. After we pick up the woman, I'll pay Mottling a private visit. It's about all I can do."

"Couldn't you make Niki talk?"

He gave me a pitying smile. "If we could use their methods, perhaps."

He left and I had no time for lunch. I was busy with the reporters and then I was closeted with Uncle Al's lawyer. When he heard that Ken's widow had taken someone else's name, he assured me that gave me enough basis to have Ken's will broken, and it would be almost automatic if it could be proven that she had entered into the marriage for some illegal purpose. After he left I was on the phone for nearly an hour. I got a yes from Garroway and Poulson and a maybe from Fitz. It felt good to be reorganizing the team. Dolson's replacement arrived, a lean man with a snow plow jaw.

There were some Washington brass with him who needed reassurance, and I did the best I could. They were miffed that Mottling was out, and I wished I could tell them more of the score. I wanted to see how far their eyes would bulge. But Tancey had told me to keep my mouth shut.

I talked to Joan on the phone and told her I would pick her up at her house some time before six. I called the car rental place and told them where they could find their car.

I drew a company sedan for my personal use until I could buy something or get my car shipped up from Florida. There was the problem of disposing of the beach house, after it had been used for a very short honeymoon.

When it was time to go see Niki, I checked with Tancey and he said his arrangements were all made.

My palms were sweating on the wheel of the company car as I drove out to the Lime Ridge house for the last time. I knew I would never go in there again. After the estate thing was fixed up, it would go on the market. It would make a nice house for somebody who didn't know what had happened in it. I would build Joan a house.

There was no wind and the late afternoon sun was low and bright as I drove in. Victoria let me in. She seemed nervous and glad to see me. I wondered how much they had told her, and how much she had guessed.

Niki was in the living-room. She came toward me and took my hands in hers. She looked regal and lovely. "Darling!" she said. "This is a celebration, you know. Can I be as bold as brass?"

"Of course."

"Victoria is going out later. I'll cook for you. I have good wine. I want us to forget everything tonight. Everything but us, darling."

She held her chin up and half-closed her eyes in a way that clearly indicated her desire to be kissed. She released my wrists and gave me a look of quick annoyance and moved away from me.

"Will you make martinis?" she asked.

"I'm sorry. I can't stay. I've got a date."

"Break it."

"Can't. Sorry."

She tilted her head. "I *must* say, you're looking and acting very, very strange, Gevan."

"I feel strange."

"With me? Or is it that you're worried about the job and all?"

"It's you, Niki. I don't know how I should react to you."

"I thought I made that clear. And not in a ladylike way, either." Her smile was lascivious. I felt utterly no response to her hints, to her warmth and ripeness. Joan was too much with me.

"I came to say good-by, Niki."

She snorted. "I'm not going anywhere, and after that vote today, it doesn't look as though you are."

"You're leaving. Not as Niki Webb, or Niki Dean. As Mary Gerrity."

She was facing me and for a long time her features were absolutely immobile, frozen in a look of habitual, delicate lust. Her features smoothed into a puzzled smile.

"Am I supposed to understand that? Is it supposed to mean something to me?"

"That isn't any good, Niki. You know it and I know it. So let's drop it. Before they take you, I'd like to know why. I planned to enjoy this, to enjoy taking your mask off, but I don't. I just feel—very, very tired."

"Have you gone mad?"

"Please don't, Niki. It's over. They know all about it. All about Dolson and LeFay and Mottling and Fitch and the rest of it. They've fixed the D4D's that were gimmicked. LeFay and Fitch are in custody. Tancey told me a half-hour ago they've picked up two more, the two who with LeFay tried to dump us in the river. They know Ken and the Brady girl were murdered and why. So it's over."

She walked slowly to one of the couches and sat down, her hands slack on her thighs. "You did it," she said.

"Some of it."

"I said I could handle you. I should have remembered from before—you're the only person who has ever made me fell uncertain of myself, insecure. Maybe it's because I was closer to being in love with you than with anybody else."

"But never in love with anybody, ever."

"No, Gevan. Never."

"How did you get on—your side of the fence?"

"You wouldn't understand if I told you."

Tancey came in, almost apologetically. He had two men with him and a husky police matron. "You'll want to pack something, Miss Gerrity."

Niki-Mary got up obediently. She gave me a long, opaque, unreadable look, and turned away from me. The matron went with her. She did not speak. I knew I would not see her again unless I saw her while testifying.

I walked to the windows. Tancey, behind me, said, "You're lucky, Mr. Dean."

"I suppose so."

"Look here. This is what I mean." I turned. He showed me a small chromed automatic. He said, "This was down between the cushions where she was sitting. I can't understand why she didn't use it on you. It would have helped ease the defeat. It would have made sense to use it— from their point of view."

I thought I knew why she hadn't. But I couldn't be sure. I could never be sure, because even if I asked her, I knew she could give me no clear reason. I walked out, thinking of what might have been. No victory is absolute. The victor always loses something.

I knew I would be late picking up Joan, but I drove back to the plant and parked, with the motor turned off. The last of the sun made flame in the windows. I listened to the deep voice of the production areas, listened to the shrillness as metal was peeled back from high-speed cutting edges.

After the sound and the look of the place had filled me and strengthened me and brought me back from the edge of gloom, I turned the car around and headed for Joan's house.

As I got out of the car Joan came hurrying down the steps. Some of her bandaging was gone and the rest was concealed under an absurd hat. She said, "They wanted you to come in and so on and be social, but that can come later."

It was good to see her and be with her. I got behind the wheel. I kissed her. We drove downtown.

"A genuine date," she said.

"For real."

"You're gloomy, Gevan. It was bad, wasn't it?"

"Bad?"

"With her, I mean. With Niki."

"How did you know I went out there?"

"I just know. It's all right. I know you had to. I'm glad you did."

"It wasn't the same, looking at her, after you."

"I know that too."

I laughed. "My God, you're smug."

"Of course. And now take me to the Copper Lounge and buy me something strong."

The late editions were out. My picture was on the front page. So was Lester's. Joan said they were crummy pictures of both of us. We went to the Copper Lounge. All gloom was gone. I was with my girl. We took a table for two and Hildy Devereaux did her last cocktail turn and Joan told me she thought Hildy was lovely, but I better not voice the same opinión or both my eyes would soon match perfectly. She suggested I wear dark glasses in the office because there was nothing dignified about a president with a black eye.

Hildy came over to the table and I got up and introduced them and the waiter brought an extra chair.

Hildy admired my eye. Then she saddened and said,

"That poor slob of a colonel, Gevan. That depressed me. And it nearly ruptured Joe, having it happen in the hotel. But, as usual, they kept the name of the hotel out of the paper."

The two girls talked politely. They kept their nails sheathed, but I had the feeling they were on guard. Finally Hildy stopped talking and stared at Joan and then at me.

"My God," she said, "I'm getting dense. You look like a couple of Halloween pumpkins."

"Does it show that much?" Joan asked.

"That much, Miss Perrit." Hildy sighed. "I was going to take a hack at him myself."

"Too late," Perry said sweetly.

"Seems to be." Hildy grinned. "All a girl has to do is turn her back and some sneaky character moves in."

"Oh, I've been working on this for four years," Perry said.

They kept talking. I stopped listening. Hildy's choice of phrase, "sneaky character," had triggered something in my memory. I went back over my talks with Hildy and I remembered.

I interrupted them. "Hildy, the Colonel is dead now. You said something about some little man who wouldn't want the Colonel to do any sounding off while drunk. I asked you about him and you hedged the question. What little man was that?"

She frowned and looked uncertain. "Well—I guess I can tell you now. The Colonel told me to keep it to myself. It was an FBI man. He'd come in once in a while and drink alone. I noticed that the Colonel would stand next to him at the bar, and one time I saw him slip the Colonel something. So the next time Dolson started bothering me, I asked him what was going on. He got upset and said I shouldn't mention it to anybody, ever. He said it was an FBI man and he had to give him secret information."

"What did the man look like?"

"One of those dark quiet little guys you never pay any attention to. The next time I saw him I took a better look at

m. One of his ears was funny. I can't remember which
e. The right one, I think. The lobe was gone."

"Did you swallow that, about him being an FBI man?"

"It seemed sort of funny to me at first. I thought Curt
olson was trying to be a big shot or something, but later I
und out that he was telling me the truth."

"How?"

She shrugged. "Oh, it was one of those things. I got
ngry after everything was closed. Three o'clock one
orning, it was. Joe took me to an out-of-the-way place
wn the valley where they have good hamburgers. I saw
e FBI man with that Mr. Mottling from your company.
hey were in a booth. It had high sides. I went to the girls'
om so I could walk by them to make sure."

"Did Joe see them too?"

"I guess he did. But I didn't talk about it. Not after what
urt said to me. You know. Secret stuff. I guess he was
porting to Mottling. I recognized Mottling because he
ed to come in now and then and have a drink with the
olonel after they started getting along well."

I excused myself and said I would be right back. It took
teen minutes to locate Tancey. I asked him if LeFay had
ything wrong with his ear.

"Yes. The lower lobe of the right ear is missing. Why?
at's a funny thing for you to know."

"Have you picked up Mottling?"

"He's out. I've got two men staked out at the Atheltic
ub waiting for him to come back. They'll phone me when
comes in."

"I think you can pick him up, officially."

There was a long pause. "One witness?"

"One definite and one probable."

"Can you get them over here?"

"Yes."

"I'll be here at the house."

"Can I send them over instead of coming along myself?"

"Don't you want to sit in on it?"

"Not tonight, Mr. Tancey. I've got other plans."

There was another pause. "She's a very pleasant girl. Congratulations."

"Thank you, Mr. Tancey."

I hung up. Maybe he wouldn't be able to make anything stick. But Mottling's effectiveness was over.

I went back to the lounge. From the doorway I saw my girl. I kept my eyes on her as I walked between the tables. She looked very good. Her smile was for me. I liked the way she sat. I liked the meaning she gave everything. I thought of her, and the work ahead, and how everything would be, and how the end of the day would be the best part. I walked faster. I put my hand on her shoulder. It was good to touch her. She seemed to lean against my touch. I sat down and faced Joan and for a moment I couldn't decide what I should tell her first.

ABOUT THE AUTHOR

John D. MacDonald was graduated from Syracuse University and received an MBA from the Harvard Business School. He and his wife, Dorothy, had one son and several grandchildren. Mr. MacDonald died in December 1986.